"I'm staying."

Jakob reined in the thoughts that reared up at the image of sleeping under the same roof as Amy. She didn't need that now. What she needed right now was a friend. That might be all she'd *ever* want from him.

"You really don't have to stay, you know." She looked at him, her eyes dark, the gold highlights subdued. "You've done what you came to do. I've crawled out of my depression. I'll call Mom tonight and confront her. I promise."

"And I'm going to be here when you do." He wasn't going to let her drive him away. "If you don't want me to listen in, I won't. That's your choice. But when the call is over, you shouldn't have to be alone."

The chin came up again. The defiance was back in her eyes. "I'm used to doing things alone."

"Maybe so." He held out a hand. "But this time you don't have to."

Her stare fell to his hand as if it was the snake in the Garden of Eden. Tempting, but also terrifying.

They'd touched so rarely. He waited to see what choice she would make.

Dear Reader,

I was actually a history major in college. And, yes, I've written a few historical novels along the way, but what's come to intrigue me most is the more recent past. I'm always fascinated by what moves people to act the way they do. I've come increasingly to believe that most of our behavior, not to mention those extremely influential little voices we all have in our heads, has roots in our childhood. If, say, you're getting out of a bad marriage but grew up in a stable, happy home, do you quit trusting all men? Not usually. Turn it around, though, so that Dad was unreliable, cheated on your mom, failed you when you needed him—then probably you never did really trust men.

The logical corollary is that our parents are the people they are because of their childhoods. And so often, we don't know our parents as well as we think we do. Heck, it's not like any of us tell our kids everything, either! Even when no one is trying to hide anything in particular, a lot goes unmentioned. Sometimes those mysteries would help us understand a parent better, and by extention ourselves.

My own father is gone now, and my mother's memory is failing, which means there's a lot I'll never know about them. It's gotten me thinking more than ever about the questions I never asked.

The time capsule was the perfect story idea for me. Lots of innocent stuff went in it, but also a few real secrets. In the case of my heroine, the mysteries of her past and her mother's have kept her from being able to imagine sharing her life with anyone. But here's a secret her mother never wanted her to know, one that shatters their already difficult relationship and remakes it into something that might be better...or might not. This particular secret also produces a shocking change in Amy Nilsson's relationship with a man she had never imagined herself loving...

Hope you enjoy the book and come to care about these people as much as I did!

Janice Kay Johnson

P.S. I enjoy hearing from readers! Please contact me through my publisher, Harlequin Books, 225 Duncan Mill Road, Don Mills, ON M3B 3K9, Canada.

From This Day On

Janice Kay Johnson

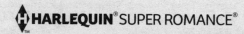

ISBN-13: 978-0-373-60791-4

FROM THIS DAY ON

HARLEQUIN®
www.Harlequin.com

Printed in U.S.A.

ABOUT THE AUTHOR

The author of more than seventy books for children and adults, Janice Kay Johnson is especially well-known for her Harlequin Superromance novels about love and family—about the way generations connect and the power our earliest experiences have on us throughout life. Her 2007 novel *Snowbound* won a RITA® Award from Romance Writers of America for Best Contemporary Series Romance. A former librarian, Janice raised two daughters in a small rural town north of Seattle, Washington. She loves to read and is an active volunteer and board member for Purrfect Pals, a no-kill cat shelter.

Books by Janice Kay Johnson

HARLEQUIN SUPERROMANCE

1454—SNOWBOUND
1489—THE MAN BEHIND THE COP
1558—SOMEONE LIKE HER
1602—A MOTHER'S SECRET
1620—MATCH MADE IN COURT
1644—CHARLOTTE'S HOMECOMING*
1650—THROUGH THE SHERIFF'S EYES*
1674—THE BABY AGENDA
1692—BONE DEEP
1710—FINDING HER DAD
1736—ALL THAT REMAINS
1758—BETWEEN LOVE AND DUTY**
1764—FROM FATHER TO SON**
1770—THE CALL OF BRAVERY**
1796—MAKING HER WAY HOME
1807—NO MATTER WHAT
1825—A HOMETOWN BOY
1836—ANYTHING FOR HER
1848—WHERE IT MAY LEAD

SIGNATURE SELECT SAGA

DEAD WRONG

*The Russell Twins
**A Brother's Word

Other titles by this author available in ebook format.

CHAPTER ONE

WELL, THAT WAS WEIRD.

At first only puzzled, Amy Nilsson flipped the crisp white envelope over, as if the backside would offer any illumination. As she'd expected, the only printed information was on the front: a return address of Wakefield College in Washington State, and her mother's name and address. Her mother's full name, Michelle Cooper Doyle, followed by Class of 1980.

To the best of Amy's knowledge, her mother had graduated from the University of Oregon. If she'd ever attended any other institution, she hadn't said so. She'd never so much as mentioned Wakefield.

Mom's mail had become one of Amy's responsibilities when she moved into her mother's house to care for it while she and Amy's stepfather were abroad for two years. Ken Doyle, her stepfather, had accepted a visiting professorship at the University of New South Wales in Australia.

Probably it was dumb, but Amy had been convinced that living in Mom's house, living her life, in a way, would give her insight into who her mother was. And how pathetic was it to realize your best chance of getting to know a parent was in absentia? Michelle Cooper Doyle was so closed off emotionally, she felt increasingly like a stranger to Amy. And yes, the whole living-in-the house strategy was working to some extent—she inadvertently made small discoveries almost daily about Mom.

Sadly, the mail had been a huge disappointment so far. Mom was handling bills online. What little came for her was junk. A gardening magazine seemed to be her sole subscription.

But now, something out of the ordinary. A real clue.

Maybe, Amy cautioned herself.

The scent of fresh-brewed coffee filled the kitchen. She dropped the handful of mail onto the table atop the *Oregonian* and concentrated for a few minutes on pouring coffee, dressing it up with sugar and one percent milk and toasting a bagel. She felt like a kid eyeing packages under the Christmas tree. Anticipation was half the fun. Amy wrinkled her nose, thinking it. Sure, right. In her experience, gifts were as often socks or underwear as they were anything fun or exciting. Chances were, *this* package was nothing but a solicitation for money.

Yes, but why ask her mother if she had no connection to the college? And…why did someone there think Mom had attended?

Then she sat back down in the dining nook,

where she could see her mother's rose garden through small-paned French doors. Amy had sworn, cross her heart and hope to die, that she would take care of the garden in exchange for living in the house.

She briefly admired the roses, still in full bloom and looking pretty darned good, if she did say so, thanks to the soaker hoses she was religiously turning on every evening, as well as the last application of manure tea. Making it was one of her newly acquired skills.

Setting aside the newspaper, Amy tossed most of the mail into the recycling bin she kept beside the table. Square in front of her sat the mysterious envelope from Wakefield College, which had the formal look of an invitation.

So much for anticipation. *Open it, already!* Sliding her finger beneath the flap, she suppressed a tinge of guilt. In theory, she was supposed to forward anything that looked personal to Mom. But really, she convinced herself, how personal could this be?

It actually was an invitation, she discovered. An astonishing one that had her reading and rereading. Former students of Wakefield College, who as English majors had put an item into a time capsule almost thirty-four-and-a-half years ago, were invited back to the campus for the capsule's premature opening. Apparently the relatively minor earthquake that had shaken eastern Washington and Oregon had damaged the foundation of one of the buildings on campus. Although less than thirty-five years old, Cheadle Hall was to be torn down and replaced. Upon reflection, college administrators had decided to open the time capsule now rather than put it in the foundation of the new building and wait until the planned fifty years had passed.

Amy kept grappling with the fact that the college thought her mother had been on campus thirty-four years ago, putting something—who knows what—into this time capsule. And yes, when she grabbed the envelope again, it was definitely addressed to her mother, Class of 1980. Cooper was Mom's maiden name. Doyle was her current last name. There was, of course, no mention of her former married name, Nilsson.

It seemed undeniable that Michelle had attended Wakefield for at least a couple of years. Which meant either she'd lied about having graduated from the U of O, or she had transferred after—what?—two years at Wakefield? Three? And why had she never mentioned it?

Amy reread every scrap of text yet again, searching for answers. The fact that the college knew her mother's married name suggested that she'd stayed in touch. Why had she done so if she'd chosen not to finish her undergraduate education at Wakefield? And why had she left a high-end liberal arts college to finish her education at a big state school? Money?

Lots of questions, no answers.

If this was a clue, Amy had no context for understanding it.

She could email her mother, but Mom never liked talking about the past, and especially her childhood or young adult years. Mom got impatient whenever Amy asked questions about her marriage to Josef Nilsson, too.

"For goodness sake!" she'd exclaimed the last time Amy had tried to learn more about her dad from her mother's perspective. "Any relationship is between the two of you. It doesn't have anything to do with me." She had cast a suspicious glance at Amy. "Why are you asking? Did he say something?"

Since she talked to him maybe three or four times a year, Amy could reply with complete honesty, "No."

End of discussion.

But…Wakefield College. Where did *it* come into her mother's history?

Doing some math in her head, Amy frowned. Her mother had to have met Josef somewhere around the same time the capsule was set into the foundation of this Cheadle Hall. Amy had been born early the next year. So probably that was why Mom had transferred to U of O—because Dad was there. That made sense. The mystery was why the subject of Wakefield College had never come up at all. No, Amy and her mother were not close, but she'd still have thought that, at some point, Mom would have said, "I went to Wakefield for a couple of years." Especially since it must have meant something to her, or she wouldn't have given the college her married name and address so she'd continue to get mailings.

More than weird.

Amy eventually went out for groceries. As always, she browsed the store's magazine section carefully. A freelance writer, she regularly published articles in half a dozen of the magazines that were displayed. She was always trying to come up with the right angle to get in at others.

Today, though, she remained distracted, even unsettled, for reasons she didn't altogether understand. Wasn't this what she wanted? She'd believed she could solve the mysteries of her own life if she understood her mother better. Here was an opening. So why did she feel…hesitant?

Oh, boy. Was it possible to want something, and not want it, too? The truth was, *she* had never liked thinking about her childhood, either. Her mother and she had that much in common.

She had been deeply hurt by her parents' divorce when she was six. She had adored her father. Dad had been the loving parent of the two, but somehow all that changed after the divorce. Her bewilderment at the way he distanced himself had become anger. Every-other-weekend visits gradually dwindled until, by the time she was a teenager, she wasn't seeing him more than a couple of times a year—a few weeks in the summer, Thanksgiving or Christmas, sometimes spring break. By then, she'd been in full rebellion.

Her mother had never been an affectionate woman; Amy had since realized she was the kind of woman who should never have had children at all. Probably she'd realized that, too, because Amy had no sisters or brothers, unless she counted her half brother, Jakob. Which she preferred not to. He'd apparently resented her existence from the minute she was born, and their relationship had never gotten any better. Until three months ago, she hadn't seen or heard from him in years, although she got occasional updates on his life from her father.

Founder, owner and CEO of an outdoor gear empire, Jakob lived in Portland. After Amy moved into her mother's house several months ago, he'd called to acknowledge that they were now in the same city. They had spoken politely about getting together but hadn't made any plans. He hadn't called again, and she didn't expect he would. She had every intention of making an excuse if he ever did suggest they get together for a cup of coffee or dinner. Her memories of Jakob were not, on the whole, positive.

That evening, Amy told herself it was only curiosity that prompted her to phone her father. He had relocated to Phoenix when she was about ten, one of the reasons her visits with him had been pared to two or three times a year.

"Amy!" he said, sounding surprised but pleased. "How are you?"

They chatted for a few minutes about work, weather and a few items from the news before a pause in the conversation gave Amy her chance.

"Something came in the mail today that surprised me. I didn't realize Mom ever went to Wakefield College."

There was a small pause. She couldn't decide if it was significant.

"Yes, she decided to leave after her sophomore year."

"Because she met you?"

"No, I happened to get a job in Florence that summer. We met in May, right after she got home from Wakefield."

Was it her imagination that he was speaking carefully, as if thinking out what he wanted to say?

"What kind of work were you doing?"

He laughed. "Construction, what else? I worked on building a new resort. Not so new anymore."

Amy did know that her mother had grown up in Florence, famous for miles of sand dunes above the Pacific Ocean on the Oregon coast. "You don't think it was because of you that she decided not to go back to Wakefield?"

Again he hesitated. "She said she didn't want to, anyway. But I guess she couldn't have gone back no matter what. Frenchman Lake is a pretty small town. I'd have had a hard time finding work there."

They had been married that August, barely three months after meeting. Mom had only been twenty, Dad twenty-three. They hadn't had to tell Amy she was the reason for the wedding. Accidental pregnancies often worked that way.

"Why the questions?" he asked now. "What did the college want? Money?"

"No." She explained about the time capsule. "It might be interesting to see what Mom put in it. I could go to the opening in her place." She hadn't known she wanted to attend until the words were out.

"Are you sure that's a good idea? Your mother values her privacy."

She didn't like feeling defensive. "I'm assuming whatever she put in is sealed. I wouldn't necessarily have to open it."

"Then why go at all?" her father asked, reasonably. "Chances are they'll mail anything that doesn't get picked up. You can send it on to her."

"That's true." So why feel deflated? "I'll think about it."

"Good." His voice had relaxed. "Jakob tells me you talked."

"Yes, he called. He suggested getting together, but we haven't managed yet."

Her father didn't question the absurdity of that excuse. In three months, two single adults who were truly interested in meeting up could certainly have managed to find a few free hours. Dad had to be aware that Jakob and Amy had never had an easy relationship.

The call ended with her feeling unsatisfied by what he'd told her. If pregnancy didn't explain Mom's decision not to return to Wakefield, what did? Why had she never, even once, mentioned that she'd gone there?

Over the next few days, Amy wrestled with her conscience. She had no doubt at all about whether Mom would want her to see whatever she'd put into that time capsule. This was the woman who repelled the most casual question about her past. But the knowledge triggered old anger for Amy. Other people talked casually about their parents.

Yeah, my mom went to Fillmore Auditorium all the time when she was a teenager. How cool is that? She even admits she took LSD. Or, *Mom says she loves Dad, but she still wishes she'd finished college before they got married. She insisted on telling me about every crappy job she ever had. In gory detail. Which I guess worked, because no way am I dropping out for some guy.*

Hearing the voices of friends, Amy thought, *Me? I didn't even know where my mother went to college.*

She had no idea whether her mother's reticence

had the same reasons as her own, which she did understand. Amy had spent her adult life blocking out growing-up years that had been mostly painful. She did holidays with her mom and Ken, who was an intelligent, kind man. That was pretty much the sum total of her relationship with her mother.

She'd actually been surprised when they asked if she would consider housesitting for them. It would be nice to think she was the only person they trusted, but the truth probably had more to do with the fact that, thanks to the ups and downs of her writing career, she pretty much lived on a shoestring and they knew it. They were doing her a favor. Two years with no rent was the next best thing to winning the lottery. She'd be able to save money. Maybe even do something wild and crazy like take a real vacation.

Her thoughts took a sideways hop. Speaking of money, was there a possible article in the time capsule? Of course the alumni magazine would undoubtedly be running one, but there had to be a tack she could take to intrigue readers who had no connection to Wakefield. The hopes and dreams of teenagers, captured so many years ago and now being revealed, unaltered. The reactions of former students as they were reminded of who they'd once been. She toyed with the notion that there was something dramatic in the capsule, a revelation that would provide a dramatic story for the *Atlantic* or the *New Yorker*.

She smiled wryly. Dream on. Okay, for *Seattle Met*, maybe.

It would be interesting to see a list of names of the attending alumni. Given the college's reputation and national ranking, some well-known public figures had undoubtedly graduated from Wakefield.

Oh, well, she had a few weeks to decide whether she really wanted to go. In the meantime, she had to concentrate on researching an article she *knew* she'd get paid for.

Deciding she wouldn't get dressed at all today— the boxer shorts and camisole she'd slept in were comfortable and cool—Amy took the coffee to her stepfather's study, where her laptop had replaced the one he had taken with him.

A few minutes later, she was almost engrossed enough to forget the peculiar fact that her mother had, by her silence, lied about her college years.

JAKOB NILSSON DROPPED his phone on the end table and reached for the remote control. He didn't immediately touch the mute button to restore sound on his television, however. Nothing much was happening in the Mariner game he'd been watching, and he was still trying to figure out what his father had wanted.

Dad was a straightforward kind of guy. Blunt, even. Out on a job site—he was a contractor—he could best be described as a sledgehammer. So why had he just talked in circles?

The purported message had been that he thought it was a shame Jakob and Amy weren't acting the part of close and loving family members, given that they probably didn't live a mile apart. Jakob had pointed out that he hadn't so much as *seen* Amy since—he'd had to stop and think—Thanksgiving five years ago. He hadn't mentioned that the only reason he remembered the occasion at all was that it had been so awkward all around. At the time, his marriage was deteriorating. The fact that Susan was sulking had been obvious to all, casting a pall over the gathering. She hadn't bothered being polite to his stepmother—yeah, Dad was on his third marriage—or to Amy, who looked as if she'd rather be anywhere at all than at Dad's house for a not-so-festive holiday meal. Jakob wasn't sure why she'd shown up that year, when she didn't most.

Before that… He really had to search his memory to nail down the previous time he'd seen Amy. A Christmas, he thought. Her mother had just remarried, he remembered that, and she'd gone back east with her new husband to celebrate the holiday with his aging parents. Amy hadn't looked real happy to be at Dad's that time, either. Jakob would have followed his usual pattern of making an excuse once he heard she was coming, except what could he do? It was Christmas, and Susan wouldn't have understood.

Jakob couldn't even say *he* understood. He only knew his relationship with his half sister had been prickly from the beginning—his fault—and by the time they were both teenagers, uncomfortable. He didn't let himself think about why. Water under the bridge. He no longer had any reason to dodge her, but no reason to seek her out, either.

Still, the conversation with his father had been bizarre. While he meditated, Jakob tossed some peanuts into his mouth, chewed, then chased them down with a swallow of beer.

Dad wanted something besides a warm and fuzzy relationship between two people he knew damn well couldn't even tolerate each other. It had to do with Amy's mother and with a time capsule opening. Jakob wouldn't swear to it, but he kind of thought he was supposed to talk Amy out of going to collect whatever her mother had put in it.

He grunted at the idiocy of the whole line of conjecture. Yeah, sure, he was just the guy with the best chance of influencing Amy's behavior.

When Mariner player Gutiérrez knocked the ball over the head of the Texas Ranger shortstop, Jakob restored the sound long enough to follow the action. Gutiérrez made it to second. The next player up to bat struck out, though, bringing the inning to an end, and he muted the ensuing commercial. His thoughts reverted to their previous track.

Why would Dad think Michelle had put anything of even remote significance in that time capsule? Jakob was speculating on why it mattered if Amy got her hands on whatever that was when he thought, *Oh, shit.* Unlike Amy—he hoped unlike Amy—he had been old enough to understand some of what Michelle and his dad were fighting about before they separated and then divorced. Now he did some math in his head and thought again, *Shit.* His father knew something. Maybe not for sure, but enough to want to keep Amy away from that time capsule and what was in it.

Dad wasn't using his head, though. Hadn't it occurred to him that if neither Michelle nor her daughter showed up to claim her contribution, the college would undoubtedly mail it to Michelle at her address of record? That address being the house where Amy currently lived and where, apparently, she was opening the mail.

Whatever secret this was, neither Jakob nor his father had a prayer of keeping it out of Amy's hands.

Thinking back to the conversation, he guessed his father didn't really *know* anything. He was only uneasy.

Jakob considered calling him back and saying, *Hey, what's the scoop?* But he doubted his father knew how much he'd overheard all those years ago.

And maybe misunderstood, he reminded himself. He'd only been nine years old when Dad and he moved out. His confusion over what he'd overheard was one reason he had never said anything to Amy. He hated her anyway, he'd assured himself at the time. After that, as they got older, he didn't know what he felt about her, only that they weren't friends, and they weren't sister/brother in any meaningful way.

They still weren't.

Yeah, but his interest had been piqued. It wouldn't hurt to give her a call, would it? Take her to dinner, maybe, if she didn't make an icy excuse. He found he was curious to know what she was like these days. His impression five years ago—even nine or ten years ago, when they'd shared Christmas Day—was that Amy had passed to the other side of her wild phase. She'd removed most of her piercings and let her hair revert to its natural chestnut color. Her makeup had been toned down considerably, too. She'd become an adult.

He knew she was a reasonably successful writer now. He'd actually bought magazines a few times to read her articles, which he had to admit had been smart, funny and not much like the angry teenage girl and then young woman he'd known.

Maybe he'd like her now.

The thought was insidious and made him feel edgy for no obvious reason.

Call her? His hand hovered over his phone. Or don't?

AMY WAS JARRED from the paragraph she'd been reworking by her telephone ringing. She glanced at it irritably. Friends knew not to call her past about seven o'clock in the evening. That's when she did her best work.

But her eyes widened at the number that was displayed. It was local, and she was pretty sure she recognized it. After a momentary hesitation, she picked up the phone.

"Hello?"

"Amy." The voice was deep and relaxed. "Jakob."

"Jakob." Her thoughts scattered.

"Dad called this evening. He was telling me about this time capsule thing. I'm being nosy."

"It is a little strange." She hesitated then thought, *Why not?* "Did you know my mother ever went to Wakefield College?"

"Can't say I did, not until Dad mentioned it tonight. You mean you didn't know, either?"

"I'd swear she never mentioned it. I assumed she'd done her entire four years at the University of Oregon. But apparently not."

"Have you emailed and asked her about it?"

The all-too-familiar anger stirred again. Why would she ask when her mother would either not answer, or only tell her it was none of her business?

"No. She and I never talk about the past. And I'm sure it's no big deal." *I am lying,* Amy realized. To her, knowing her mother had put something in the time capsule *felt* like a big deal. "I just thought it was interesting, that's all. It even occurred to me that there might be an article idea in the opening of the capsule."

He got her talking about the possible article, mentioned one of hers he'd read, which flattered her more than it should have, and finally suggested they actually have dinner together.

"It would make Dad happy to know we'd done something."

He'd played the guilt card deftly, she thought, but found herself tempted, anyway. Who else could she talk to about this? Jakob at least knew some of the background and seemed to be genuinely interested. He sounded like a nicer guy than she remembered him being, too.

Amy made a face. Yes, it was possible she'd been ever so slightly prejudiced against him. So, okay, he tormented her throughout her growing-up years, but maybe that wasn't so abnormal for an older brother. Especially one dealing with his father's remarriage followed by the birth of a baby sister who supplanted him, in a sense.

He presumably *had* grown up.

"Sure," she said cautiously. "When did you have in mind?"

JAKOB HAD THE next evening in mind, as it turned out. Either he didn't have an active social life right now, or a cancellation had provided an opening in his schedule.

They'd agreed to meet at the restaurant, and he beat her there. Amy was glad she'd checked it out online and therefore dressed appropriately. It wasn't the kind of place she usually dined. Her all-purpose little black dress fit in fine, though, and the four-inch heels lent enough sway to her hips, she was vaguely aware that a couple of men turned their heads when she passed. Good. She'd been determined to look her best for this reunion. Jakob might be her brother, but she sure as hell didn't want him looking at her with disdain the way he had the last few times they'd seen each other.

The maître d' led her straight to a window table where Jakob waited. He spotted her when she was on the other side of the room and rose to his feet, watching her as she came.

The minute she set eyes on him, she felt sure a cancellation explained the fact that he had been free to have dinner with a mere sister tonight. This was a man who could have all the women he wanted, whenever he wanted.

He got his height and looks from their father. Amy hadn't. She'd forgotten how Jakob dwarfed her. Or maybe not—perhaps her subconscious had prompted her to wear the tallest heels she owned.

Jakob was also ridiculously handsome, his features clean-cut, his nose long and narrow, his cheekbones sharp enough to cast a shadow beneath. He had dark blond hair that was probably a little longer than business-standard, but lay smooth except for a curl at his collar. His eyes had been a breathtaking shade of blue when he was a kid, but had become more of a blue-gray by the time he reached adulthood. He looked as Scandinavian as his name suggested.

She did not. Amy had inherited her mother's brown eyes and hair that was neither brown nor red nor anything as interesting as auburn. Mom was a brunette, but apparently a great-aunt was a redhead so it ran in the family. Nobody had curls like Amy's, though. That cross was hers alone to bear.

"Amy." Jakob smiled and held out a hand. Not his arms, thank heavens—nobody in their family hugged, and she didn't want to start with him.

"Jakob."

They shook, his big hand enveloping hers. It felt warm, strong and calloused, which was interesting considering he presumably sat behind his desk most of the time.

Or maybe not. He'd always been the outdoorsy type, and given his business—sporting goods—he likely tested some of the products himself. Lord knows there were plenty of mountains within a day's drive for him to climb and forests for him to hike into.

She was reluctantly aware that he had, if anything, gotten better looking with the years instead of softening around the middle or starting to gray or whatever, the way you'd expect. He was thirty-seven, after all, which ought to be edging past his prime. Part of her had been hoping for the teeniest hint of jowls, a few broken blood vessels in his nose…something.

No such luck.

The maître d' seated her and then presented a white wine to Jakob, who approved it. Left alone with their menus, Jakob and Amy looked at each other.

The experience was more than strange. They hadn't been alone together—focused solely on each other—in almost twenty years. She had hardly seen her brother after he'd left for college, when she was fifteen. At Christmas once or twice, maybe. One summer, she remembered, he'd worked in Tucson and, oh, gee, just never managed to get home while she was there. The summer after that, Colorado. Amy hadn't gone to her dad's the summer before she herself started college. Not seeing Jakob had been fine by her. Better than fine.

Now she thought, *He's a stranger. I don't know him at all. Never knew him.*

"I'm not sure how we managed to avoid each other so completely for so many years," he said, as if reading her thoughts.

"Determination and motivation." Amy sipped the wine then glanced at it with surprise. It had as little in common with the kind of wine she usually drank as she did with her brother the stranger.

His mouth crooked. "I was a shit to you when we were kids, wasn't I?"

"You were." She found herself smiling a little, too. "I don't suppose you were exactly thrilled when I came along."

"You could say that. I don't remember much about it. I was only three when you were born, after all. But I was already dealing with the shock of suddenly having a new mother who didn't seem very interested in me, and next thing I knew she wasn't fat anymore, and there you were, squalling and ugly and I could tell my daddy was totally in love with you."

Well, Dad got over that, she thought tartly, downplaying the hurt.

"It's a wonder older siblings ever like the younger ones," Amy said reflectively.

"You so sure they do?"

They shared a grin.

He nodded at the menu. "Better decide what you want to eat. Our waiter is looking restless."

The restaurant specialized in steaks but had a few alternatives. She chose salmon, baby potatoes and a Caesar salad. Once the waiter had departed, Amy looked at Jakob again.

"So what's the deal? Why did Dad call you about this time capsule opening?"

"I have no idea."

Amy felt sure he was telling the truth. Or mostly the truth.

"I'm not sure *he* knew," Jakob continued. "I suppose that's what caught my interest."

"Were you supposed to distract me so I wouldn't go?"

"He didn't come out and say so, but that's the impression I got."

"What could she possibly have put in it that Dad doesn't want me to see?" She'd only asked herself the same question a couple dozen times in the past two days. "It's not likely to upset me even if Mom did something completely scandalous when she was a student. Even if that something scandalous got her kicked out of Wakefield." Now, *that* was a new thought, one that explained why Amy's mother had deleted the college from her personal history.

No, wait. If that was true, why would her mother have updated the college records with her married name and current address?

Because on some level she wanted official forgiveness or at least the legitimacy of being treated like any other former student? And maybe, it occurred to Amy, the reason Mom had been able to keep Wakefield a big secret was that, in fact, the college never *had* sent her any mailings. This could be the first, necessitated by the fact that she had been included in the time capsule thing. They might have gotten her information from some other alum with whom Mom had stayed in touch, say.

"You know," Jakob said, "I've barely seen your mother since I was—I don't know, nine or ten?"

She nodded. "By then you were already making yourself scarce when Mom and Dad traded me back and forth, weren't you?"

A truly wicked grin flashed. "Yeah, but sometimes that's because I was behind the scenes setting up my latest prank."

She glared at him. "The snake in my bed was the worst." A memory stirred, much as the coiled snake had. "No, I take that back. The time you hid in the closet dressed all in black with that monster mask was the scariest."

"Yeah." To his credit, he looked chagrined. "Dad was seriously pissed that time. He put me on restriction for a month. I was the star pitcher for my Little League team, and I had to drop out."

"Which made you hate me even more."

"Possibly." He sounded annoyingly cheerful.

It felt really odd to be reminiscing with her former tormenter. The bitterness she'd always felt seemed to be missing. In fact, she realized at one point during the middle of the meal, it felt odd to be reminiscing at all. Had she ever talked about her childhood with anyone, besides the superficial level that was exchanged with new friends, college roommates and whatnot?

No.

Jakob, she figured out as they talked, hadn't exactly had the ideal childhood, either. First his mother was killed in a car accident, then his father married a woman who had no interest in mothering the little boy. Grand entrance: cute baby sister who entranced Dad. A divorce, another change of school. Then yet another move, this one to Arizona, followed by his father's third marriage when Jakob was seventeen.

"I'd forgotten you were still living at home when your father remarried again," Amy said thoughtfully.

"I spent as little time there as possible."

"You don't like Martina?"

He shrugged. "She's fine. I never actively hated her. Truthfully, it was never *her* at all."

Amy nodded her understanding.

"She had the sense to stay hands-off, so we've developed a decent relationship. She's good for Dad, which is what counts."

That might be, Amy couldn't help thinking, except that Jakob had chosen to make a life a good distance from Phoenix. Of course, that could have more to do with the fact that the young Jakob Nilsson had been hooked on mountain climbing—or at least the *idea* of mountain climbing—and had immediately headed for Colorado and college in Boulder, within easy reach of a whole lot of impressive peaks he could scale.

"What about your stepdad?" he asked. "Is he okay?"

"Ken's a good guy. In fact, I like him better..." Appalled, she stamped on the brakes. Oh, man.

Had she almost told Jakob, of all people, that she liked her stepfather better than her own mother?

Yes, indeed.

They stared at each other, his eyes slightly narrowed. He'd heard the unspoken part of her sentence, loud and clear. Amy didn't like the sense that Jakob saw deeper than she wanted him to.

"So." Intent on her face, he kept his voice low, the reverberation jangling her nerves. "You think you'll go to that time capsule thing, or not?"

"Why do you care?" That sounded rude, but was real, too. Why was he interested?

His shoulders moved in an easy shrug. "Like I said, now I'm curious. I was kind of thinking, if you wanted company, that maybe I'd go with you."

She had to be gaping. "You've got to be kidding me."

His grin was irritatingly smug. "Nope. What's family for?"

Amy rolled her eyes, which seemed the expected response, but she also had the really unsettling realization that she had absolutely no idea what family was for. Or maybe even what family *was*.

Jakob was implying that it meant having somebody to stand beside you. The notion was downright foreign. Amy couldn't have even said why it was also strangely appealing. It shouldn't have been, not to a woman who never considered surrendering her independence for anyone, for any reason.

"Do you mean that?"

His eyebrows rose. "That I'd come with you?"

"Yes."

"Yeah." He looked a little perplexed, as if he didn't know why he was offering, either. "Yeah," he repeated more strongly. "I mean it."

"Okay," she heard herself say. "I haven't made up my mind yet." Why was she pretending? Of course she'd made up her mind. In fact—had there ever been any doubt? Trying to hide her perturbation, she offered, "But if I do decide to go… You can come if you still want to." She'd tried so hard to sound careless, as if she were saying, *Suit yourself, doesn't matter to me.* Instead…well, she didn't know how he would interpret her invitation or the way she'd delivered it.

"Good" was what he said. Jakob's eyes were unexpectedly serious. "We have a deal."

So not what she'd expected from the evening. But…nice. Something warmed in Amy despite the caution she issued herself: if he ran true to form, her darling half brother was setting her up for a fall. The splat-on-her-face kind.

He was signaling the waiter and she understood that the evening was over. He had whatever he'd wanted from it.

She just didn't quite get what that "whatever" was.

CHAPTER TWO

JAKOB SNEAKED A glance at Amy, who was gazing out the passenger-side window at the stark red-brown beauty of the Columbia River Gorge. She might be fascinated, but he suspected she was pretending. She was a Northwest native, and had seen the admittedly striking but also unchanging landscape before.

He couldn't quite figure out why he'd insisted on coming on this little jaunt. His being here didn't have anything to do with his father. In fact, he hadn't talked to Dad since the one peculiar call. Just yesterday, his father had left a message that Jakob hadn't returned. Maybe because he didn't want to tell him that Amy was going to the damn opening—but maybe because he didn't want to try to explain his own part in this, when he didn't get it himself.

The one part he did understand was why he'd insisted on driving. Polite man that he was, he had walked her to her car the night they'd had dinner together. She drove, he discovered, an ancient, hatchback Honda Civic. He recalled running his hand over a rust spot on the trunk.

Two days ago, when they discussed final arrangements, he had suggested that his vehicle might be more reliable.

"Just because my car's old doesn't mean it's unreliable!" she had snapped.

"We'll be making a long drive across some pretty barren country. Not where you want to break down."

"I didn't break down when I drove down here from Seattle."

He knew stubborn when he heard it. Unfortunately, that was one trait they shared. A family one?

"How many miles does it have?" he asked.

There had been a noticeable pause before she answered. "One hundred and fifty-four thousand."

He seemed to remember muttering something that might have been obscene.

When it got right down to it, though, what kept him stubbornly repeating "I'll drive" had been the appalling image of trying to wedge himself into the damn car.

When Amy had surrendered at last, she said grudgingly, "I guess since my car doesn't have air-conditioning, it might be better if we take yours."

His mouth twitched now into a smile he didn't want her to see. For God's sake, it was supposed to top a hundred degrees in eastern Washington this weekend! Imagining how they'd be sweltering right this minute made him shake his head.

Jakob suddenly realized she was looking at him, eyes narrowed.

"What was that expression about?" she asked, sounding suspicious.

"Just feeling glad we have air-conditioning," he admitted. "It's hot as Hades out there."

"Nobody likes someone who says 'I told you so.'"

Jakob grinned. "Did you hear those words coming out of my mouth?"

"Close enough." Amy was quiet for a minute. Then she shrugged. "The glove compartment pops open every time I go over a bump. Usually the stuff in it falls onto the floor."

"You're telling me I'd constantly have a lap full of…what? Maps, registration, flashlight?"

"Um…hand lotion, dark glasses, ice scraper, receipts." She pushed her lower lip out in thought. "Probably a couple of books, too. I always keep something in there in case I get stuck in traffic, or finish the book that's in my purse."

He flicked her a glance of disbelief. "Finish the book *when?* While you're driving?"

She frowned severely at him. "Of course I don't read when I'm driving! Just when I'm at red lights, or we're at a standstill on the freeway. You know."

He groaned.

She sniffed in disdain.

After a minute he found himself smiling. "Wouldn't have mattered if you'd won the argument anyway, you know."

Her head turned sharply. "What do you mean?"

"When I arrived to pick you up, you'd have been bound to have a flat tire." He paused, that smile still playing on his mouth. "Or two."

The sound that burst out of her was somewhere between a snarl and scream. "Oh, my God! I'd almost forgotten. That was one of the meanest things you ever did."

This time his glance was a little wary. At the time, he'd thought it was funny. *Funny* was not, apparently, how she remembered the occasion.

"I was so excited when you emailed and promised to take me with you to the lake with some of your friends. I told all my friends how I was spending spring break in Arizona, and that my so-cool fifteen-year-old brother wanted to do stuff with me." Her glare could have eaten a hole in a steel plate. "I showed my friends pictures of you. I didn't tell them how awful you'd always been. I thought—" her voice had become softer "—you actually wanted to spend time with me."

Jakob winced. He'd had no idea his invitation, issued via email under his father's glower, had meant anything to her. By then, he had convinced himself Amy hated him as much as he did her and would be glad if something happened that got her *out* of having to spend the day with him.

She'd arrived that Friday and his father had fussed over her, sliding a commanding stare Jakob's way every few minutes, one that said, *You will be nice.* Predictably, that had made his teenage self even more hostile.

Dad had just started seeing Martina, though it was another year and a half before they got married. She'd loaned her bike for the projected outing. When Jakob and Amy went out to the garage come morning, one of the tires on Martina's bike had been flat. Examination showed a split between treads. He'd immediately said, "Wow, the guys are waiting for me. Bummer you can't come." After which he took off.

His father had suspected him but never been able to prove he was responsible for the damaged tire. Dad had worked Jakob's ass off that summer, though, and he hadn't objected too much because, yeah, he'd slipped out to the garage at 3:00 a.m. and slit the tire with a pocketknife.

"I'm sorry," he said now, and meant it. He didn't like knowing he might have really hurt her. "Teenage boys aren't the most sensitive creatures on earth. Dad was forcing my hand and I didn't like it."

She shrugged. "Yeah, I figured that out eventually. I lied when I got home and told all my friends about this amazing day with you, and how this really hot friend of yours acted like he wanted to kiss me." She grinned infectiously. "Which would have scared the crap out of me, you understand."

He laughed in relief. "No surprise. Some of us hadn't worked up the nerve to kiss a girl yet."

Amy eyed him speculatively. "You? You've always been so good-looking, and I don't remember you ever going through, I don't know, one of those gawky phases. You didn't even get acne, did you?"

He shook his head. "I actually think I was in one of those awkward phases that summer, though. I was sullen all the time. You were blinded because I was older."

"Maybe." She looked away, back out the side window. "Twelve was a hard age for me. Puberty, you know, and middle school."

He nodded, although he wasn't sure she saw him. This whole conversation felt astonishingly comfortable and yet really strange, too. In their entire history, they had *never* had a real conversation of any kind. Unlike most siblings or even stepsister and stepbrother, they hadn't banded together against their parents. He'd waged his campaign of torment and she'd fought back as effectively as a much younger, smaller and weaker opponent could. Jakob felt a little sick at knowing how unrelentingly cruel he'd been.

Which brought him back to brooding about why he had volunteered for this ridiculous expedition. Yeah, he'd been taking it a little easier these past couple weeks, after the successful launch of a store in Flagstaff. He'd given some thought to finding a friend to join him in a backpacking trip this week.

Sometimes he needed to turn off his phone and disappear into the mountains. Instead…here he was.

Amy stayed silent for a while. He kept sneaking looks at her averted face.

She'd changed, and yet…she hadn't. As a kid, he'd thought she looked like some kind of changeling, as if a little fairy blood had sneaked in. Pointy chin, high forehead and eyes subtly set at a slant. Her eyes weren't an ordinary brown, either; they had glints of gold that intensified when she got mad. She'd always been small. Not so much short— he guessed she was five foot four or five inches tall, but slight, with delicate bones. None of that had changed, even though there was nothing childish about her now.

He'd always been fascinated by her hair, too. When she was a baby and toddler, he'd spent a lot of time staring at her curls. He had never seen anyone with hair quite that color, or quite so exuberant. Not that the word *exuberant* had been in his vocabulary then. One of his earliest memories was getting yelled at when all he was doing was touching her hair. He'd been experimenting to see if the curls bounced back when he straightened them. Michelle had told Dad he was pulling Amy's hair. He still remembered the flash of resentment at being falsely accused.

Good God, he thought, there he'd been, three years old, maybe four—Amy hadn't been a new-born by then, but not walking yet, either—and the seeds of their discord had already been sown.

He surely did hope she didn't remember what he'd done to her hair when she was a lot older.

She had beautiful hair, the color hard to pin down. He'd finally figured out it was because she had strands of seemingly dozens of colors all mixed together. Everything from ash to mahogany, and just enough of a sort of cherrywood to make you think she was a redhead even though she wasn't exactly. She didn't have the Little Orphan Annie thing going—her curls weren't red enough, and they weren't tight enough, either. When she was a teenager Amy grew her hair long enough to pull back in some kind of elastic. And in a couple of her school pictures, she'd obviously straightened it, which must have been a battle royal. *Her* hair wouldn't have taken it sitting down.

He smiled, thinking about it.

"Every time I look at you, you're smirking," she said, surprising him. Her tone was mock-resigned.

Jakob chuckled. "I was imagining how hard it must have been to straighten your hair for your senior picture. You don't do that anymore, do you?"

She wrinkled her small, rather cute nose at him. "Lord, no. The only times I got away with it were when I was aiming for a very specific time. I had about an hour-and-a-half window of opportunity before curls started popping out like, I don't know, anthills in the sand. *Boing, boing.*" She surveyed him in disfavor. "You have no idea how much I envied you your hair, do you?"

"Me?" he said in surprise. "It's straight. It's blond. It's boring. Yours has life."

She seemed to hunch her shoulders the tiniest bit. "I would have liked to look more like Dad. You do."

Jakob was glad to have the excuse of concentrating on passing a slow-moving RV right then so he didn't have to address her comment immediately, or directly.

Once he had his Subaru Outback in the eastbound lane, he glanced at Amy. "My mother was blonde when she was a kid, too, you know. Her hair darkened like mine has. A little more, I guess. I thought of hers as brown."

She nodded. "I've seen pictures."

Yeah, he guessed she would have. That's all he had of his mother, since he hadn't been even a year old when she was killed in a car accident. For a young guy like his dad, who worked construction, finding himself the single parent of a baby must have been a major cataclysm. In retrospect, Jakob couldn't blame him for remarrying the first chance he got. Unfortunately, Jakob had been an adult before he achieved any understanding of his father's choices.

"We're getting there," he observed.

They had crossed into Washington State when the Columbia River swung in a horseshoe, first north and then east, the highway separating from the Columbia to take them along the Snake River north of Walla Walla and Waitsburg. He saw a sign for Frenchman Lake—25 miles. Half an hour, tops.

"I made reservations."

She'd already told him that. She sounded nervous, Jakob realized. In fact, her hands were knotted together, squeezing, on her lap.

"Did I tell you that creep Gordon Haywood refused to talk to me?"

"Yeah." He smiled. "You can't totally blame the guy for not wanting to be hit up by a journalist when he's trying to enjoy a walk down memory lane."

"'Hit up'? I have thoughtful, provocative conversations with people I interview."

"Do you accuse them of smirking?"

"You're my brother," she said with dignity. "That's different."

He laughed out loud. "Good to know I get favored treatment."

Amy didn't rise to his comment. She was quiet for a good ten miles, but Jakob kept an eye on her. "Was this a really stupid idea?" she blurted.

From his point of view? Maybe. Jakob couldn't help feeling a little uneasy at this tectonic shift in their relationship.

But for her? He thought about it for a minute. "No," he said at last, with certainty that surprised him. "This matters to you. You may not even know why, but it does. I assume you're trying to figure out some things about your mother. You could have waited placidly back in Portland until whatever she stuck in the time capsule appeared in your mailbox. But passive isn't your style. Charging ahead and demanding what you want is a better fit. That's all we're doing here."

She frowned at him. "You make me sound like a bitch."

"No. You were a feisty little girl, and unless you've changed more than I think you have, you're a feisty woman. That's a good thing, not bad."

"Oh." She fell silent again for a few minutes. "Okay. Thanks, Jakob."

The gratitude sounded less grudging than usual. Amusement lifted one side of his mouth when he glanced at her. "You're welcome."

"I meant…not only for what you said. For coming along, too. I'd have been okay making the trip by myself, but…it's nice that I didn't have to."

"I figured that. I expect to have a good time." He frowned a little himself as he realized the truth of what he was about to say. "I'm already having a good time."

Her expression was skittish and distinctly wary. She didn't say anything else. Neither did he.

AS FAR AS Amy could tell, Jakob hadn't lied—he seemed to be enjoying himself.

The college had organized all kinds of activities. Jakob was enthusiastic about most of them and assumed she would be, too. He dragged her along on the wine-tasting tour, although her idea of how to choose the right wine was picking the one that was on sale. He bought a bunch of wines, too, and lovingly carried them up to his hotel room so they wouldn't reach boiling temperature in the back of his SUV, parked in the sun.

He persuaded her to come along when he played golf, too. She had to concede the game—sport?— sort of looked fun. If she'd had unlimited free time and funds, she might have been tempted to take it up. Jakob admitted that, while he enjoyed a round now and again, he most often played because businessmen negotiated and networked out on the country club course. They also judged each other in part on how far below par they played, so he'd made sure he was good. He was so good, in fact, that he won the tournament staged by the college, which seemed to embarrass him.

They skipped the evening reception at the college president's house and ate at a restaurant, where he talked about his business and persuaded her to tell him about her writing. Amy was still astonished to know that he had bought magazines only to read the articles she'd written. She'd figured she was out of sight, out of mind, as far as he was concerned. It was disconcerting to discover he'd been at least a tiny bit interested in her life.

Over dessert and coffee, they bickered like the sister and brother they were. Most disconcerting of all was that Amy couldn't remember the last time she'd had a dinner date anywhere near as much fun.

Afterward, they'd arrived barely in time to nab seats in the back of a small auditorium to hear Senator Gordon Haywood, of Utah, speak. She had to admit the guy had charm and something probably best described as charisma. She didn't like his politics, though, and was still irritated that he'd refused to give her the interview. She might get an article out of the opening of the time capsule, but was beginning to doubt it. If she'd been set on it, she should have spent the weekend talking to alumni, not riding in a golf cart and sipping wine. What a waste, she thought. A free-ranging conversation with possible presidential contender Gordon Haywood would have been an easy sale to any number of publications.

Now, on the final day of the weekend's festivities and despite the blistering heat, Jakob leaned back against the substantial trunk of a big tree, arms crossed, seemingly prepared to enjoy the main event, too. He wore chinos, sandals and a bright red T-shirt. She'd forgotten that he had always loved bright colors.

Amy had stationed herself several feet away, needing a little separation for reasons she didn't understand. Her arms were crossed, too, tightly. It was silly to feel on edge like this, but she did.

Great moment to have a revelation. *Maybe I don't* want *to know who Mom was, before I was born.*

Did I really think it would help me to know why she became a woman who couldn't love her own child?

Because the answer was a resounding no. She still harbored more anger at her mother than she'd acknowledged even to herself. There probably wasn't an explanation on earth that would make her go soft with sympathy and understanding.

And the truth was, given that Mom had intended to major in English, she and most of the other students had likely put their very best writings into the time capsule. Since she had ultimately majored in sociology with a minor in Spanish, whatever Mom had written at nineteen or twenty was probably less than a marvel of literature.

Fidgeting, Amy glanced at Jakob to see him watching with seeming amusement and interest as the college president triumphantly pulled the capsule out of the foundation of the damaged building. He hefted it onto a table set up for the purpose on the green sward that seemed to form the heart of the campus. The crowd surrounding them cheered and clapped.

Amy couldn't seem to stay still. She shifted her weight from foot to foot and tapped out beats with her fingers unheard even by her. She'd find herself watching this face, or that. A couple of times, her gaze intersected with that of a man who stood with Madison Laclaire, the director of alumni relations who'd organized the event. He was paying more attention to the crowd than he was to what was happening up front. There wasn't even a flicker of expression on his face when his eyes met Amy's. Was he some kind of security?

Why do I care?

Amy knew perfectly well she was only trying to distract herself.

"Rob Dayton."

She quivered with a kind of alarm when she realized the college president had begun to call out names. A tall, skinny guy without much hair stepped forward to take an 8½-by-10-inch manila envelope. There was some good-natured teasing as he retreated with his contribution.

"Linda Gould." Lars Berglund, the president, glanced around, but no one responded and he set aside this envelope. The next couple, too.

"Ron Mattuschak." A stocky, graying man claimed this one.

Now Amy stood absolutely still, as if she'd miss hearing her mother's name if she so much as twitched. She didn't even look at Jakob.

Half a dozen names later, it came.

"Michelle Cooper Doyle."

What if this was a truly awful, horrible idea?

I don't have to open it.

A knot in her throat, Amy went forward. A handsome man with silver hair and bright blue eyes, President Berglund handed her an envelope with a murmured, "I'm sorry your mother couldn't be here."

She said something—probably a thank-you—
and walked quickly back to the tree where Jakob
waited, his eyes keen on her face. He was no longer amused by the proceedings, she realized on one
level. She had no idea what her expression showed,
but whatever it was had him concerned. The fact
that he was paying such close attention warmed
her. She was suddenly very glad she hadn't come
alone.

Not until she had reached him did the realization of what she held in her hand kick in. The envelope was heavier than she'd expected and harder,
too—a book? she wondered. There was room for
it to slide around in there, unlike a sheaf of papers
that would have fit just right. Her fingers flexed as
she became conscious there was also a softer lump.
This didn't feel like a short story.

Tension built in her chest.

For no good reason, she and Jakob stood there
dutifully, trapped by good manners much like con-
cert goers too polite to walk out midperformance,
while name after name was called, and people went
forward one at a time. She noticed that the alumni
director took one of the envelopes. The hard-faced
man at her side did, too, which meant he wasn't
here as security after all. Amy couldn't help noticing that his expression became even more remote
after he accepted the envelope for Joseph Troyer.
She understood how he felt.

At the end, Berglund upended the capsule and something small fell out.

"A petrified Tootsie Roll," the president said, and the grand occasion ended with a laugh.

"Do you want to get some lemonade or a cookie?" Jakob had stepped closer without her realizing it.

Amy wasn't hungry, but she was thirsty, she realized. No surprise, as hot as it was out here. "I wouldn't mind a lemonade."

He grabbed a couple of cookies, too, and wrapped them in a napkin. They walked across the field toward the street where he had parked. Voices of the small crowd they had left behind were an indistinct buzz in her ears. She was hardly aware that they passed students—even though once she had to dodge a Frisbee. Ten seconds later she couldn't have said who'd thrown it. Reaching Jakob's red Subaru was a relief.

They opened the doors to release the heat and he got in, started the engine and cranked up the air-conditioning. Amy stood there, the weight of the package feeling more significant than it could possibly be.

"Hop in," Jakob said, and she complied, fastening her seat belt and then staring down at the envelope.

I don't have to open it.

She almost snorted. Right. Sure. She'd wasted an entire weekend to come to the glorious opening of the time capsule, and she was not going to open the package her mother had put in it. Who was she kidding?

She slid her thumb under the flap and the glue gave way. Wildly curious now, she reached in and pulled out…yes, a book of some kind. No, an academic datebook, the kind you wrote assignments in. And a small bundle of cloth with pink flowers on a white cotton background.

The tension swirling inside her coalesced into dread. Panties. That's what she held in her hand. A pair of her mother's bikini underwear.

Amy stared down at them, unable to think of a single good reason Mom would have put them in this envelope to be saved for fifty years.

Her hands moved fast, but clumsily, as she stuffed both items back into the envelope. Desperate to no longer be touching it, she put it in the canvas messenger bag at her feet.

She and Jakob sat in silence for a minute or two that felt longer. Her hands were balled into fists now.

"Amy?"

"I shouldn't have opened it," she said in a stifled voice.

"What do you want to do?"

She made herself look at him. "Will you take me home?"

"Yeah." His voice was very gentle. "Of course I will."

"DAMN IT, AMY." Jakob had insisted on carrying her duffel bag in and now didn't want to leave. "I can tell you're upset. You don't have to be alone."

"I need to be alone if I'm going to look at it." She knew she was begging for understanding. "It's probably nothing. Some kind of joke."

He didn't look as if he bought that any more than she did.

"But, in case..." She stopped. "I need to respect her privacy."

"All right," he said after a minute, still sounding reluctant. His broad shoulders moved, as if he was uneasy. "Maybe you should call your mother instead. Wait and see what she says."

"She'd tell me to throw it away." Amy knew that, as if she could hear her mother's voice, sharp and alarmed. She also knew that she couldn't do any such thing. She'd come this far. She had to *know*.

He opened his mouth, and then closed it. She wondered what he'd been about to say, and why he'd had second thoughts about saying it.

"All right," he said again. "Will you call me? Let me know what you found? Or at least that you're okay?"

"Sure," she said, having no idea if she meant it or not. "I'll call."

He left finally, not looking happy. Amy didn't care. She was entirely fixated on the yellow-orange corner of the manila envelope poking out of her bag. She felt like she imagined a member of the bomb squad did as they carefully approached an IED. She couldn't *afford* to let herself be distracted. Something bad would happen.

She waited until the sound of the engine diminished as Jakob drove away from the house. The street was quiet. Although evening approached, the heat of the day lingered and she hadn't seen any neighbors out working in their yards. Later, when it cooled off, lawn mowers might be fired up. Right now, she had never been more aware of her aloneness.

She felt most comfortable alone. That's what a lonely childhood did to you.

You know you're going to do it, so why are you dawdling?

Good question.

Amy made a production out of pouring herself a glass of white wine first, although she kept a cautious eye on the corner of the envelope as if it might explode if she turned her back on it. Then she sat at the table, took a sip of wine and made a face. Ugh. Hanging out with someone like Jakob, who had good taste and plenty of money, could ruin you for real life.

She took another swallow anyway before reaching for the envelope, opening it and dumping the contents onto the table.

Staring at them, she was quite sure the panties hadn't been *clean* when Mom put them in the envelope. The crotch was stained and sort of crunchy-looking. Amy's stomach lurched. She turned her attention to the datebook.

It was, she discovered when she opened it, exactly what she'd assumed. It started in September, with the beginning of the academic year. Her mother's handwriting was recognizable but immature, more given to rounded lines and swirls than it was now. Mom had liked exclamation points, too. She'd noted assignments, dates of quizzes, when papers were due, but also used it as a diary.

Maybe it was cowardice that had Amy starting at the beginning rather than going right to the end. She never read the last page of books the way some people did. That seemed justification enough for her choice to proceed chronologically.

Amy read the first entries carefully. Her mother had been really excited to be back for her sophomore year. Partly, she'd been glad to get away from home. She had hated, hated, *hated* her summer job—half a dozen exclamation points—waitressing. Amy made a face. Coincidentally, she had worked as a waitress one summer, too. Apparently she didn't give off the right vibes, because she got lousy tips and she had vowed to dig ditches the next summer if she had to. Anything else.

Mom developed a crush on a junior, whom she didn't remember having noticed the year before. He was a transfer student, she eventually discovered. Joel. No last name given. Amy had begun skimming by that time. Michelle Cooper and this Joel did some flirting. He kissed her at a frat party not long before Christmas break.

Amy was flipping pages more and more quickly. Joel's name kept popping up. Another guy asked Mom out but she didn't want to go.

He's okay, she wrote, *but I don't like him that much.*

By spring it was apparent that Joel was seeing other girls. Michelle wrote about how she was sure he liked her. She couldn't understand how he could make out with her in his dorm room one night and then lie with his head on some other girl's lap the very next day in plain sight on Allquist Field.

The other guy—Steven—was determined. He was in one of Michelle's classes and always managed to sit next to her. He talked her into having coffee at the Student Union Building a couple of times. She still didn't sound enthusiastic, but finally she wrote, *It's stupid to just sit in my room.* Steven had asked her to have dinner with him and attend the opening night of the spring musical put on by the theater department.

Amy turned the page. Her heart clenched at the sight of blank pages. Nothing for the entire week, not so much as a note about a class assignment. That couldn't be the end, could it? She turned the page.

The following week, there was two lines, the scrawled handwriting ragged.

He raped me. But who will believe me?

The next week: *I can't go to my Econ. class, not knowing he'll be there. I've been to some of the others, but I watch for him all the time. Yesterday I saw him crossing the field and I felt so sick I ran back to my room and hid for the rest of the day.*

Finally, *I don't think I can make myself come back to school here. I don't ever want to think about what happened again. But I can't completely pretend, can I?*

She wrote about how what she put into the time capsule could be a kind of funeral offering for herself. *The old me is dead.* She had intended to throw away the panties that had his sperm on them, but when it came time to do laundry each week, she couldn't make herself touch them. Now she had decided to stuff them into the envelope along with the diary.

There was one last line.

This, she concluded, *is what happened to me at Wakefield College. This is what I choose to say: Steven Hardy raped me.*

Amy stared at that last line, and at the date when her mother wrote it. *Oh, God, oh, God.* Heart drumming, she counted on her fingers. Her mother had always said she was premature, and she'd never thought much of it because it was true she was small at six pounds fourteen ounces. That was the weight on the little card that had come home from the hospital, so she knew it was true. But considering she had stayed small and skinny and matured into a slight woman, that wasn't undersized for full-term, was it?

If her mother had lied, if Amy had in fact been full-term…the timing was right.

Steven Hardy was her father. The man who had raped the young Michelle Cooper.

She felt as if she'd walked into a plate glass window. Bang. Dazed, she knew.

No wonder Mom couldn't love me.

Amy ran for the bathroom, and barely made it before the acrid bile rose from her stomach.

CHAPTER THREE

JAKOB WENT HOME to his condominium, wishing he'd been able to talk Amy into dinner, at least, before he left her. As scrawny as she'd always been, she wasn't ever very interested in food. He knew damn well she wouldn't eat at all if she was upset by whatever her mother had put in that envelope.

He swore out loud, then scanned the contents of his freezer. Pizza was easiest. He turned the oven on, continuing to pace restlessly while he waited for the preheat buzzer.

He hadn't gotten a real good look at what Amy pulled out, but he knew a pair of women's panties when he saw them. Why in *hell* would the woman have put a pair of her own underwear in the time capsule?

His pacing took him to the wall of windows that were the reason he'd bought the condo. He was looking down at the Willamette River, dark but for glimmers of gold reflected from downtown lights. To him, the river always looked primitive despite the way humanity had caged it. He loved driving down to Champoeg and seeing the Willamette the

way it had looked to early settlers, broad and powerful, floating between banks of deep forest.

The oven buzzed; he put in the pizza and set the
timer. He made himself sit down and respond to
emails he'd mostly ignored over the weekend. But
his attention was only half on them. He kept seeing the shock on Amy's elfin face when she pulled
the last damn thing in the world she could have expected from the manila envelope.

As usual, he'd dropped his phone on the kitchen
counter when he came in the door. Not so usual,
when he went to the john he took it with him. He
kept staring at it, as if he could will it to ring. *Call.*

Apparently that didn't work, because it stayed
stubbornly silent. He wanted to phone her, but she'd
expressed herself too bluntly for him to mistake
the message: *Thank you, but I want to be alone. I
don't need you now.* It wasn't as if they were close.
Jakob frowned. Close? They were strangers, and
that was mostly his fault.

He had the momentary sense of standing on the
edge of a dark, terrifyingly deep abyss. He didn't
like thinking about Amy, because those thoughts
always brought him to this place, one that felt more
like fear than he wanted to admit. As always, he
found himself mentally backing away from it.

No point in revisiting their relationship. Fact was,
he'd never acted like a brother did to a dearly beloved, or even barely tolerated, sister, and she had
every reason in the world to resent him at the very

least. The wonder was that she'd actually accepted his offer to accompany her to Frenchman Lake.

If something did upset her, why would she turn to him? She probably had good friends, maybe even a guy she was seeing.

Yeah, but then why hadn't she asked that guy or her best friend to go with her this weekend? She could have said "Thanks but no thanks" to Jakob then and even gotten a little secret pleasure out of rebuffing him.

Maybe she didn't have any good friends who lived nearby. Yeah, she'd gone to college here, but then moved away. Amy had only been back a few months.

He reluctantly admitted to himself that she had needed him because she didn't have anyone else.

And because she needed family? He winced at that word in reference to Amy and him.

Nope, he told himself, not going there.

She'd promised to call him. He took another impatient look at the clock on the microwave. 8:39 p.m. Over two hours since he'd dropped her off.

Call, damn it.

IT TOOK SOME doing, but Amy found her baby book in a box on the shelf in her mother's closet. She didn't even know what she hoped to learn, but she was desperate. Anything. A clue. Somehow she was holding her fear and horror at bay. She'd taken a huge leap by assuming her mother had lied to her all her life.

Please let me be wrong.

The closet was vast. When Mom and Ken bought the house, it had had four smallish bedrooms upstairs, and in common with many houses of this era the few closets were grossly inadequate. Especially for a woman who loved shoes.

So the first thing they did was have walls torn out, and the floor space that had been two of the bedrooms was used to enlarge what had been the only upstairs bathroom up here, along with creating a second bathroom and a giant walk-in closet. The remaining small bedroom was for their very occasional guests. Like Amy. So far in her stay, the only reason she'd stepped foot in Mom and Ken's bedroom was to run the vacuum cleaner around and whisk a feather duster over the blinds and the top of the end tables and dressers.

And yes, she'd known her mother had a thing about shoes, but not the extent of it. In her search to find anything about her childhood or origins, she'd been excited to find underbed rolling containers. Not so much when she pulled them out to find all four of them held shoes.

Wow, Mom. What a waste of money.

Amy didn't bother with the dresser. Like her mother would keep daily reminders of her unwanted daughter among her socks, jeans or lingerie, where she'd see it every day.

Oh, ugh. Don't wanna think about Mom's lingerie.

She also ignored Ken's section of the closet, which took up about a quarter of it. She could see the gaps where he'd removed clothes and shoes to take to Australia for the two-year stay. It was harder to spot gaps in Mom's side, because she owned a truly ridiculous amount of clothes as well as the shoes.

Banker-style cardboard boxes marched along a high shelf. Amy dragged a chair in and took them down, one at a time.

Tax returns and files about expenses on the house. Slap the lid on, heave box back onto shelf.

Next.

Bank statements. Credit card slips. Receipts. Amy had always known her mother was obscenely well-organized, but this was ridiculous. Did she keep every scrap of financial information forever?

Amy had reached a corner. She could only remove this box because she hadn't put the previous one back in place. It weighed less, she realized right away as she lifted it down, which meant it wasn't packed with dense files as the other ones had been.

She stepped carefully to the floor, set the box on the seat of the chair and lifted off the top.

For a long moment she stared without comprehension. Then an involuntary sound escaped her and she reached out.

Her blankie. *Oh, my God,* she thought, *I'd for-*

gotten it. How could I? How she'd loved this blanket—no, really more of a comforter, with batting inside. The back side was flannel, worn thin by her childish grip. The front was a cotton fabric in swirled lavender and darker purple imprinted with white horses leaping over puffs of white clouds. Some machine quilting kept the three layers together.

She lifted it out of the box and held it close, burying her face in the soft folds the way she'd done as a child. Her smile shook as she remembered the major temper tantrums she'd thrown when she couldn't find "horse blankie." How funny that she couldn't even recall when she'd lost interest in it. She'd had no idea what had ever happened to her much-loved blankie.

Mom had kept it? Amy was knocked off balance by the unimaginable.

After a minute she set it aside and took out another of her childhood treasures, a stuffed puppy that wasn't as white as it had once been. She wound up the key on the bottom. Tears dripped down her cheeks when it played the familiar tune, "(How Much Is) That Doggie in the Window?"

Oh, Mom. Had she felt anything when she packed these things away? Or had she briskly assumed Amy might want them someday when she had her own children, and never given them another thought?

There were other toys here, too, including a couple she didn't remember at all. One was a plastic rattle with tiny tooth marks in it. Hers. Finally, at the bottom of the box, were the baby book and a photograph album. Those, she decided to take downstairs to the kitchen table.

She had trouble making herself open the cover of either book or album. Seeing the contents with new eyes was going to hurt.

Baby book first. There was a time she'd thought the fact that her mother had filled it out so carefully meant she must love her daughter. By the time Amy was a teenager, she knew better; the precise entries, the school pictures glued to appropriate pages, were only another manifestation of Mom's anal personality. Give her a form to fill out, and she was a happy woman.

The details were undeniably all there.

The card from the hospital was attached to the first page. Yes, Baby Girl Nilsson had indeed weighed six pounds fourteen ounces.

Before she went further, Amy booted up her laptop and went online to a site that had a chronology of child development. Then she compared the dates Mom had noted for "first smile," "rolled over," "sat up alone" and so on with the chronology. Amy had been early each step of the way. Perhaps because she was little and wiry, she'd barely bothered with crawling, instead walking at eight months and running not much later.

She closed her eyes momentarily. How could she ever have believed she was premature?

She flipped back to the first page, where her mother had written her name, the hospital where she was born, her birth date. Amy's gaze snagged on two lines that were blank. Mother. Father.

Yet another thing she'd never noticed. A *huge* thing, given Mom's personality.

She was almost numb by now. Not entirely; a tsunami was building somewhere deep inside, ominous in its power, but it was still subterranean enough to be ignored.

There were lots of photos of her in the album, mainly, she knew, because her father—*oh, God, not my father*—had enjoyed taking pictures and had adored her.

A few included Jakob, fewer still Mom or Dad himself. Those were the ones she stared at the hardest, with eyes that burned. She didn't look like anyone else in the family. A part of her had always known that, but justified it. There was the aunt with red hair. She *did* have brown eyes, like Mom...only they weren't at all the same shade of brown as her mother's. Kids didn't always look like their parents, she had told herself.

She bore absolutely no resemblance to anyone else in her family, including her only biological relative, her mother.

The tsunami lifted, as if launching itself. She must look like *him*. The horror was more than she could hold inside. Amy shoved away from the table, staggering to her feet when the chair crashed backward. She felt filthy, contaminated, ugly. Why hadn't her mother aborted her?

But she knew that, too. Mom wasn't a regular churchgoer, but she still wore a gold cross on a fine chain around her neck. She had been raised Catholic. Abortion wouldn't have been on the table as an option.

The part of Amy that was still thinking understood what her mother had gone through, how she had reasoned. She couldn't take her disaster to parents who had been stern and strict. The only truly acceptable choice to her was marriage. So she had latched onto the first guy who came her way, slept with him, lied to him, let him think the monstrous *thing* she was going to bear was his.

And then she got lucky, because Amy was small enough that Josef hadn't guessed the baby wasn't his. But somewhere along the way he had begun to wonder.

Or had he? Amy asked herself with near-clinical detachment. Perhaps instead something had happened. Blood type would have been a dead giveaway. Amy had given blood and knew she was B positive. She was willing to bet that Mom wasn't... and neither was Josef Nilsson. Yes, that would have done it. So then came the yelling that the adults had silenced when she came into a room, the intense, hissing arguments that she could almost hear clearly through her bedroom wall at night. Only a kinder-gartener, she had pulled her covers over her head and huddled, not wanting to make out words.

No wonder the man she had believed to be her father had gradually lost interest in her! Looking back, she knew he had tried. Really, he had been kind. It was for her sake that he'd maintained the facade. But even then, at six and seven, at ten and twelve and fifteen, she had known something was wrong.

She had known that neither parent truly loved her.

And her brother Jakob sure as hell hadn't.

Oh, God, she thought in shock. He knew. He must know.

He'd endured her weekend visits, and she wasn't even his sister. No wonder he'd resented her. Despised her.

She stood in the middle of her mother's kitchen, almost catatonic. A soft, keening sound came from her throat. Her very existence felt like an abomination. She wanted to wipe herself out.

Every time her mother looked at this child born of rape, she must have felt violated all over again.

Able to move again, Amy backed away from the table that held the baby book with all those careful notations, the album filled with pictures that reinforced how *different* she was. Empty stomach or not, sickness rose inside her, pushed by the huge swell of emotions she couldn't let herself feel.

This time when she ran, it was for the shower, where she scrubbed herself over and over, not stopping even when the water ran cold.

JAKOB CIRCLED THROUGH the alley and saw Amy's small white car parked beside the garage that he assumed held Michelle's and Ken's vehicles.

So she was home.

He had started calling yesterday. Her phone rang, but he always ended up at voice mail. She ignored messages. He tried email. No response. He hadn't gotten a damn thing done at the office yesterday or today, worrying about her. By last evening, he'd been pissed. To hell with her. He'd offered his support, she didn't want it. Her privilege. No skin off his back.

That didn't keep him from trying to call his father. Who didn't answer, either.

Jakob kept remembering the way Amy stared down at the women's panties in her hand, and anger vaulted back into worry and then into something even more compelling. He was going to feel like an idiot if she was absolutely fine, didn't need him. She might have been busy, that's all, entertaining friends or working.

Feeling like an idiot was a risk he was willing to take.

He rang the doorbell and got no response. After an interval he rang it again, then started pounding. An old guy was out in the front yard next door, using hand clippers to nibble away at a hedge that was already trimmed to perfection. He straightened and glared. Jakob didn't care.

"Amy," he bellowed. "I know you're in there. Open this door."

He heard noises inside at last. Fumbling with the locks. Then the door opened a crack.

"What?" she snarled.

Oh, man. She didn't look good, even though he was seeing only a slice of her face. What he could see was wan, freckles he'd hardly known she had standing out like splotches of paint.

Jakob planted a hand on the door and pushed her inexorably backward despite her obvious alarm.

"What are you doing?" she cried in panic. "I told you, I want to be alone."

"And I've left you alone," he said grimly. "Apparently, for longer than I should have."

He slid inside the opening and felt a new jolt of shock. "You're sick."

Her glare was surly. "I am not."

He bit off an expletive. "You look like hell. Damn it, Amy…!"

Her hair, that beautiful mass of red-brown curls, was a thicket of tangles, flattened on one side, kinked on the other. Amy's eyes were huge in a face that he would swear had lost flesh in only two days. It was six in the evening and she wore wrinkled flannel pajama bottoms and a tank top that was faded and stretched out. Her arms, long and skinny, were wrapped around herself as though they were all that held her together.

The defiant stare stayed in place, but as he watched she swayed on her feet.

He swore again and reached for her. She scrambled backward.

"Don't touch me!"

Was she *afraid* of him?

"You're ready to keel over."

"I'm not. I'm fine. I'm…" She apparently derailed. Her eyes became increasingly glassy. "I'm…"

"Sick."

"I'm not! I'm fine, I'm…"

"Either sick or in shock." So what if she was afraid of him? Jakob grabbed her arm. "Where's the kitchen?"

"What?"

He made a decision and marched her toward the back of the house. She stumbled beside him but seemed to have run out of protests.

The kitchen, he saw, had been entirely remodeled at some point with white cabinets, granite countertops and a copper rack for pans. A table sat in a breakfast nook in front of French doors. He pulled out a chair and let Amy drop into it.

"When's the last time you ate?"

Her face held no comprehension. "Ate?"

Answer enough. Jakob opened and closed cupboard doors and the refrigerator until he had the ingredients for a primitive and quick menu. Soup and sandwiches. He dumped a spicy corn chowder he liked himself into a saucepan and started it heating while he assembled cheese sandwiches and heated a small frying pan to grill them.

"You can't make me eat," Amy said sulkily.

"Watch me," he told her.

"Why are you here, anyway?"

"You promised to call. I got worried." He stirred the chowder.

"I didn't want to talk to you."

"Yeah, I figured that out." A fire was burning in his belly. He kind of hoped some food would put it out. "Tough shit," he added after a moment.

Apparently that silenced her. Her head bent and she stared down at her hands, clasped childishly on her lap.

Jakob got out bowls and plates, flipped the sandwiches and stirred the soup one more time, not once looking at Amy, but aware of her with every cell in his body. He was mad again, and self-aware enough to guess it was a cover for everything else he felt.

Finally, he dished up and set her food in front of her. "You going to tell me what you want to drink, or should I decide for you?"

Her chin shot up. "Wine."

"Milk," he decided, and poured them both glasses. Thank God she didn't buy skim. He could live with two percent.

He sat down kitty-corner from her with his own sandwich and soup. Maybe it would help if they weren't looking right at each other. "Eat," he ordered her, and started in on his food. Out of the corner of his eye, he saw her stare at the food as if she didn't know what it was, then finally pick up the spoon. After some hesitant sips, she began to eat faster and faster until she was all but gobbling.

Good.

The meal settled him down some, too. Without a word he got up and set the coffeemaker to brewing, then sat again.

"Okay," he said. "Now we talk."

She'd worked up enough spirit to glare. When she opened her mouth, Jakob interrupted.

"It's not going to do you any good to say 'I don't have to.'"

"I don't understand why you care."

He fell back on the old standby. "We're family."

And finally she quit fighting. The pain in her big brown eyes was so vast, his stomach clenched.

"No," she said. "I don't think we are. And you know it, don't you?"

So, why do you care? she wanted to beg him again.

But maybe she didn't want to know. Because… he was here, and whether she was willing to admit it or not, she'd needed someone. Anyone at all.

"Tell me what you learned," he said, not addressing her accusation. There were lines on his forehead that hadn't been there. Despite the neutral tone, she thought he wasn't only here out of obligation.

Maybe she was kidding herself, but she was going with it for now.

"I'll show you," she said, after a minute. Two days ago, she had swept the manila envelope and its contents along with her baby book and the photograph album into a reusable shopping bag—Mom had a whole drawer full of them, neatly folded—and hid it at the back of the coat closet under the staircase, which she went to retrieve.

She returned to find he'd piled the dirty dishes in the sink and was pouring coffee. Amy dropped the bag with a thud in the middle of the table. She pulled out her mother's datebook.

"Cream? Sugar?" Jakob asked.

She put in her order and he brought both mugs to the table, then retook his seat. Amy shoved the datebook toward him. "I read the whole thing. You can go right to the end. It pretty much tells the whole story."

He looked down at it for a minute, as if reluctant, then opened it to the back. The pages for April, May and June were blank, of course; by then, the datebook had been entombed in the time capsule. He reached the page that held Michelle Cooper's final statement, read silently.

Amy knew what it said by heart. The part about how the old me is dead. And finally, *This is what happened to me at Wakefield College. This is what I choose to say: Steven Hardy raped me.*

Jakob muttered an obscenity and looked up, a

storm of emotions in his eyes. Anger was the only one Amy was certain she'd picked out.

"You think this—" he glanced back down at the open page of the book "—Steven Hardy is your father." The emotions had roughened his voice, but it was also astonishingly compassionate.

"Yes." The single word sounded so small, so stark. She couldn't look at him anymore. Instead she gazed, as she had done most evenings since she had moved into her mother's house, at the garden and the roses she hadn't watered since she left for eastern Washington.

"Do you have any other evidence?"

"Yes." She had to clear her throat. She pulled out the baby book. "I was born small enough that no one questioned Mom's claim that I was premature. But I went through this and compared my milestones with the standard charts. If I really was premature, I should have been behind. I wasn't. If anything, I was ahead from the very beginning. If my birth weight was evidence that I was premature, I should eventually have gained on my contemporaries, but I didn't. The truth is, all through school I was in the bottom twenty-five percent in weight. I still am. I'm skinny."

His gaze flicked over her and he nodded. "You're small-boned," he said slowly. "Slim."

She appreciated his kindness in making *skinny* sound a little more appealing.

"And then there's the family album." She opened

that next, turning pages until she found a picture taken, at a guess, not long before the divorce. All four of them were in it. She scooted the album over so he could see the picture.

He looked in silence for a long time. Without looking herself, she knew exactly what he was seeing. Not only the fact that she didn't *fit,* but also the tensions that were visible despite smiles for the camera. There was something anxious on her face, bewilderment in her eyes. The adults might be smiling, but they weren't touching. Josef's hand lay on his son's shoulder. Jakob's expression was stony. Michelle stood behind Amy, but wasn't touching her, either. There was a distinct distance between the two children, too. Body language all but shouted the news that this family was splintering.

"Not a good moment in our lives," Jakob observed at last.

"Funny, I remember looking at the picture and not seeing that. I think I've been guilty of a lot of self-deception."

"Maybe." He waited until she had to turn her head and meet his eyes, closer to gray right now than blue. "But you don't *know,* do you?"

"I do," she said sharply.

"You're still guessing."

She narrowed her eyes. "But you already knew, didn't you?"

He hesitated. "No. I heard things that made me

wonder, that's all. Remember, I wasn't very old. Mostly, I put what I heard out of my mind."

The slightest change of intonation in his voice there at the end suggested he was lying, although she didn't know why he'd bother. After a minute, though, she nodded, as if in acceptance.

"You were only eight. No, I guess nine at the end."

"Their yelling freaked me out."

"Me, too," she admitted. "I pulled the covers over my head at night. Sometimes the pillow, too, when they got especially loud. I knew I didn't want to hear what they were saying. I was so scared."

Jakob laid a hand atop hers on the table. His was big and warm and comforting. She stared down at it until, to her disappointment, he removed it.

"I didn't like your mother," he said gruffly, "but change is always scary for kids. I felt safe when we were a family. Sometimes I worried Dad would leave me behind if he moved out."

"Like he did me." Amy swallowed. "I wanted to go with him so bad."

"I think he believed your mother needed you, that she loved you."

She snorted. Not with a lot of authority, but still… "Sure. Right. Get real. He didn't want me, because I wasn't his kid. And yes, he was nice enough to keep pretending for my sake, but even then I could tell. He didn't look at me the same. I knew, but I didn't want to know. Now, well…" Amy shrugged. "I guess denial only takes you so far."

Jakob sat there frowning at her. "What have you been doing the past two days? Hiding out?"

She tried a smile, even if it didn't come off very well. "Yeah, I suppose. I felt…" A huge lump clogged her throat. *Felt* was past tense. *Feel. I feel.* "Sick," she finally acknowledged. "I always knew that Mom…" She gave something like a laugh. "I was going to say, Mom didn't love me. But it was worse than that. Especially when I was little. It was as if she couldn't stand to touch me. She'd shy away from me if I tried to cuddle. I learned not to try." *Oh, that sounds pathetic.* She managed a shrug. "It's not like I didn't survive. Maybe I'm tougher because she wasn't touchy-feely. In all honesty, I don't think she would have been even if I'd been a planned pregnancy. Her parents were rigid and cold."

Jakob nodded. She'd forgotten that he had, of course, met them.

She sighed. "I'll bet *they* didn't do a lot of cuddling, either."

Jakob's expression was troubled. Looking at him, she felt as if a band was tightening around her chest. He was a really beautiful man, with that lean face and strong, prominent bones. His hair was disheveled, even spiky tonight. It seemed darker in this light, but the hint of stubble on his jaw glinted gold. As a child, she had so wanted them to be close. She'd taken comfort in knowing he was her brother, that however funny she looked she still shared his blood. Maybe if she had kids of her own, the Scandinavian genes would reassert themselves. *Nope,* she thought sadly, *no such genes here.* Hers were…who knew?

"You never suspected?" he asked. "Your mother never said anything?"

"Like, by the way, your *real* father is this creep who raped me when I was only nineteen?"

"Uh…I was thinking more along the lines of saying that she was pregnant already when she met my dad, but he's a good guy who took responsibility for you."

Amy huffed out another laugh. "One of the things she wrote in that diary—" she nodded toward the book that still lay open to the final, devastating passage "—is that she didn't ever want to think about what happened again. Then she said, and I quote, 'But I can't completely pretend, can I?' And she was right, because she was stuck with me. A living, breathing manifestation of the worst thing that ever happened to her."

Jakob visibly winced.

"Hard to put it all out of your mind once you realize you're pregnant," she continued, her tone hard. "Did you know Mom was raised Catholic? I think we can assume if she hadn't been, I wouldn't have seen the light of day."

He sat forward abruptly. "Jesus, Amy, don't talk like that."

"I've had two days to think about it. Wouldn't most women who had been raped want to abort the baby?" She saw that he couldn't deny her conclusion. "But Mom was stuck between a rock and a hard place. Specifically, her religion and her parents. Your dad gave her an out."

He closed his eyes and scrubbed a hand over his face. He looked older when he was done. "No wonder he was so angry."

"No kidding."

"I tried to call him last night. When I hadn't heard from you. He hasn't returned my call yet."

"You were going to ask him if he knew what was in the time capsule?"

"Yeah." Jakob grimaced. "I was going to ask him if you were his kid."

"I suppose the panties raised a few questions in your mind."

"You could say that." His eyebrows drew together. "DNA testing wasn't available that long ago, was it? Did she say what she was thinking?"

"Only that she never washed them because she couldn't bear to touch them. She says in there that they and the diary were a sort of funeral offering. That the woman—girl—she'd been was dead."

They were both quiet for a minute after that.

Jakob let out a long sigh. "You know what you have to do, don't you, Amy?"

She gazed at him in alarm. "What do you mean?"

"You have to talk to your mother. We could be completely wrong about all of this. The pieces could fit together in a way you're not seeing at all."

"You know I'm not wrong."

"That doesn't mean you should sweep it all under the rug, even if that's what she did. You won't be able to come to terms with it until you hear her side of what happened, why she made the decisions she did."

Amy crossed her arms protectively. "What makes you think she won't keep lying to me?"

"Why would she? You're not a child anymore. I imagine she kept the secret partly, or even mostly, for your sake. You're in your thirties now, and it's tough to take in. Imagine if you'd found all this out when you were sixteen."

Amy shivered a little. Of course he was right, but that didn't mean she wasn't still mad at her mother. Which wasn't the worst part, she realized. Most painful was the fact that, as a woman, she understood and sympathized with her mother. A second shiver was more of a shudder as she thought about having to bear a child of rape, keep her, raise her, pretend to love her.

Could I?

She honestly didn't know.

"I'll call her once I've absorbed all this."

Jakob shook his head, his expression implacable.

"Nope. We'll figure out the time difference and you'll call her tonight, while I'm here."

"What?" she snarled. "You think I'll collapse if I don't have you here to support me?"

He actually had the nerve to smile. "No, I think you won't do it at all."

"My privilege."

"I want to know, too," he said simply.

She should have asked why. What difference did it make to him? Did he want permission to go back to ignoring her?

But she couldn't do it. Some veiled emotion in his eyes made her uneasy. Did he suspect some other truth? If so, she couldn't deal with it.

Anyway, maybe he was right. She *should* demand answers now, while the tide of anger still carried her. Wimping out wasn't her style. She wasn't about to start now.

"Fine," she snapped. "I'll do it. But not because you say I have to."

He chuckled, deepening the creases in his cheeks.

Amy wanted to punch him.

CHAPTER FOUR

JAKOB'S PHONE RANG only a minute after he and Amy had finished calculating the time difference with Sydney, Australia. He looked at the number then answered.

"Dad."

Posture having gone rigid, Amy closed her laptop.

"Hope you were calling to tell me you talked your sister out of that time capsule nonsense," his father boomed in the voice that served him well on job sites.

Jakob winced. "Hold on, Dad." He pressed the phone to his belly and said quietly to Amy, "Do you want to talk to him? I can put this on speaker and tell him I'm with you."

"Well, that would be cozy." Snarky seemed to be her fallback mode, but he saw the anxiety in her eyes when she lifted her head. "Call me a coward, but I don't think I'm ready to talk to him. I know I'll have to eventually, but…not now."

"All right. You can eavesdrop if you want," he offered, even though he didn't much like the idea of luring his dad into confidences he didn't know were being overheard.

She shook her head and started past him. "I need to shower."

"Amy." He said her name softly, but she stopped, her back to him. "Ask me if you want to know what he says. I won't keep secrets from you."

She nodded jerkily and kept going.

Swearing under his breath, Jakob lifted the phone back to his ear. "Dad?"

"Who was that? Did I get you at a bad time?"

"No, this is fine. A woman. She's, uh, going to take a shower."

"Lady friend?" His father sounded pleased. "You haven't mentioned one recently."

Jakob didn't say, *That would be because there hasn't been one in a while*, even though it was the truth. He liked sex as well as the next guy, but with the big four-oh looming on the horizon, he'd begun to tire of the effort it took to get some. Dating was mostly a huge waste of time.

He also didn't say, *Nope, I'm with Amy. She's upstairs stripping and getting in the shower right now.* He didn't even want to *think* about that, never mind say it aloud.

"No, it's been a while." Vague was good, he congratulated himself. "And no, I didn't head Amy off. In fact, I went with her, spent the weekend in Frenchman Lake."

Deafening silence.

He made his voice hard. As a businessman, he had it down to a fine art. "You knew what was in that goddamned time capsule, didn't you, Dad?"

"Why the hell are you taking that tone with me?" Josef blustered. "How would I know?"

"There was a reason you didn't want her to go. Tell me what you know."

Another pause. "What was in the capsule?"

"You tell me first."

His father muttered something Jakob took for profanities. "I don't know what she put in there. She said some cryptic things about it, that's all. Stuff about how in fifty years, the Wakefield College people would find out there was a dead body in there. Made no sense, but I got to say, it made me nervous."

"There were no bodies, but maybe the next best thing." Jakob stared out the French doors at an idyllic garden, golden in the evening light and too pretty for his current mood. "I remember your fights with Michelle. I heard you accusing her of trapping you."

"You were a kid. Why would you remember anything like that?"

He turned his back on the garden and took a few steps into the kitchen, where he could lean a hip against the counter. "Be straight with me, Dad."

After a long silence, Josef said, "I don't want Amy to know any of this."

"The horses are already out, Dad. Too late."

He could hear his father breathing. "Oh, hell," Josef said finally.

"So you know?" That enraged Jakob. Hadn't it occurred to either his father or Michelle that a secret like this had the potential to be more destructive than the truth ever would have been?

"All I know is, Amy isn't mine."

Jakob found himself reeling even though he didn't move a muscle. All these years, and now he knew.

She's not my sister.

The part that stunned him, and yet didn't, was that his primary emotion was relief. Relief so potent, it poured through him like a drug injected in his veins.

"You're sure?"

"I'm sure," Josef said gruffly. "She fell off the monkey bars at school. Had what turned out to be a mild concussion, but she also bled like crazy from a cut on the head and her nose, too. At the hospital they checked her blood type. I knew her mother's and I know mine. Amy doesn't have either."

Well, that seemed definitive.

Not my sister. Not my sister.

The relief could have been a full chorus singing, full-throated. He staggered back to the table and sank onto a chair.

"Why didn't you ever tell me?"

"Because I couldn't tell her." His father cleared his throat. "She's a sweet girl. She didn't deserve to find out something like that. I love Amy. As far as I'm concerned, she's my daughter."

"You didn't trust me."

"When you were a kid? Hell, no!"

"As an adult?" Jakob kneaded the back of his neck.

"You didn't have anything to do with her. What difference did it make?"

A grunt escaped him. For the first time ever, he faced his own truth. From the time she was twelve or so and getting a figure, he had always felt things for Amy that were mind-blowingly inappropriate for a brother to feel. He'd been pretty sure she wasn't his sister—but not a hundred percent. What if the sprite he was lusting for *was* his half sister? The horror and guilt had just about killed him.

Right this minute, it was his father he would have liked to kill.

He unclenched his teeth. "I always suspected. It mattered, Dad. My suspicions got in the way of any kind of relationship we might have had."

And what kind of relationship would that *have been?* an inner voice taunted him. He ignored it.

The shower upstairs had shut off some time ago although he hadn't yet heard her footsteps on the stairs. "I've got to go," he said to his father.

"Like hell you do! What was in the time capsule?"

"I think it's Amy's right to tell you or not. It's

not good, though, I'll say that much. She's having a hard time dealing with it."

A pause extended. "Will you be seeing her?"

"Yeah." Any minute.

"Tell her I love her. I always have."

Jakob felt himself relax infinitesimally. That helped. It definitely helped. "Okay, Dad," he said. "I'll do that."

He didn't hear her coming at all. The first he knew, he caught a hint of movement out of the corner of his eye and there she was in the doorway.

She stared at him defiantly as she walked across the kitchen. Jakob was struck by how stiff she was. Usually she was as light as air, hardly seeming to touch the ground. It occurred to him that he never had been able to count on hearing her approach.

"He's gone?"

The phone lay in front of him on the table. She was looking at him, not the phone.

"Yeah."

"Are you going to tell me what he said?"

"I told you I would."

The relief had metamorphosed into something else. Jakob had no idea what he was feeling now. All he knew was that, for the first time in his life, he was letting himself fully see her as a woman. As such, he was almost sorry she'd showered and changed out of the thin tank top and low-slung pajama bottoms into jeans and a sacky sweatshirt. The jeans did a heck of a job molding hips that weren't quite boyish, though. And he realized that, though he hadn't consciously noticed earlier, when he pushed his way into the house, he had definitely been aware of her breasts. They weren't large, but he'd been able to make out their shape just fine. He imagined them nestled in the palms of his hands and was damn glad he was sitting down, because he was getting aroused.

Guilt jabbed, but he stomped on it. *Not my sister.* He couldn't help wondering if the seismic shift had fully hit her yet, and if so what the realization meant to her.

Oh, hell, what was he thinking? She was dealing with her mother's lies, with his father's lies, with the knowledge that she was very likely the product of rape, and he was rejoicing because he didn't have to feel guilty anymore for wanting her.

What she needed right now was a friend. A brother. The understanding sobered him. That might be all she'd ever want from him. If it was, he would give her what she needed. There were too many years when he'd hurt her as much or more than Michelle and his dad had. He owed her.

"Sit."

She sat, but indignantly. "I'm not a dog."

His grin came despite his plunge in mood. "No, you're not."

Her spine didn't touch the back of the chair. Her neck stretched so long it had to hurt, and that pointy chin thrust out. "So?"

"He found out you weren't his when you fell off the bars at school. I'd kind of forgotten about that."

She frowned. "I knocked myself out."

"And bled. A lot, according to Dad. I don't know if they were thinking transfusion or what, but they checked your blood type."

Amy compressed her lips. "I thought it might be something like that," she said after a minute.

"According to him, that's all he knows. Your mother never admitted anything to him. Maybe if she'd told him, they could have patched the marriage together."

"I can't imagine. Finding out he'd been used like that? It would be hard to get past it."

He gave a noncommittal grunt. Yes. No. Depended on how much a man loved a woman. Speaking of…

"He said when I saw you to tell you that he loves you. Always did."

She made a small, pained sound. For the first time, she bowed her head and seemed to be fighting for control. Finally she nodded. Acknowledgment, or acceptance? Jakob couldn't tell.

"You really don't have to stay, you know." She looked at him again, her eyes dark, the gold highlights subdued. "You've done what you came to do. I've crawled out of my depression. I've eaten, showered, gotten dressed and my resolve is solid. I'll call Mom tonight. I promise."

"And I'm going to be here when you do." He

wasn't going to let her drive him away. "If you don't want me to listen in, I won't. That's your choice. But when the call is over, you shouldn't have to be alone."

She mumbled something.

"What?"

The chin came up again. The defiance was back in her eyes. "I said, I'm used to doing things alone."

"Maybe so." He held out a hand. "But this time, you don't have to."

Her stare lowered to his hand as if it was the snake in the Garden of Eden. Tempting, but also terrifying.

They'd touched so rarely. He waited to see what choice she would make.

O_H, GOD. C_URLED on one end of the sofa in the living room, Amy listened to the first ring. The second. Apprehension had her in a vise. *Ring.* Had they screwed up their time calculations? Or Mom and Ken could have gone out and Mom forgotten her phone. She could be outside gardening. Although wasn't it winter there? Did that mean days were short? Fifth ring.

Jakob lounged in an armchair, feet stacked on the coffee table, and watched her.

"Hello? Amy?"

Her breath left her in a whoosh. "Mom?" She sounded strangled.

Jakob put his feet on the floor and sat up.

"My goodness. I had to run for the phone. I didn't expect to hear from you. Is something wrong?" Her mother sounded her usual crisp self, perhaps mildly anxious. God forbid Amy had to report that the house had burned down.

It was weird knowing she was half a world away, in an entirely different hemisphere, yet the phone reception was so clear they might have been calling across town.

"In a way," Amy heard herself say. "Something came in the mail from Wakefield College."

There was a very brief pause. "From where?"

"You remember the earthquake in eastern Washington that happened just before you left? It damaged a building on the Wakefield campus. The time capsule was in the foundation."

Jakob leaned forward now, his elbows resting on his thighs, his eyes keen on her.

Her mother didn't say a word. Amy felt compelled to fill the silence.

"The college decided to open the capsule instead of putting it in the foundation of the replacement building. They made an event of it. I thought it would be interesting to go."

"You surely didn't open something so private." Shock altered her voice to one that was unrecognizable.

"I didn't expect it to be so private. Other alums were holding readings on the lawn and laughing at the short stories they thought were so profound when they were twenty years old. They didn't know *my* mother buried her young self in that capsule."

The hitch of breath might almost have been a sob. "You had no right!"

"To think I might like to know my mother, a woman who is a complete mystery to me?" Amy hadn't known she could be so cutting. She made herself stop and breathe raggedly. "Steven Hardy is my father, isn't he? Not…" *Dad* was the word that froze on her tongue. "Not Josef."

"That's a terrible thing to say! What happened to me doesn't have anything to do with you," her mother exclaimed. "You were premature, that's all."

Anger carried Amy. Anger, and Jakob's steadfast, calm presence.

"You've lied to me all my life and you're still lying. Why bother now?"

She found herself listening to silence. "Mom?" Her mouth fell open. "She hung up on me."

Jakob swore. His eyes were intensely, vividly alive. She couldn't look away from him as she set down the phone. Amy was stunned, although she didn't quite know why. How foolish to have expected her mother, of all people, to meekly surrender and admit to the sins of the past.

"Give her time," Jakob said. "You hit her pretty hard."

Amy laughed because she refused to cry. "*I* hit *her* hard? What was I supposed to do, say 'Mommy, is there anything you'd like to tell me?'"

The phone rang. She jerked and looked down at it. Oh, God, it was her mother's number. She hesitated, then reached for it.

"Mom?"

"I never wanted you to know," she said so low it was barely intelligible. "I tried not to remember."

"But you couldn't help it, could you?" Amy's bitterness bled into her voice. "Every time you looked at me, you remembered."

"That's not true!"

"It is true." She sounded hard; wished she felt the same. "I could always tell. I just didn't know why."

"You're my daughter," her mother whispered.

"I'm also *his* daughter."

"No! You're not. Never. Josef has been a good father to you."

"He was," Amy agreed, "until he discovered I wasn't really his. Then he changed. You know he did."

"He loves you."

Wasn't that telling? Not once had her mother said, I *love you.*

"I'm surprised he doesn't hate me, given the way you used him."

Silence was her answer. Story of her life.

"Did you ever tell my *real* father that you were pregnant?"

"He's not your father!" her mother snapped. "Not in any sense of the word. And of course I didn't tell him. I never spoke to him again. I never wanted to see him again."

Amy disregarded the faint softening she couldn't help feeling. She understood, oh, she did, but forgiveness was something else again.

Throat choked, she said nothing.

"You aren't thinking…?" her mother said, her horror stark. "Promise me you won't approach him! Swear!"

The terrible desire to lash out overcame Amy. "Don't you think that's my decision?" she said, almost gently but knowing the rage wasn't hidden.

One push of the button, and her mother was gone. *My turn.* Amy turned off her phone. Her hands were shaking, she saw with distant surprise. She couldn't bring herself to look at Jakob.

"That was petty," she mumbled.

"No."

She blinked and lifted her head. His face was carved with lines of concern. "I was trying to hurt her."

"I know. But what you said was also true. Whether you ever approach this Hardy or not *is* your call, not hers."

"I'm not really thinking about doing that."

"No, I don't suppose you are yet." His expression changed with startling abruptness and he rose to his feet, circling the coffee table swiftly to sink onto the sofa beside her and wrap her in his arms. That was the moment Amy realized the face she pressed to his chest was wet with tears. She was crying and hadn't even realized. *I am such a mess*.

But maybe, for once, she had an excuse. Amy let herself lean on Jakob, clutch his T-shirt in both hands and weep, taking comfort from the heat and strength of his big body. The fact that he wanted to hold her was a miracle. She wouldn't question it, not now. He was here when she needed him.

My brother.

Except, of course, he wasn't. The reminder swirled in her head, knowledge confusing her at a moment when he was acting like her brother in a way he never had before. Something else to think about later.

He was rocking her slightly. She felt his hand stroking her hair. Probably, she thought on a weird bubble of amusement, the way he'd have soothed a frightened dog. She'd have to ask him if he had one.

She didn't know how long she cried, but eventually she ran dry. Some of the pain inside had washed away, leaving…nothing. Cautiously she poked around internally and decided that she was numb. Anesthetized.

Then she expanded her senses to become aware that Jakob had propped himself in the corner formed by the back and arm of the sofa and had stretched out his legs so that she could all but lie on top of him. Now his hand moved in circles on her back. His fingertips gently kneaded. She thought that must be his bristly jaw pressed to the top of her head. She could hear the deep, slow beat of his heart.

Amy sniffed, wiped her nose on the soft fabric of his shirt and began to separate herself from him. Either he was reluctant to let her go or it took him a moment to realize what she was doing, because his arms tightened before finally loosening. She sat all the way up and awkwardly scooted away from him.

"Better?"

She made a face, but also took stock. "I guess I am," she said with mild surprise. "Um…I think I'd better go do some repairs."

Cold water could only accomplish so much, she found. A few minutes later, she gazed at herself in the mirror. Ugh. With her redhead's skin, she was not an attractive crier. Her eyes were so puffy, they could barely be seen through slits, and she'd acquired some hideous, uneven red blotches. At least she'd scraped the damp tendrils of hair off her face and brushed the whole mess back into a ponytail. Short of hiding in here for the next hour, there wasn't much she could do but go out and face Jakob, though. And, hey, it wasn't as if he hadn't already seen this face.

He wasn't in the living room, she discovered. The sound of a cupboard door opening and closing led her to the kitchen. The teakettle was already murmuring. She saw him rip open a couple of packets and dump the powder into two mugs.

"Cocoa?"

He turned to face her, giving her a quick, hard scan. "Found it in the cupboard."

"It's not mine. I think Mom or Ken left it."

He shrugged. "It seemed appropriate. Neither of us need caffeine at this time of night."

She was embarrassed by the wet spots on his royal blue T-shirt. "You're soaked."

He glanced down. "A few tears won't hurt anything."

"Some of that is probably snot," she said, chagrined.

Jakob laughed quietly. "Yeah, I kind of guessed. Snot never hurt anything, either."

"I suppose not." This conversation felt unbelievably weird.

The kettle worked up to a whistle and he poured boiling water into the mugs then carried them to the table. Amy sidled past him and sat down. She inhaled and was surprised at how good the cocoa smelled. She had a suspicion her reaction didn't have as much to do with taste as it did memories.

"Mom used to put a marshmallow on it."

"I didn't find any."

"I never actually liked marshmallows." She frowned. "Except on cocoa, I guess."

He nodded, quite seriously. "On cocoa and s'mores."

"Oh, boy. I haven't had a s'more since I went to summer camp. I couldn't have been more than eight or nine."

"I still carry the ingredients when I backpack." Jakob grinned. "I have a sweet tooth."

"I remember." That wasn't all she remembered. She scowled at him. "Right before the divorce was the first time I got to go trick-or-treating. You stole part of my candy."

His eyes crinkled with amusement. "To save you from getting sick. You were too little to eat that much."

"What a big heart for an eight-year-old boy."

A smile playing on his mouth, he pressed an open hand to his chest. "That was me."

"I'm surprised you didn't steal my whole bucket and tell everyone I didn't remember where I'd hid it."

He laughed out loud. "Crossed my mind, but Dad would have made me split mine with you."

"You were a creep, you know?" So, okay, she was laughing, too, which was another thing that felt weird given everything happening inside her.

His smile vanished as if she'd turned off a light switch. "Yeah." He cleared his throat. "I know I was."

Amy eyed him warily. "It was…nice of you to stay tonight."

"Pure nosiness."

"Sure."

They sipped in silence for a few minutes. It was very late now. Maybe the cocoa had a tranquilizing effect or the effect of all those tears was catching up with her, because Amy began to feel sleepy. Time to wonder if Jakob intended to go home at all.

"You can stay if you want. The sheets on Mom and Ken's bed are clean."

"All right," he said slowly. "If you're okay with it."

"Why wouldn't I be?"

Some shadow slid through his eyes, passing too quickly for her to identify. "No reason." He paused. "Don't suppose you're ready to talk about any of this."

She shook her head. "I think I'm going to conk out. Maybe tomorrow."

Jakob nodded, pushed his chair back and took their empty mugs to the sink. "If you want to go on, I'll make sure the house is locked up and turn out lights."

"Okay." Wow, she didn't know what had happened, but it was all she could do to plod toward the staircase. Her feet felt encased in cement blocks as she climbed the steps. She was doing well to brush her teeth and loosely braid her hair, get into clean pajamas and fall into bed. Her eyelids were so heavy, switching off the lamp seemed like too much trouble.

She was almost asleep when she felt a soft touch on her cheek—fingertips?—then heard a quiet "Good night," and knew even through closed eyelids that the room was plunged into darkness.

Amy hugged the gentleness of the touch to her as she sank into oblivion.

SLEEP ELUDED JAKOB. The damn mattress was too soft, for one thing. He liked his to be hard. A faint scent seemed to cling to the bedding, too, one that he finally realized summoned memories of Michelle.

Funny, you'd think he'd have called her "Mommy" when he was little. She was in his earliest memories. Maybe she'd insisted on "Michelle." That part, he didn't recall. Only that he'd never even thought of her as his mother.

Looking back, he wanted to say she was a cold bitch, but had to amend the thought right away. Not a bitch, but the cold part was definite. She was always…pleasant. Brisk, efficient. He'd had warmer encounters with couriers who'd raced into the office to throw a package at him than he ever had with his stepmother. She did what she had to do—he had memories of her packing his school lunches, putting dinner on the table, even driving him places like Little League practice. She didn't go to parent-teacher conferences, though, or school open houses. It was more as if she was perfectly willing to deal with him as part of the everyday organization of the household, but not to accept him on any personal level.

He grunted. There never had been any possibility of the little boy he'd been feeling anything but resentment for the baby girl who had cast him into the shade. Thinking back, he couldn't believe his father could have been so oblivious to his small son's misery.

Jakob tensed. Had he heard a sound from across the hall? No surprise if Amy had a nightmare tonight. But he lay rigid for some time, listening, and didn't hear anything else. He must have imagined it.

Letting his muscles go loose, he speculated on what effect all this was going to have on her. Was she secure enough to shake it off, realize it was history and really had nothing to do with the woman she had made herself into? He was undecided. She was no weakling, that was for sure. Her instinct was to come out fighting. He was surprised, in a way, that she'd let her mother's revelations hit her so hard she'd sunk into a depression these past couple of days.

Yeah, making any kind of assumptions about Amy was dumb. He didn't really know her, did he? Maybe she was emotionally all over the map. It could be that what he thought of as her feistiness was something only he brought out in her. He'd given her enough reason over the years to have earned her hostility.

Brooding, he changed his mind. Of course he knew her. The little girl she'd been, anyway. Lonely, he saw in retrospect, but also spirited. One memory stuck in his head. She'd gotten in a scratching, clawing, hissing fight in kindergarten. Her mother wasn't available to pick her up, so Dad had done it. Jakob heard about it and sneaked upstairs, where she was confined to her bedroom. A vivid scratch had marred her cheek and her lower lip had poked out so far he thought at first it was swollen. There might have been a glint of tears in her eyes, but even then she had too much pride to let them fall.

That got him speculating on how often she *had* let herself cry over the years.

When their parents split up? Yeah, probably. But he was guessing it wasn't the norm for her. She'd seemed too appalled when she went stiff in his arms tonight. Or maybe it wasn't the tears—maybe it was discovering herself in her hated half brother's embrace that had horrified her.

Not her half brother. No blood relation at all.

Thank God. Not that he had any concrete plans to act on their new status as two single, unrelated adults. It would be unbelievably awkward. No, that overwhelming relief had more to do with the past, with the awareness of her he'd never quite been able to suppress. Yes, he'd done his best to shut it down, but Jakob didn't like to imagine what he'd be feeling right now if he had found out she was, in fact, biologically his sister. He didn't know if he'd ever have been able to look himself in the mirror again. He'd had a hard enough time over the years dealing with the ugliness of those moments when he'd noticed her in a way he shouldn't.

With a groan, he laid his forearm over his eyes. At this rate, he wasn't going to get any sleep at all tonight.

AMY OPENED HER eyes and stared without comprehension at the digital clock beside her bed. Did it really read 11:38? Night? Morning?

Morning, of course—the blinds couldn't entirely block the sunlight.

And…did she smell *bacon?*

A door seemed to open in her head and remembrance flooded in. Jakob pushing his way into the house, bullying her into eating, telling her straight out what his father had said, holding her without complaint when she cried.

Jakob, who had slept across the hall from her.

Of course he would have wanted to have breakfast before he left for work—or for home to shower and change first—but she was quite certain she hadn't had any bacon in the house. She didn't eat much meat, and never bothered with anything but cereal or occasionally toast for breakfast.

Uh-huh, and why did she care how he came by the bacon?

How do I feel?

Amy cautiously moved her arms and legs at the same time as she made herself think about things her mother said, things she said.

She'd meant every one of them.

My father is a man who raped my mother.

Oddly enough, the knowledge didn't feel as terrible today as it had when she first read her mother's diary. It seemed to have settled into her, become part of her, the marrow of her bones.

Because it matched how she'd always felt about herself? If even her own parents couldn't love her, how could she help but know there was something dreadfully wrong with her? Now she had her answer. *He* was what was wrong with her.

Amy found she still didn't want to think about him. Her mother, the man she'd thought was her father, Jakob… They gave her enough to brood about.

Skipping the shower, she decided on yellow yoga pants and a thigh-length, thin orange top with a scooped neck low enough to allow it to slip off one shoulder. Barefoot, she padded downstairs. Even though Jakob was long gone, there was comfort in knowing he had spent the night. Maybe they could really be friends. Who'd have ever dreamed?

Two feet into the kitchen, she stopped abruptly. Jakob sat at the table, a laptop in front of him. The French doors were open wide behind him. He looked up, smiling.

"You're still here." Oh, brilliant.

"I'm here again," he corrected her. "Went home to shower and get out of the snot-soaked T-shirt. Plus, you didn't have much food in the house."

She looked at the dishes in the sink. "You mean, I didn't have bacon and eggs."

"Or bread."

Oh, yeah. "I guess I'm overdue for a shop." Something she'd intended to do as soon as they got back from Frenchman Lake, but had forgotten along with her appetite.

Jakob pushed back from the table. "Pour yourself some coffee. I'll make breakfast for you."

"I usually have cereal."

"Dry? We finished the milk last night."

"That's your fault. I wanted wine," she mumbled, sulky.

He only laughed. "Scrambled or over easy?"

"Um…scrambled, I guess."

Somehow she found herself planted in front of a plate that held a pile of fluffy scrambled eggs, several strips of bacon and two slices of some kind of whole grain toast with jam she was pretty sure hadn't come out of her refrigerator, either.

"I can't possibly eat all this," Amy argued, but started in.

Having poured himself a fresh cup of coffee and resumed his seat, Jakob only smiled. He seemed to be focused on his laptop, which let her eat without self-consciousness. To her astonishment, she polished off the entire plateful of food.

"Good girl," he said, and she realized he'd been watching after all. "How are you this morning?"

She really had to think about that. "I don't know," she finally admitted. "Why aren't you at work? Surely Mr. CEO is expected to show his face at the office most days."

"Mr. President, actually." His mouth had barely quirked, but the smile sounded in his voice. "As such, I can take time off when it pleases me."

She met his eyes, which she couldn't help noticing were quite startlingly blue this morning. "I'm not suicidal, if that's what you're worried about."

"Never crossed my mind."

"You're sure?" It hadn't occurred to her, but why else had he pushed his way in last evening? "You didn't have an attack of guilt because you imagined that offering to go with me to Frenchman Lake means you encouraged me?"

His eyebrows rose. "That never crossed my mind, either."

"If you weren't encouraging me, why *did* you offer to go?" Gee whiz, maybe she should have asked that question *before* she accepted his offer. Hindsight was a wonderful thing.

He stared at her for an unnerving length of time. A muscle twitched on one side of his jaw. "I felt… protective," he said at last, very slowly, as if he was as disturbed by his answer as she was.

"Protective," she repeated. Astonishment and an emotion that felt like wonder so shook her, she grabbed for the more familiar anger. "Was it like the time you locked me out of the house just when it was getting dark and lied and told Mom and Dad I was upstairs in my bedroom?"

Guilt altered his expression. "You remember that?"

"Yes!"

"Is it too late to say I'm sorry?"

"Yes!" Fuming, she snatched up her dishes. "Just for your information, I'm fine. I don't need a baby-sitter, okay? Feel free to go home."

He watched her stomp over and deposit the dishes with a clatter on the counter beside the sink.

"So maybe I do feel guilty. So guilty I'm going to dig in my heels and stay."

"Stay?" She whirled to face him. "Stay how long?"

"I don't know." He hesitated. "I packed a bag. Maybe for a day or two."

"Why?" It came out as a whisper.

"Because I think you need to talk." He frowned, once again looking discomfited. "So we can get to know each other." His eyes searched hers. "Don't you want that, Amy?"

Her mouth opened and closed. She discovered she could not tell a lie. Not now, not to him. So she opened the dishwasher and began loading it.

CHAPTER FIVE

FOR THE FIRST couple of hours, she did her damndest to pretend he wasn't there. Jakob could tell he'd shaken her.

Truth was, he was a little unsettled by his own behavior. What was going on here? If she wasn't his sister and he wasn't going to hit on her, what *was* he doing?

Being a friend, he decided, falling back on his belief that he owed her. Of course, it was a little more complicated than that. Nosiness definitely played a part. This was her history, but it was his, too. Dad and Michelle hadn't only lied to Amy, they'd lied to him, as well. He found himself so enraged when he thought of his father, he knew he was in no frame of mind to talk to him again right now. He'd already deleted a couple of messages without even listening to them.

He worked at the kitchen table, scrutinizing sales figures on products he was considering replacing, keeping an ear cocked for Amy, who had disappeared into the small home office at the other back corner of the house. She had announced that she had to work, and disappeared.

Midafternoon, he got hungry. "I'm going to make a sandwich," he called. "You want one?"

"No." Silence. "Thank you," she added grudgingly.

He grinned, guessing what an effort it was taking for her to be polite to him, the enemy.

His hands paused in the act of taking bread from the wrapper. Did Amy still think of him that way? As her enemy? He hoped not. He was almost sure she didn't. She had confided in him, and she wouldn't have done that if she truly detested him, would she?

He laid on the vegetables atop slices of turkey and Havarti, and washed down the sandwich with a dark, local brew he'd recently discovered. It felt decadent to feel free to have a beer in the middle of the day. He might order one or a glass of wine during a business lunch when everyone else did, but then he'd do little more than take a few sips. He didn't like to cloud his thinking.

The slice of the tiramisu cheesecake he'd picked up at a bakery on his way back to Amy's went down just fine, too. It was so good, in fact, he raised his voice again. "I have a cheesecake."

She didn't answer. He shrugged and was putting it back in the refrigerator when she appeared.

"What kind?"

He told her.

"I love cheesecake."

Jakob put a slice on a plate and handed it to her. She grabbed a fork from the drawer, hesitated, and then all but stomped over to the table, where she plopped down in what he was coming to think of as "her" place.

"What are you working on?"

He explained. "I'm looking at items for spring. We solidified stock for winter long since. I'm considering dropping a line of lighter-weight sleeping bags, for example, in favor of these down ones in brighter colors." He turned the computer to show her one illustrated with a shell in sunshine yellow with darker swirls. "Nothing wrong with the ones we carried, but sales are falling and the manufacturer is sticking to the traditional navy, forest-green, red for variety. Our goal is to attract younger buyers. They want something more exciting."

"I thought Boulder River Sports Company catered to the back-to-nature crowd. I'd think they want colors that would blend in."

He felt a ridiculous smile growing on his face. "How do you know who we cater to? Have you visited one of my stores?"

"The one in Seattle." Her glance was almost shy. "The one here in Portland, too."

"You were curious," he said, delighted.

Her chin came up. "You were, too."

"I admitted I was." He filed away the knowledge that she'd followed his career, just as he'd followed hers, then answered her question. "You're right. Mechanized sports aren't our thing. We don't carry alpine ski equipment or snowboards, we're not going for snowmobilers. We're after hikers, climbers, runners, Nordic skiers, windsurfers, people who are careful to respect nature even as they enjoy it. Doesn't mean they're stodgy or don't want to be stylish."

Amy nodded. "I've actually bought some clothes from you when I found them on sale."

"Yeah?" He pushed the laptop back and crossed his arms on the table. "What brands did you buy?"

"Mr. President goes into product survey mode."

"Something like that." He smiled openly and thought she might be blushing a little.

"Mountain Hardware, prAna, Horny Toad. Those were all new brands to me. Um, Moving Comfort."

He guessed from the deepening color in her cheeks that she'd bought sports bras from Boulder River. Moving Comfort was a popular brand. From the list, it was obvious she'd shopped Boulder River more than once or twice, too.

"What draws you?"

She frowned, taking his question seriously, which he liked. "I prefer stretchy. Fabric that moves. Colorful. For winter I like hoodies. Oh, and thumb holes in long sleeves, when I can find them." She made a face. "Surely you don't decide what women's clothes your stores will carry."

"I have buyers, but I approve every product,"

Jakob said flatly. "I keep an eye on the clothing lines to make sure they don't deviate too much from our core business. If a woman wants to wear one of our dresses to a nightclub, that's fine, but I expect the dress to be lightweight, packable, the one that same woman would choose to carry if she's backpacking across Europe. I check out recommendations to start carrying a new brand very carefully. Freedom of movement, durability and ease of care come way ahead of style."

"You're hands-on."

"Very." He allowed himself a wry smile. "*Controlling* is the word some people might use."

She looked offended on his behalf. "You started the company. You're entitled. Plus, Boulder River has expanded successfully even when the economy sucks. You wouldn't be where you were if you delegated too much."

"Thank you," he said, and meant it.

Her flush had definitely deepened. "I have to go back to work."

Her retreat looked more like flight to him. Not that he'd have said so.

Later he talked her into going out to dinner. Once he found out she hadn't yet discovered Apizza Scholls, he dragged her across town to the Hawthorne neighborhood.

"Best pizza on the west coast," he promised. They shared a veggie plate and the New York White Pie, a mouthwatering mix of mozzarella, pecorino Romano, ricotta and lots of garlic. Jakob was gratified by the pleasure she took in the meal.

He had the impression she was trying to pick a fight while they ate, though, and wasn't a hundred percent happy to find out they mostly agreed on politics, local and national, the right to die, gay marriage, U.S. drug policy and every other controversial issue she could dredge up. It got so Jakob, amused, would have agreed with her even when he didn't just to aggravate her.

"Well, this is no fun," she finally declared.

He laughed. "What? You wanted to peg me as an arrogant, money-hungry, elitist, corporate stuffed-shirt? Haven't we spent enough time together this week for you to know better?"

Amy wrinkled her nose at him. "If I keep poking and prodding, I figure the jerk I remember will show himself."

"Thanks."

"You've changed." Her gaze was unexpectedly intense. "I mean, more than most people do. Me…" She shrugged. "I'm still myself. You know?"

He considered that. "Yes and no. You've gotten past the in-your-face rebellion."

"Most people do by the time they reach their thirties."

"True," he conceded, studying her. "I guess you got tired of having all the metal on your ears clank every time you shook your head."

She fingered one ear. "I have some tiny scars."

"Tattoos?"

"One on my butt. Probably a mistake. Someday it'll sag."

He immediately wanted to see it. Was it a dainty little accent, or something bolder? Oh, damn—the very idea turned him on.

"No sagging yet," he remarked, careful to sound only casually interested. "Why's that? I haven't seen you exerting yourself."

"I run. And do yoga." Humor glinted gold in her eyes. "It's my effort to achieve serenity."

"Ever tried mountain biking?"

She went quiet. "I'm not much into biking."

God. He hoped like hell that wasn't his fault. "Because of the flat tire?"

"The what?" Amy focused on him. "Oh, that. Of course not. I used a bike to commute to a job for a while in Seattle, until I got hit by a car. Some jackass who took off. I broke an arm. What really scared me, though, was that my helmet split in half."

"But it protected your head the way it was supposed to."

"I guess so." She gave a half defiant, half resigned, one-shoulder shrug. "It freaked me out, though. Plus, my bike was toast. I went back to riding the bus."

The Amy he saw right now, the one who'd just told that story, was quintessentially *her,* Jakob realized. Brassy in one way, wanting to thumb her nose at the world and him in particular, but also vulnerable. He liked the veneer, but the sometimes shy, uncertain, lonely person he could see underneath made him feel uncomfortable and unfamiliar emotions.

He was probably the one who got quiet after that. They didn't talk much during the drive back to her mother's house. He parked on the street again and nodded at the suspicious old guy who was whittling away at the hedge again.

"Hey, Mr. C.," Amy called, and the neighbor came really close to cracking a smile.

Waiting while Amy unlocked, Jakob reflected on how everybody had always *wanted* to like Amy. Maybe it was her soft underbelly they could see, maybe the sprinkling of freckles on that small nose, maybe a smile that always seemed to surprise her. He didn't like thinking she'd never been really happy and still wasn't. One thing he was sure about—her mother was wrong in believing Amy hadn't needed to know the truth that defined her life. Answers might allow her to understand why her childhood had been so damn dysfunctional. Maybe now she'd be able to move on.

He grimaced behind her back. If that wasn't psychobabble, he'd never heard it.

"I should get some more work done," she announced even before she had the front door shut behind them.

"Why don't we talk?" Jakob suggested.

Her eyes shied from his. "We've been talking. All evening."

"You know what I mean."

"I'm not sure what there is to say."

"You've got to have a million thoughts going through your head."

She hesitated. "Maybe. Jakob, aren't you getting tired of my drama yet?"

"Nope." Not even close.

Amy heaved a sigh. "Fine."

She agreed she wouldn't mind another cup of coffee, and let him go off to the kitchen to make it. Seemed she didn't have a lot of qualms about taking advantage of free domestic help when it was on offer.

They sat on the sofa, Jakob at one end, Amy at the other. He stretched out as comfortably as he could and watched her tuck one foot under her so that she was facing him, cradling the mug of coffee between her hands.

"Do you think Mom really didn't want me to know because she thought I'd be hurt?" she asked abruptly.

Oh, man. Maybe he wasn't all that qualified for this talk.

"I don't know," he admitted. "You've got to remember, I don't know her. Not the way you do."

"But that's just it." She leaned forward. "I don't. I've been realizing how much I've learned about my mother since I moved into this house." She looked around, but he could tell she wasn't really seeing anything in particular. "Notes she wrote to herself. The way she files. Her garden. It's not that I've been digging in her closet or anything like that," Amy added hastily. "But you can't help noticing things about people."

"What have you learned?" he asked, curious.

"She's obsessively organized. I kind of knew that, but not the extent of it. Even her garden. She didn't do much gardening until she and Ken bought this house. But when Mom decided to take it up, she didn't go at it halfheartedly. Not her. She bought books—I swear there's an entire bookcase of gardening books upstairs. No landscape designer. See, that would have been ceding control. Most people would say having a designer would take the fun out of it, but Mom? I don't think she has fun. And no surprise, she didn't go for a cottage garden. It had to be English manor classical, all straight lines, symmetry, exact spacing. It's beautiful, but you know she'd napalm some poor plant that came up from seed in the wrong place."

"Maybe she learned her gardening style from the guy next door. He's got that hedge terrorized."

Amy giggled. "Mr. Cherpeski? You've got a point. Oh, boy, I'm glad Mom didn't put in a hedge. I might have had to decline the offer of two years of free housing."

"For fear of letting it run wild?" Jakob gave a slow grin. "Mr. C. might have been flattered if you'd begged him to take it over. Uh, how are you and your mother's garden getting along?"

"So far, I'm following her instructions to the letter. Remind me to show you her instructions. They look like some college professor's lesson plan for a year-long course. I mean, we're talking a binder here."

"You grew up with her. How did you miss this?"

It was as if he'd opened a Pandora's box of a different kind. Amy talked until she was hoarse about her mother. Why the absent woman who owned this house wasn't the same person as the mother Amy remembered. Unlike most people, he had the advantage of remembering Michelle, who put together fine school lunches but who he'd swear had never once asked him how his day had gone when he came in the door.

All the time Amy talked, Jakob watched the shifting expressions on a face that wasn't pretty in a conventional way, but still made him think of fairies in 19th century children's books. And he wished like hell she'd tug the neckline of her shirt up so it didn't expose her delicate collarbone, bare shoulder and too much creamy skin.

"What I don't know," Amy finally concluded, "is whether she's the way she is because of the rape, or because of her parents." She huffed out a breath. "Probably both. They were really stiff. When my grandparents visited, I didn't have to worry about being smothered in hugs or having my cheek pinched."

He tore his gaze from the upper curve of her breast. "Michelle might have been channeling her own mother when it came to parenting."

"Like we're doomed to? I hope I'm not." There was something wistful in her eyes. "Maybe I'd better not have kids." She shrugged as if to be sure he knew she didn't care. "Not that it seems to be happening, anyway."

"You should have kids." His voice came out rough. "You won't be anything like your mother."

Amy's startled gaze met his. "How do you know?"

"Because *you* aren't anything like her." He knew that much. "You're genuine. Emotional, honest. Fun to be with. Polite even when you're mad." Jakob let himself smile. "You give a guy a second chance."

"Twenty-five years later."

"Who's counting?"

He loved her laugh. It was pretty close to the earlier giggle. What would she have been like if she'd been appreciated and adored from the beginning, instead of having a cold fish for a mother, an older brother who resented her very existence and a father who emotionally abandoned her, leaving her bewildered?

Less complicated, certainly. Maybe not as interesting, he realized, disconcerted by his own conclusion.

"Where were you when I needed you?" she

asked. Lightly, not as if she meant it, but he felt the jab, anyway.

"Being an idiot."

She was quiet for a minute. "You haven't had kids, either."

"No. Susan and I hadn't even seriously talked about it. A clue to the state of our marriage, I guess."

Amy's expression was grave. "I only met her a couple of times."

"You didn't miss much." Irritated with himself, he made a sharp, impatient gesture. "That's harsh, and I don't mean it. But she wasn't what she presented herself to be. She was supposedly big on mountain-biking and kayaking. A vegan chef, completely passionate. She'd chew me out about what I ate. Talked about all these adventures we could have, like buying a catamaran and sailing across the Pacific. I finally figured out that she knew who I was when we met, supposedly by accident, at a bar where I was hoisting a few for a friend's bachelor party. She liked the cool look of Wilderness Girl, but once we were married she quit actually wanting to head into the wilderness. When I got her there, she was a whiner. The vegan thing was a phase. So was being a chef. She liked doing fun things with her girlfriends. Her happiest moment was when the *Oregonian* did a spread on us because I was a 'rising entrepreneur.'" He felt like an idiot even saying all this. Toward the end of his five-year marriage, he had the feeling an alien had taken over the woman he'd married. More likely, he'd just plain been taken. "Unfortunately, the company was expanding fast and I had to pay a shit-pot full to get free of her."

Amy had listened as if she really wanted to know. "I'm sorry. I guess, um, Susan is one of the reasons you're so insistent on the women's clothing Boulder River carries being about more than how it looks."

Her comment took him by surprise. "Maybe," he said after a minute.

"Well, at least you tried. Me, I always shy clear of a relationship getting serious. It doesn't feel like it's meant to be, not for me."

He heard again in her voice that determination not to be an object of pity. *Who, me?* she always seemed to be saying. Why would she want to be cherished, valued, appreciated? It could be she even believed herself. It didn't cross most people's minds to want what they'd never had.

But damn, Jakob hurt fiercely for her at the thought, at her casual dismissal of any dreams.

"You thought figuring out your mother would help you understand yourself."

She bent her head and gave another of those shrugs. The slouchy neckline slid lower. She was too small for anything he could call a cleavage, but he could see a distinct curve now. "Sounds dumb, doesn't it?"

"No, it makes sense."

That earned him a startled look.

"Dad's left a couple of messages. I've deleted them."

"He left me one, too. I just…didn't listen."

"You think you'll want to talk to him?" Jakob asked.

"Oh, eventually. He was nice to me."

"You're not pissed at him?" he asked, sounding edgy even to his own ears.

"Are you?"

"You think? He lied to me, too, you know."

She nodded at that. "Yes," she blurted. "Yes, I am mad. He meant well, but not knowing what was wrong was awful. I thought…it was me. You know?" She swallowed and looked away. "I guess it *was* me, in a way."

"No, damn it." He could tell his anger had broken through in a big way, because there was shock in her eyes. "What changed about you after you fell off those monkey bars? Nothing. Not one thing. I get why he was angry at your mother. But if he loved you, he loved you. Being a parent isn't all about passing on your genes."

"He should have figured it out sooner," Amy said in a stifled voice. "Just look at us. How could we be brother and sister?"

"I've known full siblings who didn't look much alike." He said it to be kind, because the truth was, in their family she had looked like the baby left in a basket on the back step.

She snorted, a rude but still somehow feminine sound that almost made Jakob smile despite the grimness of the topic.

"I thought Mom might call again."

"She hasn't?"

Amy shook her head. "I wonder if Ken knows. About the rape, I mean."

"If she didn't tell my dad, I doubt she's told anyone."

"No. This must have been a really unpleasant surprise for her."

He grunted his agreement. "She was pretty emotional. I didn't know she could be."

Amy made a face. "There was all that yelling when we were little."

"Mostly Dad yelling, though. Your mother usually kept her voice low."

She shivered. "I'd forgotten."

"Are she and this Ken happy, do you think?"

"I actually do. He's really smart, but so easygoing all he does is tease Mom if she gets sharp with him. A few times I've seen her blush and look at him as if…" She stole a look at Jakob. "You know."

"She has the hots for him."

"I was thinking more that she's in love with him."

"The two things kind of go together, don't you think?"

"I wouldn't know. I've never been in love."

Don't go there, he warned himself, while knowing he wouldn't be able to resist. "But you've had the hots for guys?"

"I'm thirty-four years old. Of course I have." She drew her knees up and wrapped her arms around them in a clearly defensive posture, glaring at him over them. "Why would you ask something like that?"

Good question, Nilsson. Why would you?

He aimed for an easy grin. "Dad tells me about your, er, career moves. He never mentions guys."

"That's because he and I talk, like, twice a year and we don't get that personal. And if by career moves, you mean whatever crap job I'm holding to actually pay the bills."

"You're not working a crap job right now."

"My writing income is finally climbing, plus no rent," she explained. "Speaking of which, I was thinking."

He braced himself.

"I'll bet I could sell an interview with rising entrepreneur Jakob Nilsson."

Relaxing, he laughed. He didn't know what he'd expected, but not this. "Written by Amy Nilsson? You plan to explain our relationship?"

She opened her mouth and then closed it. "I guess that's easier said than done."

"Yeah, I'm afraid it is." He hesitated. "You considered writing about what you're going through? Finding out who your father is?"

"You mean, finding out my father is a monster?" Her eyes flashed gold sparks.

"If that's the case."

"If?" Her entire body tightened. "What? You think there's a possibility there was some other guy in between?"

"No, of course not. I can't see your mom being into casual sex right after she was raped. Besides, both our parents were pretty definite." Jakob hesitated, knowing he was stepping onto treacherous ground. "What I mean is that, at some point, you might want to find out more about the guy. It wouldn't be that hard, you know. He didn't come out of the bushes wearing a mask. Your mother knew him. She told you his name. He was a student at Wakefield College."

He'd have sworn she was vibrating.

"He raped her."

"Yes, he did," Jakob said, his voice heavy with regret, "and I'm not making excuses for that. I'm only saying you might want to research him. That's what you do."

Those furious eyes were still flashing fear and anger. "Did you look him up online?"

"No." He was glad to be able to answer honestly. "I won't do that, Amy. I swear. A decision like that is yours to make." What he didn't tell her, and wouldn't, was that he had a suspicion he knew who her father was. He hadn't verified the possibility and could be wrong. But he'd recognized the name immediately. Only the fact that she was new in Oregon had kept Amy from doing the same.

For a long, quivering moment she stared at him. Then she seemed to collapse, curving inward. She laid her forehead against her crossed arms. "I almost did it today." The voice that emerged was muffled.

"You almost typed his name in to see what would come up."

"Yes."

"Why didn't you?"

"Because…" She lifted her head, expression desperate. "I don't know. It feels like betrayal."

"Of your mother."

She swallowed and nodded.

He wanted in the worst way to put his arms around her. It was killing him not to be able to. If he'd been her brother in truth, he could have held her when she needed someone. If they'd had a dating relationship, ditto. As things were… The boundaries were beyond fuzzy. Worse yet, he had a bad feeling he and Amy didn't see those defining lines in anything like the same way.

"Acting on what you learn about him isn't the same thing as informing yourself," he suggested, not sure that wasn't bullshit, but sensing she wouldn't feel whole until she did learn everything she could about the man who was her biological father.

"I'm trying not to think about him," she admitted. "I think I *want* him to be that monster in the mask, completely unidentifiable."

"No." Instinct had him shaking his head. "God, no. That's the last thing you need." He couldn't help it. He held out his hand. "Come here."

She stared at his hand the way she had last night, when he had told her he was staying. Last night she'd panicked and drawn back. This time, to his shock, she hesitated, then scooted herself sideways on the sofa so that she could lay her hand in his. He tugged her even closer, keeping his fingers folded firmly over hers. After a moment, she laid her head against his upper arm. Jakob's heart cramped at the evidence of her trust.

"What do you mean, that's the last thing I need?" she asked in a small voice.

He frowned, pushing aside his physical awareness to think how to put into words his inchoate certainty. "Like it or not, he's part of you. Is that faceless someone who you want inside you? Sheer horror, anonymous and hateful? Or would it be better to find out he's real? A creep, but at least someone who has good with the bad. Someone who is complicated, like most people." Definitely complicated, if Jakob's suspicions were correct.

"Do you know, when I read what Mom had written, I threw up? It was like I was trying to rid myself of *him*."

"Yeah, I can imagine feeling that way." He gently bumped his jaw against the top of her head. Her hair had been slipping out of its restraints all evening. Now curls compressed reluctantly and sprang back as soon as he lifted his head.

Amy didn't say anything for a long time. They sat there in surprising comfort, her leaning on him, him liking the feel of her hand, so small and fine-boned yet strong, clasped in his.

"I'll think about it," she mumbled finally.

"Think about what I said earlier. You're a writer. Isn't it how you process what you feel?"

"I haven't kept a diary in years." She gave a small, gruff laugh. "Good thing. Look what happens when you do. Other people discover your secrets."

He couldn't help a twinge of guilt at the memory of the times he'd ransacked the guest room when she was staying with them in search of her diary. Someday he might have to be honest with her about that, but this didn't seem to be the moment.

"I guess sometimes I do tackle personal stuff by writing about it," she continued. "After I got hit on my bike that time, I did a series of articles for *Seattle Met* about bike safety, the politics surrounding bikes versus cars, the attitudes of people on both sides, the real challenges of creating bike lanes and so on. It helped."

"Then do the same this time. Maybe your mother would cooperate anonymously." Amy had left Michelle's academic datebook/diary out on the table.

He'd read it more thoroughly today. "She didn't really want to go out with this guy. Why? Disinterest? Or was she reading signals she ended up disregarding? Talk to other victims. I'll bet there's a rape hotline here in Portland. Counselors. Maybe you could find some other women who'd talk to you. Even one who got pregnant. What decision did she make?"

She'd gone very still while he talked. He wasn't even sure she was breathing. Maybe he'd screwed up; maybe all this was too soon for her to think about. Being pushy was his way. Charging ahead, being aggressive, was a requirement for a successful businessman. Didn't mean that was right for Amy. Having to rewrite her entire life story had to be a shock.

But then she stirred. "You're right. I can do that. I'd have probably gotten around to thinking of it eventually, but…" Her shoulders jerked. "Thanks. If I start now, it will help give me some distance."

"Good." He let go of her hand so he could hug her. Distance might be a really good idea, he thought as he embraced her, before he did something stupid.

She scuttled, crablike, back to her corner. At the same moment, his phone vibrated. He removed it from his belt and saw that a text had come in. From his father, who hated texting. Jakob hesitated, then opened it.

Answer your goddamn phone or else I'll have to come to Portland.

After a soft grunt, he turned the phone around so Amy could read the message.

Alarm flared in her eyes. "He'll want to see me."

"Yeah." Jakob frowned. "I'll tell him to forget it."

"Maybe if I promise to call him."

He grimaced. "Dad isn't a real patient guy." After a moment's thought, he opened a screen to reply and typed deftly.

Give her time.

Amy was keeping as anxious an eye on his phone as he was. Two minutes later, it buzzed.

Already bought ticket. See you midday.

She stared at his phone. "If I don't answer the door, what can he do?"

"Keep hammering on it, the way I did?"

She scowled at him. "Fine. You won't tell him anything I said, will you? He doesn't have to know...."

"How much he hurt you?" The idea of letting his father off the hook made Jakob royally pissed. "You're just going to give him a pass?"

"Why are *you* mad? This is about me." She stabbed her thumb toward herself.

"You think I don't care about you? We have a history, too."

"Sure we do." She was spitting mad again. "You put dye in my bra when I was in eighth grade."

Well, hell. He'd actually forgotten that one, partly because she hadn't said a word so he thought maybe the dye had dried before she put the bra on.

"I thought it didn't work."

"I was too embarrassed to tell Dad! It was even worse because I only got my bra partway on before I noticed. I had one blue boob. Do you know how long it took to wear off? I begged Mrs. Storino to let me skip showers in P.E. and she said no. *Everyone* saw." Her eyes narrowed to evil slits. "Are you laughing?"

"No." He cleared his throat. "Trying not to."

"I hated you!"

He'd wanted her to. His confused teenage self hadn't known why that was so, but Jakob had no trouble stripping his motives down now. She had scared the crap out of him, and the safest course was making sure she detested him. They could not be friends, they could not hang out together. They had to be enemies.

"I know," he said quietly. "I do know. But we're not the same people anymore. We've spent the better part of a week together now." His eyes met hers. "You know everything has changed."

They stared at each other. In that moment, he felt as if he'd been stripped naked, and not in an

"I am man, I am powerful" way. Emotionally, as if he'd bared himself so that she could see straight through him.

The thing was, her eyes were wide and shocked, and he was seeing straight through into her, too.

His heart kicked up a gear, and he thought, *I am in deep shit here*.

CHAPTER SIX

EVEN JAKOB AT his most bullying couldn't make her talk to Dad, Amy reminded herself.

No, *not* Dad—she had to get that out of her head. Josef. Repeat to self…

Amy was so tempted to let herself be a coward. But the experience the past couple of days of having a complete meltdown had been an eye-opener. She wanted to believe she was stronger than that, and it was time she acted like it. Call it a vow.

Jakob had stayed overnight again last night. She couldn't quite figure out why he had moved in, and she knew she ought to confront him and say, *I'm fine. Go home. I don't need you.*

Of course she didn't. She couldn't deny that having him here had been…nice. She *would* be fine by herself, though, she told herself, now that she'd gotten past the first shock. Boy, did she wish Jakob hadn't caught her being totally pathetic. Amy cringed to think what she'd looked like when he pushed his way into the house. After a couple of days of not eating or showering, she couldn't have been a pretty sight. Gee, that might explain why he was refusing to leave her alone now. Sad, pitiful Amy, who wouldn't even eat if he didn't put the food on the table and the spoon in her hand.

So, okay, it had only been two nights. Once his dad had come and gone, Jakob would surely go home. Presumably Josef would expect to stay with his son.

Jakob had spent the morning on the phone, dealing with some kind of work problem. Or a couple of unconnected problems, maybe. First there was something about a manufacturing defect—it sounded like it might be bindings on cross-country skis—not discovered until after a brochure had gone out to everyone on the company's mailing list. Apparently, that ski package had been featured.

Jakob was brisk, solution-oriented, but Amy had no trouble hearing an undertone that told her he was furious. Maybe an hour later she had wandered into the kitchen to pour another cup of coffee and once again he was on the phone, this time sounding pretty unhappy about the performance of someone named Hughes, whose job security had clearly just gone south.

She contrasted the razor-sharp voice she was hearing with the way he talked to her. Did the people he worked with know he could sound tender? Amy was embarrassed to feel a little mushy inside at the contrast.

Mostly, she stayed out of his way. Pretending to work seemed like the best strategy. The result was, she spent a lot of time in the small home office staring at the screen of her laptop and not accomplishing anything. She couldn't concentrate on her current article—on spec, thank God, so she didn't have to worry about a deadline. Unfortunately, she was far from ready to sort out her emotions and try to put them down into words.

Twice she went on the internet and let the cursor hover over the search field. She kept hearing what Jakob had said after she insisted she wanted her mother's rapist to remain faceless, any woman's nightmare, instead of accepting that he was a human being whose existence she'd have to come to terms with.

Like it or not, he's part of you. Is that faceless someone who you want inside you? Sheer horror, anonymous and hateful? Or would it be better to find out he's real? A creep, but at least someone who has good with the bad. Someone who is complicated, like most people.

Amy actually didn't know the answer. Look at her—she had a hard enough time reconciling the anger she felt for her mother with unavoidable empathy. Muddling how she felt about the man who had raped Mom didn't seem like a great idea right now.

But curiosity ate at her, and she knew herself well enough to guess she wouldn't be able to contain it long-term. Or even for another day.

The doorbell rang and a jolt of adrenaline shot

through her. She heard footsteps, the door opening, the rumble of masculine voices.

Maybe she should give the two of them time to talk first.

Coward.

Is that so bad?

Amy groaned and pushed herself to her feet.

They had gotten as far as the kitchen. When she walked in, Josef had his back to the cupboards and had his hands braced on the tile countertop to each side. Jakob was pouring two cups of coffee.

The sight of the man who had always been her father made the ache in Amy's chest tighten to a knot that felt as if it might never loosen. A big man, he equaled his son's height but was bulkier. He hadn't gone soft at all. For the first time she saw that his hair had turned entirely white. The process hadn't been very noticeable, as pale a blond as he'd been. The hair on his tanned forearms still glinted gold, though, and the intense blue of his eyes hadn't dimmed at all. Pale lines, formed from squinting against the Arizona sun, fanned out from the corners of those eyes.

That's what Jakob would look like when he was in his sixties, except for the leaner build.

Jakob, who had seen her first, stopped in the act of handing a cup to his father. The hint of a smile on his face gave her courage.

"Josef," she said coolly. "You didn't have to come rushing up to Portland."

"Josef?" His face flushed with anger. "I've been your father for thirty-four goddamn years, and now you're going to disrespect that by using my first name instead of 'Dad'?"

"Turns out we were both wrong, though, doesn't it?" Amy couldn't seem to help taunting him, even if that wasn't productive. Behind his father, Jakob was shaking his head in a warning she refused to heed.

But Josef surprised her. He crossed his arms and eyed her shrewdly. "Is it really me you're steamed at?"

"Yes!" she yelled, feeling like a bottle of soda given a good shake just before the top was opened. "You knew! All those years, you knew."

He heaved a huge sigh, bent his head and pinched the bridge of his nose. "I knew," he said raggedly.

"I knew, too." She could not, would not, look at Jakob, who was watching her with such compassion. "I knew something was wrong. Of course, you and Mom never told me what."

Josef lifted his head to meet her eyes. His regret filled the room. "How could I? You were a little girl. My little girl. Only suddenly you weren't. Your mother pleaded for me not to ever tell you. I couldn't figure out why, but she wouldn't answer any of my questions. I still don't know who your biological father is."

Amy froze, just like that. In her fury aimed at

Mom *and* Josef, she had forgotten that, in a way, he was as in the dark as she'd been.

Jakob set down the cup of coffee in his hand and crossed the kitchen in a couple of strides. "Let's sit down," he said quietly, his hand closing around her upper arm. He steered her to the table in a way she recognized. She didn't want anyone to know, but she was shaking all over. Jakob had to feel it, but he didn't say anything. He only squeezed her arm gently, then let her go. "Dad?"

After a moment, his father pulled out a chair at the table, too, as did Jakob. Amy was very conscious that Jakob had chosen to sit at her right hand, close enough she could have touched him.

"Maybe it's time somebody told me what you two found out," Josef said gruffly.

Jakob raised his eyebrows at her. "You do it," she mumbled, and gazed down at her hands.

He looked at his father. "Michelle was raped."

"What the...?"

"Date rape," Jakob continued in a hard voice that reminded her of the one he'd used on the phone. "A fellow student at Wakefield. She lasted through the semester, but she couldn't bring herself to go to the class the guy was in. Maybe she dropped out, I don't know. She was pretty traumatized. She must have known she was pregnant by the time she met you."

"That much I'd figured out." Josef made a rough sound in his throat. "Why didn't she tell me?"

He sounded so genuinely bewildered, Amy looked up. "She must have been ashamed, don't you think? You know my grandparents. What would their attitude have been if she'd told them she'd been raped? Would they have believed her?"

He was silent for a moment, then shook his head. "No. They were old-school straitlaced. They'd have probably accused her of being a whore who had reaped what she sowed."

Tears pressed at the back of Amy's eyelids. No way would she let them fall. "That's what I think. And maybe she believed it, too. When a woman goes out with a man, did she encourage him?"

"God," he said, and ran a shaking hand over his face. Finally he looked at Amy, something like grief adding ten years to his face. "If she'd told me, if I'd been sure she loved me, I would have married her, anyway. I would have claimed you without a second thought."

Amy's throat closed up. She couldn't have said a word to save her life.

"Instead, I got to suspecting she never gave a good goddamn about me. I was just the sucker she picked to solve her problem." If anything, the lines carved in his face deepened even more. "She tried to claim that wasn't true, but a lot came into focus for me."

Ridiculously, Amy still felt the need to defend

the person she was maddest at. "I don't think expressing emotion was ever easy for Mom."

He gave a humorless laugh. "You can say that again."

She sucked in a breath. "I wanted you to take me with you when you left."

Josef said a harsh, obscene word, unusual for a man who tried not to swear around his womenfolk. "You think I didn't want to? I offered. I begged. I told her I loved you and I knew she didn't. She wouldn't hear of it. I was never sure if she was punishing me, or if I was wrong and she did love you."

Under the table, Jakob's hand closed on hers. She hung on hard.

"I don't know." Amy gnawed on her lower lip until it stung. "She's never said the words. Not once. But...why would she want to punish you? She had to have known it was her fault, that she'd done something really lousy to you."

"I never understood that woman at all," he admitted. "But damn..." He shook his head. "Rape."

"I could tell you didn't love me anymore, either." Amy hadn't known she was going to say that until the words had burst out. "I felt so abandoned."

If possible, Jakob's fingers tightened on hers. The connection to him kept her head high, the tears at bay.

"I never quit loving you." Josef's cheeks had flushed again, and she suspected that this time it was with shame. "You've always been my little girl.

You still are. But I guess I did try to hold something back. I'd lost all right to you. Your mother could have refused to let me see you, and I wouldn't have had a leg to stand on. Letting you go hurt so damn much, I guess I was protecting myself." His eyes met hers, and she'd have sworn there was a sheen of moisture on them. "I'm sorry, imp. If I'd known you could tell…" Words apparently failed him.

Oh, lord. He hadn't called her that in a long time. Amy swallowed hard. After a moment she managed a nod.

He cleared his throat loudly. "And I expect to be called 'Dad.' You hear me?"

She fought the hot spurt of tears. *Breathe. In through the nose, out through the mouth. Like that. In, out.* She won the battle at last, enough to—sort of—smile.

"Dad," she said, and he groaned and reached for her. Amy let go of Jakob's hand and allowed her father to envelop her in his powerful embrace.

"Yeah, I overheard enough to suspect," Jakob told his father that evening, after they'd left Amy's house. Reluctantly, in his case.

They'd all had dinner together after a lively debate about where to eat. Josef wasn't an adventuresome eater; Jakob had suggested Laurelhurst Market because it offered enough meat and deep-fried sides to please Dad. Better yet, it was the only restaurant Jakob knew that had s'mores on the menu. Seeing the listing had made Amy laugh and she'd ordered them. Making Amy laugh had lately become one of his paramount goals in life.

Driving her home, he'd let the two of them talk while he brooded. No, he didn't want to leave her alone. He didn't think she was ready. But there was no third bedroom for Dad, and he couldn't think how to justify handing Dad the key to his own house and saying, *You're on your own.*

No, that wouldn't have gone over well at all. In fact, the current discussion had begun when his father noticed the duffel bag full of toiletries and dirty clothes Jakob had carried in from the car to his own house.

"What the hell is that?" had been his first, combative question.

They had progressed from there.

Now his father took a swallow of the brandy he had unerringly located in a cupboard above the refrigerator. "Why didn't you ever ask?"

"You made such a point of telling me to be nice to *my sister*. Words emphasized. The whole subject felt taboo."

"I don't suppose it much mattered to you whether she was literally your sister or not," his father said thoughtfully.

Jakob grunted. It was more like an exhalation of air after someone had punched him. Didn't matter? Oh, yeah, it had mattered.

"Is that why you two don't have much to do with

each other? Because you figured you didn't have to bother with her?"

"Hell, no!" Irrationally mad, Jakob leaped to his own defense. "You think I just dismissed her?"

"Looked that way."

"That wasn't it."

"Then what was it?" His father's voice hardened. He'd never appreciated his son's attitude. Jakob had gone on restriction more times than he could count for whatever nasty prank he'd been caught pulling on Amy.

"I was jealous." That much of an admission wouldn't hurt. "You remarried, I just thought Michelle was fat and next thing I knew there was this baby and you were besotted." He grinned at his dad's expression. "And yes, I know you made time for me, too, but then it didn't feel like it. After the divorce I thought, great, at least I won't have any more competition, only then I realized Amy was still going to be showing up regularly."

"Wasn't too bad until you both got to be teenagers, though," his father said with unexpected shrewdness. "She wasn't with us as often, but she was staying longer. All I knew was, you got more vicious every time she came."

Jakob rubbed the back of his neck and tried to think what to say. Nothing came to him.

His father's eyes narrowed. "Did you ever tell her she wasn't really your sister?"

Jakob's head came up. "Hell, no! What do you

think I am?" He hesitated. "Besides, I wasn't sure. I thought I knew, but I could have been wrong."

"Goddamn." Josef finished the brandy and clunked the glass down on an end table.

You don't know the half of it, Jakob could have told him. Instead, he maintained his silence, sprawled in a big leather armchair, his own brandy scarcely touched.

"Never meant her to find out at all," his father muttered after a lengthy interval.

"What you said tonight, I think that helped."

Josef's sharp blue eyes met his. "What do you mean?"

"Insisting she call you Dad. Telling her you *are* her father."

His big shoulders moved. "It's nothing but the truth."

"She's pretty devastated."

"Is she?" He mulled that over. "Amy always fights back. That girl came out of the womb with her hands curled in fists."

A dry laugh caught in Jakob's throat. "Do you remember that scratching, punching brawl she got into in kindergarten? I was in awe. That was one of the few times I was really proud she was my sister."

His father chuckled. "No surprise you admired her over that. You were an eight-year-old boy. Her mother, now, she didn't feel the same about it."

"No, I remember." Michelle's deep freeze had been aimed at her daughter, but it had chilled everyone else in the household, too. Jakob even felt sorry for Amy, an equally rare emotion for him in those days.

"If we'd taken her with us," his father mused, "things would have been different for her."

Jakob kept his gaze on the amber liquid he swirled in his glass. He thought it might have been hell, growing up in the same house as Amy. Sharing a bathroom with her. Living with her bras hanging over the towel rack, overhearing bits of confidences she was telling her friends over the phone, maybe walking in on her in the shower.

Or maybe, it occurred to him, he might have come to really think of her as his sister. Constant exposure would have worked like a vaccine does on a virus. Maybe the real trouble was that he saw so little of her. She was virtually a stranger to him by the time they were teenagers. That made her a little mysterious. He didn't watch her maturing into a woman, he got slapped in the face with it when she appeared each time after a six-month absence.

He relaxed a little, thinking about that. Even if she'd really been his half sister, even if he'd never suspected otherwise, there might have been some... discomfort under the circumstances. Good word, he congratulated himself. He settled a little deeper in the chair.

"So now what?" his father asked, startling him out of his introspection.

He cocked an eyebrow. "What do you mean?"

"You and Amy. What's with you going to that damn time capsule opening with her?" Josef had the bullish look of a man issuing a challenge. "Then, what, you've been living with her? You don't like her, remember?"

He could have argued. Could have said, *That's not the way it was. I wanted her to hate me. Didn't mean I hated her.*

Instead, he smiled faintly, thinking about the shock on her face last night. "Everything has changed," he told his father, taking no small amount of satisfaction in repeating a line that was true even though he didn't yet know what that change would mean.

Josef sat up, his chin thrust out. "What the hell are you talking about?"

Here we go again, Jakob thought, more amused than disturbed this time.

AMY COULD HAPPILY have said her goodbyes the night before, but Josef wouldn't hear of it. He insisted she meet them for breakfast before he flew out in the morning.

Despite the fact that he'd rented a car and therefore Jakob didn't have to take him to the airport, all three of them had breakfast at Pine State Biscuits. The upside was that the famous biscuit sandwiches were fabulous; the downside was that she had to endure the scrutiny of both men, who could probably tell she hadn't gotten much sleep last night.

She was embarrassed to realize that she'd slept better the previous couple of nights because she knew Jakob was there, across the hall. Why that made anything better, Amy had no idea. She hadn't survived some terrible trauma that made her fear nightmares. Whatever trauma she was undergoing was devoid of blood and too old to have that much impact.

And yet, her eyes were sunk so deep in her head, the sockets were starting to look cavernous. She'd used more makeup than usual this morning in hopes of covering the bruises beneath her eyes, but wasn't sure it had helped much.

The first thing out of Dad's mouth had been "You look like hell."

What could she say? *"Oh, gee, thanks."*

He was still grumbling when she kissed him again right before he got into his rental car.

"You come and see me soon," he ordered her.

Her smile trembled. "I promise," she whispered, and sank into the comfort of a big hug that made her feel very young and safe again, if only for a minute.

Jakob had leaned against the rear fender of her car, crossed his ankles and said nothing after his own goodbye to his father. He waited until Dad was gone to raise his eyebrows at her.

"He's right. Did something happen last night?"

"What could happen?" she asked sharply.

"Your mother might have called again. Or you let curiosity overcome you."

Oh, boy. They both knew what she had to be curious about.

"Neither. I was restless, that's all. Didn't sleep well. There's a reason they call it beauty sleep." Amy shrugged. She studied him. "Don't you wear a suit to work?"

A smile deepened a crease in one cheek. "Sometimes. When I have meetings. As it happens, I don't plan to go to work today."

Her arms tightened around her hobo-style handbag as if it was a beloved and well-worn stuffed bunny. "Well, enjoy your day."

The smile broadened. "I thought we'd do something."

She was probably gaping. "Do something?"

"I was thinking the zoo. Or maybe the Japanese Garden."

"You're serious."

He laughed at her astonishment.

"When I can't get into the mountains, the Japanese Garden is my favorite place to go when I need to think. Haven't you been?"

Amy shook her head. "Mom's garden has been all I can handle."

"Come on," he coaxed. "Try it. You'll like it."

"Don't you ever have to go to work?"

"I don't take much vacation, and I have my phone if somebody needs to reach me."

She'd intended to go home and actually focus on work herself. *She* couldn't afford vacations. Amy had a suspicion, though, that she wouldn't have gotten any more done today than she had yesterday. Jakob's suggestion was tempting, as was the chance to spend more time with him.

"Fine," she mumbled, not all that graciously.

"I'll drive." He pushed away from the car and started for his Subaru.

After only the smallest hesitation, Amy trailed after him.

Ten minutes after walking inside the five-and-a-half-acre enclave within the city, Amy was in love. She suspected every leaf and tree trunk had been shaped and positioned as carefully as an artist laid down each brushstroke of paint, but the whole was astonishingly natural and just plain beautiful. Jakob told her the aim of a Japanese garden was to create a sense of harmony and tranquility, and she had to admit it worked.

Little of the city noise reached them. For peaceful stretches, the only sound was the crunch of their footsteps on gravel paths and the trickle of water. Maple leaves were just beginning to turn color, adding splashes of yellow and orange here and there among the soothing green. Moss-covered stone pagodas and lanterns accented vistas. Occasionally Jakob gently nudged her to sit for a few minutes on one of the strategically placed benches. They hardly talked at first.

Finally, as they leaned on the railing of an arching bridge and contemplated the upper lake, Amy sighed. "I can see why you like to come here."

He looked more relaxed than she'd ever seen him. "It's an irony since my first love is nature untouched, but if nature is going to be manipulated, they did a damn good job here. It's one of my favorite places. If I ever buy a house and actually have a yard, I want a Japanese garden of my own."

Amy smiled, feeling peaceful herself. "Are you tired of my soap opera yet?" she asked after a minute, as she had before.

"Still riveted," he assured her. "You figured out the next act?"

"You were right. I do need to know who he is."

She was aware that Jakob had turned his head and was studying her.

"You feeling okay about Dad?"

She straightened away from the railing and stretched. "To my amazement. I'm glad he came."

"Yeah, I am, too. He and I got a few things ironed out, too."

"Like what?" she asked, scrutinizing him.

Jakob only smiled. "Nothing that matters here."

They resumed strolling.

"Shall we have tea here, or go out for lunch?"

"Oh, tea, please."

A traditionally clad woman escorted them along the stones of the inner garden path, pausing to allow them to rinse their hands in a water basin.

They had to all but crawl through a tiny door into the tea room within the larger traditional house. Amy found the intimacy of the small enclosure unsettling. She reminded herself that she'd spent plenty of time with Jakob in his vehicle, which was considerably smaller. She finally decided that what made this different was that they were facing each other, seated on the mats, with no passing land or cityscape to be a distraction. In fact, there wasn't much of anything to look at *except* him. Narrow, paper-covered windows didn't give her an excuse to look away. It was hard not to be aware of his sheer size and masculinity. Her gaze kept glancing off details she didn't want to notice, like the way the fabric of his chinos stretched over strong thigh muscles, or the thickness of his wrists. His hands—she fixated on them for an unnerving length of time. He had good hands—long-fingered, huge compared to hers but also capable of holding the delicate teacup without appearing clumsy.

The tea ceremony helped her relax again. She was being silly. Of course she was aware of him physically, given that she'd barely met him before as an adult. The details that made him weren't familiar from a lifetime, the way they normally would be. She was taking snapshots, so to speak. Nothing was different here than at her kitchen table. He was being nice to her, that's all. He and his father—yes, her dad, too—were being the family for which she'd always yearned. *Be grateful,* she told herself, and quit questioning.

The silence went from feeling like a space she ought to fill to being comfortable. She momentarily closed her eyes and inhaled the intoxicating fragrance of the tea.

"I recognized the name Steven Hardy," Jakob said.

Amy went still. "What?"

"I wouldn't have said anything if you'd decided not to research him." His eyes were dark, troubled.

"You know him?" she whispered, a kind of horror creeping over her.

"No." He set down his teacup very carefully and looked at her. "It may be a common name. But there's a Steven Hardy who is in the news pretty regularly here in Portland. In fact, he has been this past week. I'm surprised you didn't notice it."

"I haven't read the paper."

"He's about the right age." Jakob hesitated. "I've seen pictures."

"Oh, my God."

"The resemblance isn't so obvious it ever struck me before," he continued, sounding reluctant, "but once I knew the name of the guy who…" He stopped. "I can see it, that's all."

"Did he go to Wakefield College?"

"I don't know. I haven't done a search or anything like that. I told you I wouldn't."

She nodded, feeling herself ease at her belief that

Jakob had kept his word. She took a deep breath for courage. "Why is this Steven Hardy in the news?"

"Ready for some irony? He's prominent in the Multnomah County District Attorney's office. He handles the high-profile cases. Word has it he's likely to replace the district attorney when he retires—except I've also read speculation Hardy may run for U.S. Representative to the House."

Amy stared at him in shock. "He's a *prosecutor?*"

He dipped his head.

"You must be wrong."

"I told you I don't know. This guy may not be your father. But…"

"You think he is."

Jakob grimaced. "Yeah. I do."

"Oh, my God," Amy said again. Stricken, she didn't know what she felt beyond shock. "It doesn't make sense." She focused again on his face. "This is why you said what you did, isn't it? About him having good with the bad. Being complicated."

"Maybe," he admitted.

She opened her mouth and then closed it before she could once again say, *Oh, my God.* That seemed to be the extent of her capability for speech.

"Maybe I shouldn't have told you now," Jakob said, sounding remorseful.

"Can we go?" She began struggling to her feet.

He rose to his so quickly, he was able to help her up. "I did this wrong."

"No, it's okay. But I want to go home now."

He grasped both of her upper arms. "To hide? Or to look him up?"

Both. "To look him up," she lied.

"You can do it now, if you want. You can use my Droid."

Of course he'd noticed she still carried an old flip phone, practically an antique.

Amy shook her head almost frantically. "No. Thank you, but I'd rather do it at home when I can be..."

"Alone?" His voice, gone brutally hard, cut her off. "Not a chance."

That made her stiffen. "What do you mean?"

"I mean you're not going to go crawl into your hidey-hole at your mother's house and be miserable by yourself."

"I will if I want to," she snapped, knowing immediately how utterly childish that sounded but not caring. "You've been nice. I appreciate it. It doesn't give you the right to..." *Be the boss of me.* Amy managed, barely, to contain yet another schoolyard refrain. "To tell me what to do," she concluded. Which wasn't actually any more adult.

"But I'm going to, anyway." His jaw had tightened in a way she'd begun to recognize meant he was angry. "If you want to research him now, this afternoon, we'll head back to your house—or we can go to mine—and do it together."

She wasn't accustomed to feeling such a bewildering mix of emotions. Churning hate and the curiosity—of which she was ashamed, and confusion, too. All that probably made her more volatile. Right now, she was blazingly angry at Jakob, but also glad he refused to let her do this alone.

The glad part upset her most of all, because it was so out of character for her.

"Come on." He boosted her out of the small, private room and just as quickly took her arm and started her walking toward the exit from the tea garden.

Short of revolting entirely and calling a taxi or planting herself at the closest bus stop, she was stuck with him until he returned her to her car. It was probably the restful atmosphere of the garden that made his hand gradually loosen its grip on her arm and her fury to lessen into mere fuming.

"Jakob," she said finally, looking straight ahead, "you've already wasted days on me. Okay, you were nosy. And ticked at your dad, too. I understand. But this is getting ridiculous."

They'd reached the car park. His fingers tightened again and he stopped her. His eyes, she saw when they faced each other, were closer to a wintry gray than the brighter blue she was used to seeing.

"*Wasted?* Is that what you think of yourself?"

To her astonishment, Amy found herself speechless. *Oh, God,* she thought. *That* is *what I think.* "I didn't mean it that way," she protested, but weakly.

His jaw flexed. "Yes, you did. And no, nothing about you is a waste of my time. I had…issues when we were kids, but I never thought of you as worthless. Not once. Got it?"

Her head bobbed. She was mesmerized by the expression on his face, even though she didn't understand it.

"This thing with your mother, with Dad, with the guy who raped your mother, we're in it together. You need answers, and we'll find them together. Don't try to get rid of me, because I guarantee you'll fail."

No masterful man had ever turned her into a bobblehead doll before, but apparently there was a first time for everything. She nodded again.

"Good," Jakob said, sounding satisfied, and once again steered her toward his car. "Your house or mine?"

CHAPTER SEVEN

SHUFFLING FORWARD WITH the rest of the people in line to get through security at the courthouse, Amy tried very hard not to fidget. She had nothing to be nervous about. The worst that could happen was that she wouldn't be allowed in the courtroom once she got that far. Were mere curiosity seekers allowed in at all? Either way, enough had been written about this particular trial, seating might be limited and the doors barred once the room was full.

And maybe that would even be a relief.

She looked at her watch for the thirtieth time, even though she had no deadline. It wasn't as if she needed to be there for the beginning of the day's proceedings, or planned to stay long, for that matter. All she wanted was to see *him*.

Jakob didn't know what she was doing today. If he had, she knew he'd have insisted on coming with her, and no matter what he said, this was one thing she had to do alone.

Friday when they'd gotten back to her mother's house, it hadn't taken five minutes to verify his suspicion. They could have used Jakob's Droid, no problem, and found the same information. There was Steven Hardy's bio, in black-and-white. B.A. Wakefield College, J.D. University of Washington. He had achieved his B.A. two years before Amy's mother had gotten hers from the University of Oregon, which made his age right.

The most difficult part had been studying pictures of him. With Jakob looking over her shoulder, Amy had located several online.

She tried to tell herself she felt no sense of recognition at all. Yes, they did share a similar hair color—she couldn't tell about the curls, because this man's was cropped short—and okay, maybe eye color, too, although it was hard to tell from relatively small photos posted on the internet. Like hers, his chin was more pointed than square. He was smiling in one picture, intense and determined in the others.

She hadn't been able to look at the pictures long.

Jakob, sitting beside her, had asked what she thought.

"I don't know," Amy said, breathing hard. "I can't see it."

His eyes were a soft gray-blue again, warm with compassion. He didn't say a word.

She had said politely, "I'm going to check my email," and he left her alone for a blessed few minutes, when she managed to quit shaking.

Her mother had finally emailed her.

Clearly, we need to talk in person.

She'd given her flight information and asked Amy to let her know if she'd be available to pick her up at the airport when she arrived on Tuesday.

Typical Mom—of course she didn't bother with expressing any regrets, any annoyance at Amy for inconveniently resurrecting the past, for sticking her nose in where it wasn't wanted.

But she was coming. Whatever that meant, Amy thought, not sure how she felt about her mother's visit. One more thing to be confused about.

She did talk to Jakob about her horribly mixed feelings, but she didn't dwell on the subject and was relieved when he didn't press her. It was too hard to explain what you didn't understand yourself.

She ended up spending most of the weekend with him. He didn't stay at the house, which was a relief to her for reasons she didn't examine, but Saturday he'd taken her on a hike up toward Mt. Hood. She had the impression he thought she needed to be kept busy.

He called the hike a stroll. Which meant athletic shoes were fine for today, he told her. "But if we're going to do more, we'll need to outfit you with hiking boots."

The *we* gave her a secret glow.

The trail was only three and a half miles long, circling Lost Lake, but for someone who hadn't done much outdoors stuff, she found the experience amazing. There were spectacular views of the volcanic mountain across the smooth water of the lake. A sturdy boardwalk had been built across wetlands Jakob referred to as a cedar bog. Stretches led through forest that felt deep and primitive to her. They ate their lunch sitting on a rock on the lake shore, dangling bare feet in the icy cold, astonishingly clear water. She'd been entranced by the tiny fish darting around the rock and also, more privately, by the sight of his feet, long, bony and masculine.

Jakob, she thought, had enjoyed her pleasure, and she had the sense the outing had quieted some restlessness that was building in him.

She asked him on the drive back to the city, and watched as his fingers flexed on the steering wheel.

"Yeah," he said finally. "I need to recharge sometimes. Usually I load up a pack and head into the backcountry, where there are fewer people."

The Lost Lake trail had been surprisingly busy, Amy would concede. Most of the time they had been able to hear other voices. The trailhead was close enough to Portland to make it an easy day's outing, and the hike short enough for families. Older kids scrambled like mountain goats on the large rocks that formed the scree slope, stared in fascination into the boggy waters from behind the safety of the boardwalk railing, and squealed when they discovered how cold the lake water was. Even so, compared to city streets, Amy hadn't had the sense of being crowded.

"And I thought I was the loner," she said, making a face at him.

He laughed. "I don't always go alone. I have friends who enjoy backpacking, too."

Probably female friends, she had thought acidly, then been ashamed of herself. Their relationship wasn't...whatever that spurt of jealousy suggested.

He probably still thought of her as a sister and assumed she thought of him as her brother, even though they now knew they weren't really related at all. They had only been stepsiblings, and that was long ago.

How else would she think of him? she asked herself, but didn't allow any answers. She was very careful to turn her mind in another direction.

Sunday they'd driven west on Highway 30 to the historic port town of Astoria at the mouth of the Columbia River. Astoria, she already knew, was the oldest American settlement west of the Rocky Mountains, established when John Jacob Astor founded the American Fur Company there in 1811. She teased Jakob that he felt a kinship with Astor because they shared a name.

Mostly, they walked along the waterfront and climbed some hills to look at the gorgeous historic mansions, decorated in elaborate gingerbread and painted in mouthwatering combinations of colors. Some had been converted to bed-and-breakfast inns. She had the wistful thought that it would have been fun to stay in one. For lunch they had fish and chips and watched an enormous cargo ship led by a pilot boat across what a waitress at the restaurant told them was a dangerous river bar where powerful river currents met ocean waves.

"This is the second weekend in a row we've spent together," Amy observed, after a long, peaceful silence during the drive back to Portland.

She had been very aware of Jakob's glance.

"So it is," he said in his deep, lazy voice, the one he *didn't* use during the occasional business phone call.

"Do you plan to go back to work tomorrow?" she asked, hoping she sounded completely casual. She didn't want him to suspect her plans.

He scrutinized her again before returning his attention to the now four-lane highway. "I guess I'd better."

"Me, too."

She had already told him what she was working on, a story about motorized bicycles—the kits to convert regular bikes, tips, pluses and minuses, and the fact that, as long as the motor had less than one horsepower and the bike went less than twenty miles an hour on a flat surface, the operator didn't need to have a motor vehicle license. They were still something of an oddity, but getting to be more common. She'd interviewed people who sold the kits or already-outfitted bikes, who rode them, who'd tried one and gotten rid of it.

"Same safety drawbacks as a regular bicycle," he had observed, and she nodded. In preparation for writing the article, she'd taken several test rides—or were they drives?—and found them exhilarating. She'd also been a little panicky when she got off. Amy didn't think she'd ever feel truly comfortable riding a bike again after her accident. She was afraid this article, too, was an attempt to distance herself from the experience.

Jakob dropped her off without suggesting dinner, which left her feeling momentarily bereft and then exasperated with herself. For heaven's sake, the last thing she could afford was to get dependent on him!

On anyone at all.

Besides, being left alone meant she was free to do some further research online and sneak a few more uneasy looks at pictures of the man whose genes she shared.

She was disturbed to find that he seemed to be respected within the legal community. He was described as an effective trial attorney, but not given to melodrama. His low-key style allowed jurors to relax and focus on what he was telling them. He was known to mentor newcomers to the office of the district attorney. She read about several attention-getting cases in which he'd been the lead prosecuting attorney. One involved a serial rapist who had finally strangled a victim. Amy stared at that headline cached on the *Oregonian* site.

What if she and Jakob were *wrong?* What if more than one Steven Hardy had graduated from Wakefield within a few years of each other?

The image of a faceless monster didn't line up with the dedicated deputy district attorney's. How was it possible that they were one and the same?

The current, well-publicized trial was of a businessman alleged to have burned down a warehouse for the insurance money without realizing a homeless family was sleeping in it. A man, woman and young child had all died of smoke inhalation. Amy had missed the chance to watch Hardy in action; this week, the defense was taking their turn to convince the jury that the evidence already presented was flawed. That was fine—all Amy wanted was to set eyes on him. A part of her was convinced that she would *know,* on some kind of cellular level, once she saw him.

And she definitely wanted to do this before she had to talk to her mother about what happened.

At last she was cleared through security that reminded her of the airport and was able to ask for directions to the courtroom. She had dressed today in hopes of blending in. In her snug-fitting, dark russet suit, she could have been an attorney who belonged here. Or a journalist. They must be in and out all the time. In a way, she was one, right?

Nobody seemed to pay any attention to her. The

traffic was brisk going into that particular courtroom. Inside, the buzz of talk made her realize
the judge had yet to appear. The jury box, too,
was still empty. Maybe *he* wasn't there yet, either.
Her heart drummed as she walked down the center
aisle, pretending to scan the front rows for a seat
even though they were all full.

A railing separated spectators from the floor of
the courtroom. On the other side of it, three people sat to the left behind a table, their heads bent
together as they talked intensely. To the right, a
woman was already seated at another table but two
men stood talking. Both wore suits and she pre-
sumed were attorneys. One was a thin young black
man whose manner was as intense as his oppo-
nents' on the other side of the courtroom; the other,
not very tall, had his back to her, but her gaze settled on his reddish brown hair, and she came to a
stop, not fifteen feet from him.

The lawyer whose face she could see gestured;
the other man nodded, quick and sharp. Amy
couldn't do anything but stare, even though she
knew vaguely that she was beginning to draw
attention, just standing there.

The conversation appeared to finish. Time and
motion seemed to have slowed down, in an un-
real way that felt dreamlike. The man with hair
the color of hers turned as if to take a seat. His
glance passed without interest over the spectators,
including Amy, and he stepped behind the table and

started to pull a chair out. Then he went very still and swung back around, his gaze locking on Amy.

He and Amy stared at each other. All she could think was, *Of course he's my father. Anyone looking at the two of us would know.*

He *knows*.

Her head swam, probably because she hadn't breathed in way too long. With a gasp, she turned and fled, walking faster and faster until she was nearly running by the time she reached the huge double doors. Someone opened one just as she reached it, and she escaped into the lobby.

Amy found a restroom, hiding in a stall until she regained her composure.

No, she told herself, of course he had no way to guess who she might be. It might only be the way she had been staring at him that had caught his eye. Prominent attorneys probably got wary of crazy members of a defendant's family, or weird courtroom groupies, or whatever.

Finally leaving the toilet stall, she washed her hands and then met her eyes in the mirror. She was paler than she ought to be, which made her freckles stand out and her eyes dominate her face. And this was after she'd had time to get a grip. A few minutes ago, in that courtroom staring at her father the rapist, she probably hadn't looked quite sane.

She didn't *feel* all that sane, truthfully.

Amy was ashamed to discover that she wished Jakob was waiting out there for her. He would have

taken another morning off work and come along
if she'd asked.

I had to do this alone.

Somehow the stubborn defense didn't ring as
true as it usually would. The unsettling truth was,
he had been with her as much as she'd allowed this
past ten days. His motives might still be a mystery,
but she did know he wanted to see her all the way
through this.

She walked slowly down the broad steps of the
courthouse and to her car, parked several blocks
away. She was almost there when her phone rang,
making her jump. Amy dug it out of her purse and
looked at the number, feeling a surge of gladness.

"Hi, Jakob."

"Hey." He sounded casual enough. "What are
you up to?"

She took a deep breath. "I just left the courthouse. I had to see him."

"Goddamn it!" Jakob roared. "I knew it."

Amy stiffened, her feet stopping. "What's that
supposed to mean?"

"You had this in mind yesterday, didn't you?
Would you have told me what you planned if I'd
asked?"

She hesitated, feeling a little guilty. "I don't
know." The silence seemed to simmer. "I was, um,
just thinking about calling to see if you had time
to meet me for lunch."

"You wouldn't have done it, would you? You'd have decided you were bothering me."

The fact that he was right didn't negate how much she'd *wanted* to see him. Amy didn't say anything.

"I'm out in Beaverton at a manufacturer," Jakob said abruptly. "Any chance we can meet here? There's a place called Hall Street Grill that's good."

They agreed on a time and she told him a little shakily that yes, of course she could find it. Just as abruptly, he ended the call, and she unlocked and got into her car feeling something so unfamiliar, it took her a minute to identify it.

Wonder.

Once again, Jakob was insisting on being there for her when she needed him. He was mad at her, and still hadn't hesitated. Nothing like this had ever happened to her before.

She heard him again, rough and even a little angry. *This thing with your mother, with Dad, with the guy who raped your mother, we're in it together. Don't try to get rid of me, because you'll fail.*

He meant it.

Amy started the car and mentally calculated how she'd get on Highway 26, which would take her to Beaverton, a suburb only a few miles outside the city. There were shopping malls; she'd find something to do to kill an hour before she met Jakob.

AMY NILSSON HAD to be the most stubborn damn woman he'd ever known.

Jakob looked at her across the table in their booth, thinking how quickly she could make him mad. She had a talent, it appeared. He usually contained his anger better than this.

Still, the sight of her was having a calming effect. For one thing, this was the first time since their initial dinner together he'd seen her dressed up, and the result surprised him. Her business suit, approximately the color of her hair, was well-cut, revealing a nice length of stocking-clad legs and emphasizing a tiny waist. With her hair up in some kind of loose knot, her lashes darkened and with her often sulky mouth accented by a copper-red color, she looked as sophisticated as any business-woman he met in the course of the day. He was intrigued to see this different side of her.

The best parts, though, were that she was here, and that she had admitted to wanting to see him. So, okay, they both knew she wouldn't have called, but her admission that she'd been tempted was a step in the right direction.

To what?

He ignored the question, since he still didn't know the answer.

They had already ordered and had their drinks. "The morning paper mentioned the trial." He crossed his arms on the table. "I had a gut feeling. I should have paid attention."

"You really didn't miss much. I got all dressed up so I wouldn't attract attention." Amy waved at herself. "I thought someone might stop me before I got in the courtroom, but I guess the disguise worked."

He smiled at that.

"I walked in, made it almost all the way to the front and saw him." She shrugged as if to say, *See, no big deal*, but Jakob didn't buy it. The signs were there on her face, subtle, but he was looking for them. Tiny creases on her forehead, a tightening around her eyes, her lips more pinched than they ought to be.

"Did he see you?"

She met his eyes, and that's when he saw how shaken she was.

"Yes." She swallowed. "The proceedings hadn't started. He and another guy were still standing and talking by their table. You know. He glanced around before he sat down and saw me standing there, not very far away. I guess I was staring. So he did, too."

"He recognized you."

"How could he?" she snapped. "That's ridiculous."

"You look like him," Jakob said simply.

"So there's a resemblance. Haven't you ever seen kids that looked enough like you they could have been yours? Do you immediately think, oh, wow, that girl must be mine?"

He frowned. "No, of course not. And you're probably right. But I'm more ordinary-looking than you are. You... There's a reason Dad calls you 'imp.' I always think of words like *pixie* and *sprite* when I see you. You're exotic. He has that look, too. You almost expect his ears to be pointed."

Her mouth opened and stayed open. "Exotic?" she squeaked, a good minute later. "Ordinary?"

She still seemed stunned when their food came. "Eat," he told her, and she finally blinked and looked down at her plate.

"I take it the concept is new to you," Jakob said, between bites of his Dungeness crab melt.

"Of my skinny, freckled self as exotic? Um, you could say that." She swiped a fry through ketchup, but instead of eating it she studied him with perplexity. "You said *always*."

He cast his mind back. "There was something about you, even when you were a baby. I'd sneak into your bedroom and stare at you when you were sleeping. I got into trouble for it."

"You got into trouble over me plenty of times."

Jakob laughed. "Later, I was usually asking for it. Mostly, when we were little, I was only interested. Your mother never trusted me, though. I remember trying to figure out why, when your hair was plain brown in some light, it caught fire in others. She was suspicious whenever she caught me creeping close to touch your hair."

Her eyes widened. "Is that why you cut my pigtail off? To pay me back?"

He winced. Damn, another episode he'd hoped she would never remember. "I was mad," he admitted. "I was mad a lot by that time." He'd been… nine, he thought, and bitterly resentful because he'd thought he would have his dad to himself again after they moved out, leaving Michelle and Amy behind. "I was also still fascinated by your hair. I thought if I cut some off I could keep it, and that would give me time to study it."

She snorted. "Which was why you were stupid enough to hide my pigtail somewhere Dad would find it right away."

"Yeah." He couldn't help it. A smile was playing around his mouth. "Give me a break. I wasn't very old. I thought under my mattress was incredibly clever."

"All *I* remember is waking up in the morning and going to the bathroom. I caught sight of myself in the mirror and started to scream."

"It was blood-curdling." Okay, damn it, he was laughing again. "I've never heard a scream like that before or since."

"I hated you."

Suddenly, he wasn't amused at all. Hearing her say that again made him feel really lousy.

"I know," he said. He looked at the sandwich in his hand and discovered his appetite had gone missing.

"You still didn't like me even when we were adults."

Jolted by the sadness in her voice, Jakob focused on her to see that she had her head bent and was twirling the same French fry in the ketchup with great concentration.

"Why do you say that?" He had to clear his voice. "I was polite."

She glanced quickly at him and then away again. Her smile was small and twisted. "You mean, when you couldn't think of an excuse not to be there when I visited?"

He'd wanted to believe she hadn't noticed. "I wasn't home that often."

"You always had been the weekend before I came. Or Dad would mention that it was too bad I was missing you, you couldn't make it until the next weekend."

Hell, he thought. Where could he go with this? Keep pretending she'd imagined things, that the fact they went years at a time without seeing each other was nothing but chance?

Amy might let him get away with it, but clearly she knew better.

"Did you want to see me?" he asked carefully.

Her expression was unreadable. "I don't know. It stung, that's all. I had this feeling Dad felt obligated to pretend I was welcome, and you weren't bothering." She shrugged. "Water under the bridge."

"Things weren't how they appeared."

Amy made a scoffing sound in her throat, and the wounded skepticism in her eyes blistered him. "Maybe not with Dad. Although the jury is still out on whether he really cared."

Jakob stared at her with astonishment. "You didn't believe him."

She dropped the French fry at last and pushed her plate away. "I wanted to." Her voice came out small and gruff. "Best way to make yourself credulous is to want something."

"What a load of crap!"

She shrugged again. "Okay."

Nothing good could come of this topic, he told himself. Let it go. He summoned some willpower. "What are you going to do about your father?"

The wounded look in her extraordinary, gold-flecked eyes was obvious. "Nothing," she said after a moment. "What should I do? Embrace him as dear Daddy? I don't think so."

"I guess not." Jakob rotated his shoulders, desperate to ease some of the tension that gripped his body. "You're picking your mother up tomorrow morning."

"Yes. God. I'm not getting any work done."

He wasn't, either. He hadn't been able to concentrate a damn this morning for worrying about Amy.

"You don't know how long she's staying?"

"Not a clue. Probably no longer than she can help," Amy said dryly. "Our visits are strictly duty. This one is…different."

Duty. She'd spent a lifetime believing neither of her parents felt anything but obligation toward her. He'd seen her face when Dad insisted he had always loved her as his daughter. The hope in her eyes had hurt Jakob to see.

"Do you want me to come to the airport with you?"

"Of course not," she said briskly. "Then Mom and I would have to be polite to each other, and what good is that?"

A humorless laugh escaped him. "You're breaking my heart. You know that, don't you?"

"What?"

Jakob shook his head and reached for his wallet. "You wouldn't understand. No, I'll get this." He threw some bills on the table even though they hadn't gotten the check yet and neither of them had finished their meals.

Amy walked ahead of him out of the restaurant. He pushed open the door and, in an automatic gesture, put his hand on the small of her back to usher her through it. Big mistake. He almost groaned at the feel of subtly shifting muscles. Touching her was not a good idea. Which part of that was he having trouble understanding? He removed his hand as if the palm had been burned.

Amy gave no sign she'd even noticed he had laid

a hand on her. "I'm parked right here," she said, stopping by her beater.

"I see." Damn. Nothing about this lunch had gone the way he'd wanted it to. He didn't like leaving her this way. "I told you I had issues where you were concerned." Appalled, his common sense wanted to know what in hell he was thinking. Or whether he was.

Amy had turned to look at him. Her lips were slightly parted. Her curls were beginning to escape their confines, and she put one hand up to brush them back from her face.

"You tell me when you're ready to hear what those issues were." His voice was thick. "If you ever want to know."

The apprehension in her eyes made him feel unbelievably self-centered. She had enough to deal with. The last thing she needed was him to dump his "issues" on her. What she needed from him right now was friendship and support she could trust, not...whatever he had in mind.

She still hadn't said anything. He nodded. "I'll call tomorrow to find out how it's going," he said, trying hard to sound gentle. "Okay?"

Amy bit her lip then nodded. "Yes. Okay."

He even managed a smile of sorts before he strode toward his Outback, parked a couple vehicles away from hers. He started it, backed out and waited until she drove away. Then he bent and clunked his head on the steering wheel a couple of times, making sure it hurt.

"I HAD NO idea how miserable that flight would be without a break in Hawaii," Amy's mother complained. "If only there was three more inches of leg room."

"I'm sorry you felt you needed to come," Amy felt obliged to say. Trailing behind, she was pulling the large suitcase her mother had checked, while Mom gripped the handle of the smaller carry-on and carried a sizeable tote bag.

She gave Amy a cool glance over her shoulder. "I'm having trouble understanding why you were interested in what I'd put in that time capsule to start with, and even more trouble understanding why you felt you had the right to open it."

"You expected me to open your mail."

"Bills. Junk mail."

"If I'd forwarded the invitation to you, you wouldn't have gotten it in time."

"You could have called. Emailed."

They were both silent while stuffed in an elevator with four other people. They stayed silent as they walked down an aisle in the concrete parking garage.

Amy unlocked the trunk of her car and heaved the large suitcase in. Her mother carefully wedged the smaller one in beside it.

"Surely you can afford to replace this car," her mother said over the roof as Amy unlocked.

She didn't bother with a reality check. "It runs. Hondas can get 200,000 miles plus. Why would I replace it until I have to?"

Mom sniffed.

Inside, Amy put the key in the ignition but didn't turn it. "I was curious," she said. "Living in your house made me feel as if I was getting to know you. The thing from Wakefield came and I thought, cool, a clue to Mom's past."

Her mother's stare was incredulous. "What are you talking about? I'm your mother! You lived with me for eighteen years. To suggest you don't know me…"

"I know hardly anything about your life before I was born. You never once mentioned Wakefield College. You never told stories like most people do. I don't even remember *my* childhood that well, because you didn't tell stories about it, either. No 'remember when you were four and you said something so cute' reminiscences from you."

Mom was staring at her in shock.

Amy shook her head. "It doesn't matter. I'm only making a point. I was filling in my own history, that's all. I had no idea I was going to be taking the lid off some great secret." A secret that belonged to both of them, that Amy had had a right to know about.

No, she wouldn't feel guilty.

Her mother had withdrawn in a way entirely familiar to Amy. They didn't talk during the entire drive. Amy kept sneaking glances at her, feeling resentful at how unfazed she was by the lengthy flight despite her complaints. The crease in her linen-weave slacks was still sharp, any tousle in her expertly highlighted blond hair looked stylish, her blouse remained tucked in. No creases in her cheek from sleeping awkwardly, no rumples in those slacks that couldn't really be linen—not even Mom was that good. No signs of exhaustion around her brown eyes. Perfectly applied makeup.

No wonder I always felt so inadequate.

Only now Amy knew something new. The cool facade and formidable self-control had been created to hide terrible pain. Knowing what she did changed everything.

Disconcerted, she remembered Jakob saying the same thing. And he'd been right—Amy was stunned to realize that all of the important relationships in her life had undergone a sea change. She'd never see Mom or Dad the same again. And Jakob—well, two weeks ago she wouldn't have listed him as important in her life.

And now he was.

Mr. C. was out in his front yard when Amy pulled up, and Mom went over to greet him while Amy unloaded the suitcases. She carried them upstairs one at a time. Good thing Mom hadn't surprised her with this little visit. Otherwise she might have had to explain why she'd better change the sheets.

She had a feeling her mother was not going to appreciate knowing that Jakob was also privy to her deep, dark secret. And oh, yeah, Josef, too.

"Amy?" her mother called from downstairs. "For goodness sakes, you didn't have to carry both my bags upstairs by yourself."

Amy started down. "Are you hungry at all? I suppose you're all skewed time-wise. Um…what time *is* it in Sydney?" She hadn't paid that much attention the night Jakob figured it out so she could call.

Studying her delicate gold watch, Michelle momentarily appeared dazed. "I believe we're nineteen hours behind right now."

Something about timelines always boggled Amy's mind. She grappled with it, though. "It must be early morning there. Like 6:00 a.m.? You should be feeling ready for breakfast then. We'll just substitute lunch for it."

"I believe I could eat," her mother decided. "You needn't go to much trouble, though."

Amy ignored her and put together a salad with balsamic dressing and feta cheese. She set out sourdough rolls she'd discovered at a neighborhood bakery.

"You've taken good care of the garden," her mother said at length.

"Thank you. As long as you're here, I might

have you give me a lesson on pruning roses so I'm ready."

"Of course. It hadn't occurred to me you wouldn't know how. Fortunately, it's not that difficult." She paused. "The house is in good shape, too."

Amy laid down her fork. "Did you expect to find beer soaking the floors? Take-out pizza boxes growing mold and piled ten deep in a corner?"

Her mother frowned. "Of course not. I wouldn't have asked you to house-sit if I'd thought any such thing."

"But you don't know me well enough to be sure of my lifestyle. Isn't that right?"

They stared at each other.

"I had no idea you were bitter," Michelle said. "Or why you are."

"Bitter?" Amy considered the word. "I don't think I am. Angry, maybe, to find out I've been fed a lifetime of lies. Yeah. That's definitely a better word."

Her mother, too, set down her fork. "You think I should have told you that you were a child of rape. Please tell me how that would have made your life better."

"Better? Maybe not. More honest, though, that would have been good." This awful burning in her chest *was* anger; what else could it be? "I never knew what was wrong, why you could hardly bring yourself to touch me, why my own father didn't love me the way he should. Why I didn't look like anyone else in the family. Tell me why, after the divorce or at least once I reached adulthood, didn't you tell me you were already pregnant when you met Josef? That he wasn't my biological father?"

The skin seemed stretched tight over the prominent bones in her mother's face. "I thought you never needed to know."

"You ever heard the saying, the truth will set you free?"

"I don't appreciate the sarcasm," Michelle said stiffly.

"It wasn't sarcasm. It was truth. I'm kind of fond of it." Amy shut her mouth before she said, *Truth. You know, something you don't seem to be well acquainted with?* Nope, wouldn't help. "You know he lives here in Portland, don't you?"

All color leached from her mother's face. *"He?"*

"Steven Hardy." Amy paused deliberately. "My father."

"Oh, dear lord," Michelle whispered. "I have been so careful...! What have you done?"

Amy *felt* cruel. She had the right. She looked her mother in the eye. "I went to see him."

CHAPTER EIGHT

"How is it going?" Amy's voice broke as she repeated Jakob's question. "I've been hateful, that's how it's going."

His hand tightened on the phone. He stood on his balcony looking down at city lights shimmering on the dark water of the river and wished Amy was here. Or he was there.

"I think you might be entitled."

"Does that make it right?"

At the pain he heard, Jakob stifled a groan. "Probably not."

"We had it out this morning. Then she went to take a nap. Over dinner we talked about…nothing. I keep thinking of apologizing, then decide that, damn it, I'm not going to. I might if she did, but she seems totally convinced she did the right thing. Why would I want to know? she asked."

He winced. Didn't Michelle know her daughter at all?

"Have you told her about Dad's visit?"

"No, we haven't gone there yet. She's not going to be happy."

"Have you mentioned me?"

"Nope. The subject hasn't yet arisen."

No reason to get his feelings hurt. He turned his back on the view and leaned on the iron railing. "What *has* come up?"

"I killed all conversation dead in the water when I told her I'd been to see my biological father."

Amused despite himself, Jakob shook his head. "Good going. You didn't mention that you hadn't actually even said hello, never mind introduced yourself?"

"I got to that, once I noticed she was about to faint. Like I said, I was hateful."

"Sweetheart—" his voice had softened "—I'll say it again—you're due. Dad and your mother both deserve to feel some sting."

There was a long, drawn-out silence. He reran what he'd just said and stumbled over the endearment. Oh, damn. He'd said that out loud?

"Okay." Her voice was hushed, too. "Thank you, Jakob. Um. Will you come for dinner tomorrow night?"

"So long as you're not planning to spring me as a surprise."

Amy laughed, a low gurgle. "Out of a cake? Oh, that would be mean." She sounded a tiny bit regretful. "No, I promise. I'll warn her you're coming."

"Would you rather I pretend complete ignorance and don't say anything about the time capsule, the rape, Dad's visit…?"

JANICE KAY JOHNSON 185

"No," she said. "I'll tell her all that, too."

"All right." He smiled even though she couldn't see it. "Six o'clock work? See you then."

After ending the call, he laid the phone down on a glass-and-wrought-iron table that was out here with two chairs. After a minute, he sat in one of the chairs, tilted it back on two legs and stacked his feet on the railing. He tipped his head back to see the sky. The few stars visible seemed tiny and far away. If he'd been lounging on his sleeping bag somewhere deep in the Cascade Mountains, the sky tonight would have blazed with an astonishing panoply of diamond-bright stars against a velvet-black night. He half wished he was there, but knew he wouldn't have taken off for the wilderness even if he'd felt he could afford more time from the office. Not when Amy might need him.

Her knight in shining armor, he mocked himself. *I am playing with fire.*

He was getting somewhere near decision time. His *issues*—there was a euphemism, if he'd ever heard one—still existed, if in altered form. Did he want to stick around as Amy's brother in name if not in fact? Jakob had a bad feeling he couldn't manage it. But could he abandon her, as too many other people had done in her life?

Hell, no!

He groaned.

Making a move on her could be cataclysmic. If she freaked, he'd lose her for good. If she told his father… God. That could be ugly. He had no doubt Dad would be disgusted with him.

Baby steps, he told himself. Be subtle. Always have an exit plan. Wait until you see in her eyes that she feels the same. If that ever happened.

He became aware he was getting cold. For October, the days had been unseasonably warm. Nights had the sharp bite of autumn. Jakob wondered whether Amy would enjoy backpacking or some easy scrambles up mountains. She'd seemed to revel in the short hike they took this weekend. He didn't know when he'd last enjoyed himself so much. Most of the time, her face was completely honest. Delight, suspicion, impatience, misery or curiosity, she didn't—or couldn't—hide any of them. Jakob loved that transparency. He could trust Amy.

He kept lounging there, in the dark, wondering whether there was any chance in hell she would ever think of him sexually. As a man. And he admitted to himself that he was desperate enough to take a chance, when the moment arrived.

THE NEWS THAT both Josef and Jakob knew all did not go over well with Amy's mother.

"Jakob offered to go to the opening with me. Neither of us had any reason to suspect it would be anything but a fun weekend," Amy tried to explain.

Michelle sat on the living room sofa, her back rigid, her face frozen in an expression of anger and unhappiness. "Even if you felt privileged to pry into my past, it didn't occur to you that he was another matter entirely?"

Amy didn't like feeling on the defensive. "He's family."

"He's not family."

"He's my..." She caught herself. "Stepbrother."

"I had no idea you were even in contact with him."

"I've seen him occasionally at Dad's." Very occasionally. "When he heard I had relocated to Portland, he called. We had dinner, I told him about the time capsule opening and he offered to go with me. And no, initially I didn't show him what was in your envelope, except when I pulled everything out he saw the panties."

Her mother shuddered.

"I didn't tell him until a couple of days later. I was upset when he came over."

"And Josef. If I'd wanted him to know, I'd have told him." Michelle's tone was straight-out-of-the-freezer cold.

"Do you know what he said?" Stung, Amy made sure Mom met her eyes. "He said if you'd told him in the first place he would have married you anyway and accepted me as his daughter. All he needed to know was that you loved him."

Michelle made a sound that reminded Amy of an animal in pain. She bent her head and looked down at her hands. "I don't know if I did." The ice had cracked. Her voice was brittle, as if she'd tapped into emotions that might shatter her. "I was so frightened, I never gave myself time to think," she said with obvious difficulty. "Josef represented a way out. I thought nobody ever had to know. I could pretend it never happened." She met her daughter's eyes again. "I did try to be a good wife. It wasn't easy. I was dead inside for a long time, and the idea of sex… The rape…it was my first time, you see." She closed her eyes momentarily. "But I thought Josef was happy."

Amy was shocked that her mother was finally being open with her. They had never had an entirely honest, adult conversation. It occurred to her that she'd better learn as much as she could while she had the opportunity. It might never come again.

"You must have known my blood type wasn't the same as his," she said carefully.

"Yes, but I told myself the chances were good he'd never find out. I suspect most people can't tell you their own blood type, never mind their children's or their spouse's."

Amy nodded acknowledgment. "I still don't understand why, once he found out I wasn't his, you didn't tell him the truth. He would have understood better than when he thought you were just trying to pass some other guy's baby off as his."

"I couldn't talk about it." Mom's fingers squeezed each other bloodless in her lap. "I suppose I was the classic rape victim. Because I never told anyone, the shame burrowed deep until it was part of me. I am not like you, Amy. I did a lot wrong as a mother, but at least I didn't cripple you the way my parents did me. I may have never said this, but I've always admired the courage that allows you to defy rules." She smiled wryly. "However annoying it could be."

"You never did come down that hard on me when I got in trouble at school." Memories cascaded with the power of a revelation. Amy had been so consumed as a child and teenager by her belief that she was unloved, she'd never noticed how often her mother had gone to a teacher or the principal and insisted that Amy's side be heard. "You didn't want to be like your parents."

"God forbid. I believe I hate them," she said as if mildly surprised. "That's probably a terrible thing to say, but I have no fond memories at all."

Amy nodded. "I knew as soon as I saw what you'd written why you couldn't go to your parents."

"And so I deceived Josef."

They left the conversation there. Her mother insisted on starting the coals out on the patio while Amy chopped vegetables. When the doorbell rang, she let her mother answer it although she listened for their voices.

When they reached the kitchen, Jakob was asking civilly about Sydney.

"It's a lovely city. So far, we've been happy there." Mom sounded stiff. "Amy tells me you've been quite successful with your business. You must tell me more about it over dinner."

"Sure, but don't let me bore you." Smiling at Amy, he crossed the kitchen and bent his head to kiss her cheek. The fact that she jumped seemed to amuse him. "Thanks for inviting me."

"You've fed me plenty of meals lately."

Her mother lifted her perfect eyebrows.

"I've dragged her out a time or two," Jakob told her. "Plus, we drove out to the ocean Sunday and had lunch in Astoria."

Mom made no effort to hide her astonishment. "How...thoughtful of you."

He grinned. "Amy and I have discovered what we've been missing all these years when we didn't see each other. We've hung out together a lot these past few weeks."

"So I hear." Mom the ice queen had made a return.

Jakob only leaned a hip against the counter edge. "What are you making?"

"I marinated chicken breasts in citrus and ginger and plan to grill them. I'll serve them over jasmine rice." And yes, she knew perfectly well she'd gone to so much trouble only because he was coming over. She'd pored over recipes until she found the right one. To impress him? "Mom, do you think the coals are ready?"

Her mother stepped outside to check.

Amy poked him with an elbow. "'What we've been missing all these years?'"

He pretended to look wounded. "I thought we were going to quit hiding how close we've become."

"You're making it sound…"

"Like we've become friends?"

That wasn't what she'd been about to say, but there was no way she *could* say what she'd been thinking. Because, wow, it had crossed her mind that he was hinting at something else entirely.

As if she were in free fall, Amy knew she wished it were possible. Which was unbelievably stupid, because even if Jakob didn't think of her as a sort-of sister, she couldn't possibly be his type. What had he called her? A pixie? That didn't sound sexy, even if he'd also said she was *exotic*. Plus, she'd met Susan. Beautiful, athletic, blonde—of course—and passionate about her causes. That part had apparently been untrue, but the beautiful, athletic and blonde part, Amy could vouch for. Jakob Nilsson, outdoorsman, successful, wealthy and sophisticated, would not go for a woman who was short, scrawny and freckled. A woman who admitted to being afraid to even ride a bike anymore. *He* probably took his dates mountain biking down reckless plunges.

Free fall hadn't quite ended with her going splat on the pavement, but close enough.

Amy turned on the burner under the water in which she planned to cook the rice.

"You're in a good mood," she said.

Before he could answer, her mother returned. "I think we can put the chicken on."

Serious conversation was suspended until they were at the table, set, at Michelle's insistence, in the formal dining room.

A few bites into the meal, she carefully set down her fork and looked at Jakob. "I understand from my daughter that she's shared my history with you."

"Yes." His tone was both grave and gentle. "I'm sorry if that makes you uncomfortable."

"It does."

"Amy needed support."

She wondered if that was his entire motivation for sticking close. Did he feel sorry for her?

Probably, she thought, depressed even though she should still be grateful.

"Have you spoken to your father about this?"

"I was here with Amy when he flew up to see her. But yes, he and I have talked on the phone a couple of times." The tightness of his jaw gave away something his carefully neutral voice didn't. "I wasn't real happy that he'd lied to me about her all these years."

"You know it was for her sake," Amy's mother said.

His cool stare met hers. "Was it?"

Amy was astonished to see a flush of anger—or could it be shame?—on Michelle's sculpted cheekbones.

But her mother wasn't a woman to back down. "It's clear that you don't think highly of me."

Jakob seemed to give that some thought. "I wouldn't say that. I don't know you. I haven't so much as set eyes on you since I was a child. I do believe Amy deserved the truth about her own heritage. For medical reasons alone, she should know who her biological father is."

Michelle's chin lowered a notch. "If the need had arisen, I would have told her."

His expression held enough skepticism, Amy decided it was time to intervene, even though she couldn't help relishing having such a staunch defender. Maybe he was only doing it out of pity, but he took the job seriously.

"Mom, you never answered when I asked if you knew that Steven Hardy lives in Portland."

Her mother's gaze jerked from Jakob to her daughter. "Of course I knew. How could I help it? I didn't until I'd married Ken and moved here." A shadow of remembrance crossed her face. "I was horrified when I saw an article about him in the *Oregonian*. I hardly left the house for weeks, until Ken began to notice. I told myself at last that he was unlikely to recognize me after all these years. And that if he did, *he* was the one who should be ashamed. If we met by accident and he recognized me, he was hardly going to rush over and say, 'Remember me?'"

"No, I don't suppose he would." Amy thought about the way he'd stared at her. "He never suspected you were pregnant?"

"How could he? He might conceivably have worried, but once I disappeared I doubt he gave me another thought."

Amy wasn't so sure about that. This man was not your garden-variety rapist. If nothing else, he had to be smart, and a smart guy—even a smart twenty-one-year-old guy—had surely gotten up the next morning and thought, *Shit, I didn't use a condom.*

"He didn't, did he?"

"What?" her mother said. She and Jakob both stared at her.

Amy blushed. "Um…did he use a condom?"

"Well, of course he didn't! How do you think I got pregnant?"

"Condoms have been known to fail." Amy was very careful not to look at Jakob. Had *he* ever had one fail, or been afraid he had gotten a woman pregnant when that wasn't their intention? Even thinking about Jakob and condoms in the same scenario made her twitchy.

"I suppose that's true." Michelle appeared equally uncomfortable. "But no. He didn't. He was drunk."

"Oh." God. Amy struggled to imagine the man she saw in that courtroom both drunk and violent.

He hadn't been all that tall, she remembered noticing, maybe five foot nine or ten at most. She'd gotten her stature from him, not her mother, who at five foot seven was above average in height for a woman. His build was lean. It was easy to imagine him as a long distance runner. Quick-moving—she remembered the way he'd spun around to meet her stare. With the color of his hair, the sharp jut of his chin, the lithe movements, there was something feral about him. She could see what Jakob meant. Hardy made her think more of a fox, though, than the fey.

Hmm. Maybe being compared to a pixie was more flattering than being told she looked like some wild dog.

"Did he hurt you?" Jakob asked.

Her mother drew back as far as her chair allowed. "Hurt me? Of course he did."

He was already shaking his head. "I'm sorry, that was poorly phrased. I wondered how badly you were injured, that's all. Black eye, broken bones…" He trailed off under her mother's still shocked stare.

It seemed to take her a moment to summon the power of speech. "Are you implying it wasn't rape if he didn't beat me, too?"

"No. God, no!" Jakob exclaimed. "He's bigger and stronger than you. I have no doubt he forced you. I only wondered whether he carried enough rage to want to slug you, kick you."

Eyes nearly black with emotion, she pressed a

hand to her throat. "No," she whispered. "No. He was so drunk, I believe he passed out when he was done. I was able to…to get away and straighten my clothes before I ran back to my dorm."

"I shouldn't have asked." The lines in Jakob's forehead were carved deep. "I thought Amy needed to know." His eyes, smoky with regret, turned her way. "Maybe I was wrong."

Not for the first time in recent days, Amy found it hard to speak. She touched her tongue to dry lips. "I…suppose I did want to know. I'm sorry, Mom. Sorry to put you through all this."

Her mother looked blindly down at her plate. "There wasn't a great deal of choice once that time capsule was opened, was there?"

"If you'd been here, you'd have burned what you'd put in it, wouldn't you have?"

"Yes." Her head came up and her eyes met Amy's. "Yes. Right or wrong, that's what I'd have done. I don't think I'd even have opened the envelope. I didn't need to see…" She faltered. "I will never forget…" When her voice broke again, she abruptly stood. "Please forgive me, but I don't think I can eat."

Amy half rose, but Jakob's hand on her arm stopped her. She watched her mother leave the room, her back straight and her head held high. Wouldn't you know, she never lost her dignity.

They sat without moving and listened to the soft sound of Michelle's footsteps on the stairs, followed by the equally soft click of her bedroom door closing.

"Oh, God." Amy sank back into her chair. "Now I feel like scum."

"I'm the one who asked how brutal the rape was," Jakob said ruefully. "It didn't occur to me in time that it would sound as if I was questioning whether it really was rape."

"I hadn't even thought…"

"It's been giving me nightmares," he admitted. "I'm sorry I asked in front of you. The more horrific it was, the harder it would have been for you to accept that you have his genes and his blood."

Amy shuddered. "Isn't rape horrific, no matter what?"

"Yeah." His voice was heavy with that regret. "It is."

"He doesn't *look* like a rapist," she heard herself say, without even knowing what that meant.

"I know. I imagine that's why so many women don't report date rape."

Neither of them pursued the subject. The psychology was obvious. A woman who had agreed to go out with the man who raped her might all too easily feel as if, on some level, she'd conspired in the assault. She might share the confusion Amy was feeling because Steven Hardy didn't match her image of a monster. She had to wonder whether her mother had gone through a period of wondering if she'd sent the wrong signals. Not been firm enough the other times she'd said, *No, I don't want to go out with you.*

Would a woman be more haunted by a brutal assault by a stranger, or the shock of being attacked by a guy she thought she knew?

Amy shuddered. *Oh, Mom.*

"We haven't done justice to your dinner," Jakob said into the silence.

None of them had come close to clearing a plate.

"It's okay," she said, glad to be pulled from her thoughts. "Um...would you like coffee?"

"I'd love coffee." He stood with her and helped carry dishes to the kitchen, where they scraped food into the garbage. She put on the coffee while he covered the unserved part of the meal and put it in the refrigerator.

"You can take that home if you want," Amy offered. "I'm sure you'll be starved once you get away from the house of doom and gloom."

He laughed a little, as she'd intended. "Maybe I'll take you up on that."

By unspoken agreement, they carried their coffee cups to the table in the dining nook rather than the more comfortable living room. Their voices might have carried upstairs from there.

"Damn," Jakob said. "Are you and she getting anywhere?"

"She's been more open than I thought she would be." Amy told him what her mother had said about the shame burrowing deep, and about how she felt as if her parents had crippled her. "She said she hated them. And that while she knew she might not have been the best mother in the world, she'd tried not to do the same to me. She actually sounded as if she was proud that I was always so rebellious." She paused for a moment to marvel. Her mother, proud in any way of her? The very concept boggled her mind. "And that got me remembering the times she backed me when I was in trouble with teachers."

"So…it wasn't all bad."

"No." Admitting as much was unsettling. "I guess it wasn't."

"Anything else?" He lounged back, appearing as comfortable as if the straight-faced dining chair was a deeply upholstered leather club chair. He had a gift of stillness and ease, which couldn't be more of a contrast to her own jumpiness.

"I've started writing about it," she said gruffly. "Since Mom got here. We talk and then one or the other of us disappears for hours at a time. I can't concentrate on what I should be doing, so I've started…I don't know, spilling it all out. Probably not in any coherent order yet. I have no idea where I'm going with this, whether it has the potential to be anything I'd ever want to publish, but just getting it down does help." She gave a stiff little nod. "Thank you for suggesting it."

Jakob shook his head. "You'd have done the same without any prompt from me. You kept a diary when you were a kid."

Alarm and then outrage flashed through her. "It was a secret."

He cleared his throat.

"Oh, my God. You read it." Oh, please not when she was old enough to be in that phase when she hero-worshipped her big brother. Amy hated to think what she'd confessed to her diary.

"Uh…yeah. A few times." He looked apologetic, although she'd have sworn there was a gleam in his eyes. "You hid it in difference places when you came to stay. Finding it was a challenge."

She growled, a wordless sound of rage that had never escaped her lips in her life.

"I really *am* sorry."

She finally found words. "You jerk! Do I have any secrets from you?"

"We were kids. Your diary was boring. It was just the principle of the thing."

"Tell me the truth." She hoped her narrowed eyes reminded him of fire and brimstone. A former boyfriend had once claimed her furious stare was more effective than any hell-raising sermon he'd ever heard. "Did you read it later, when I was a teenager?"

"And mooning over some guy?" His mouth relaxed into a grin. The fire-and-brimstone thing wasn't working. "Or a succession of guys? No, unfortunately. I didn't see you that often, you know. I contented myself with pranks."

Like the blue boob that had made her life a misery for about two months.

"Every time I start really liking you..." She shook her head. "I think I must have repressed a whole lot of memories. Now they're popping out, like jack-in-the-boxes. Boo!"

He was watching her a little strangely. "All bad?"

It was definitely an echo of what he'd asked before, about her mother. "I guess not," she conceded. Remembering, she thought, would have been bad if not for the presence of the Jakob she was now getting to know.

"I kind of like what's happened with us." There was still an expression on his face she didn't understood.

Amy felt a little shy, but couldn't be anything but honest. "I do, too."

"You come to terms with the fact that we're not related?"

That made her pulse bounce. Did this have anything to do with what he'd described as his "issues"? Should she ask? But her cowardice stampeded. "We're still sort of family, aren't we?" she asked instead. Begged?

Whatever that odd expression in his eyes meant, he shut it down. "In a convoluted way, I guess."

Amy cradled the mug in her hands. "Very convoluted. Does Mom seem like a total stranger to you?"

"She seemed like a total stranger even when she was my stepmother."

"She's my mother, and sometimes she seems like a total stranger." She momentarily closed her eyes. "That's probably an awful thing to say."

"Honest, not awful."

Amy gave him a twisted smile. "My whole life feels convoluted right now. That's a good word."

Jakob leaned forward, gaze suddenly intense. "Your life is what you make of it, not where you began. You're still you, Amy. Don't forget that."

"A woman in her thirties who jumped at the chance to house-sit for her mother because it meant she'd have two years without having to pay rent. That's who I am, Jakob."

"You're a good writer. Money isn't everything."

She laughed. "Says the guy who must be rolling in it."

"Do I act as if it's that important to me?"

After a difficult moment, she shook her head. "No. I'm being bitchy."

"Why?"

Oh, damn. He was watching her again in that same, meditative way. As if…she didn't know.

"Sometimes you scare me a little." She was immediately mad she'd told him that. She leaped up and took her cup to the sink, dumping out the dregs.

The scrape of chair legs on the floor told her he was following. "You want to tell me why?" His voice sounded a notch deeper than usual, even a little ragged.

Amy shook her head hard. The silence made the back of her neck prickle.

"Okay," he said finally. "For now. You can trust me, though. You know that, right?"

Squaring her shoulders, she turned around to face him. "You won't jump out of my closet in a monster costume?"

"God, no!" Jakob sounded as appalled as she felt the minute she said that.

Amy flushed. "I don't know why that rose to the top of the list of your pranks. I'm sorry."

"You should be." He looked pissed now. "After what happened to your mother? And what you're facing now?"

"I'm sorry," she repeated, embarrassed when her voice cracked.

"I think I'd better go." He set his cup down next to the sink.

Amy swallowed. "Jakob, please."

He let out a long breath. "It's okay. I can't deny I did that to you. I meant to scare you. Maybe not as much as I actually did, though."

"That was a really long time ago. You were— what?—in about fourth grade? Boys that age aren't known for empathy."

He smiled faintly, although she had the sense humor was the last thing he was feeling. "You can say that again."

On a stirring of worry, Amy realized they were circling back to the question of the issues that had made him continue to be hateful to her even when they were teenagers. He couldn't possibly still have been jealous, could he? Not of some girl who showed up at most for spring break, maybe Thanksgiving, then a few weeks in the summer. Most boys his age would have seen her as a nuisance, nothing more.

I should ask, she thought, but felt an instinctive retreat that told her she wasn't ready.

For what?

She was dealing with enough, she told herself stubbornly.

Coward through and through.

"So, um, do you want the leftovers?"

"Sure. If you don't?"

"I'm never that big an eater."

This smile was crooked but more relaxed. "It's because there's so little of you."

Amy rolled her eyes but reached in the refrigerator for the lidded container. "He's not very big, either." Then her eyes widened as she realized what she'd said. Was he in her head all the time?

Jakob waited until she'd turned around. "I didn't know that. Only that there was something about his face."

"Doesn't it figure, I look like him. It must have been hard for Mom."

Was she ever going to be able to see herself in the mirror without picturing Steven Hardy? There was a lovely thought.

"I like your looks." Jakob's voice came out rough. "I always have."

Astounded, she stared at him. He couldn't possibly be suggesting what she thought he might be. But warmth uncurled like a cat stretching and flexing its muscles. He had said exotic. And…as a boy he'd cut off her pigtail not to be mean—well, not *only* to be mean—but also because her hair had always fascinated him.

"Really?" The plea escaped before she could snatch it back. *Oh, way to beg. Please tell me I'm ravishing, sexy, way more interesting than those ordinary beautiful blondes.*

"Really." He stepped forward until only a few inches separated them. He very gently ran his knuckles over her cheek, sending prickles as far as her toes. Then he bent forward and lightly bumped his forehead against hers. Somehow their noses touched, too, and it felt as if he was nuzzling her. "Why don't you sleep on that?" he murmured, and now there was a smile in his voice as well as an unidentifiable hint of strain.

He removed the container of food from her nerveless hand and started for the front door.

It was a minute before her feet were capable of enough movement to follow him. He finished shrugging into a parka, smiled at her one more time and left with no more than a "Lock up" lingering in the air.

Stunned, Amy stared at the closed door.

I like your looks. I always have.

Oh, my God, she thought.

Exhilaration that made her want to dance swirled with confusion and something more ominous. Apprehension? Or an emotion darker yet?

CHAPTER NINE

WHEN HIS PHONE rang, Jakob glanced to see his father's phone number and couldn't help a spurt of worry. Dad never called in the middle of a workday.

Jakob was back in Beaverton to continue the discussion about a line of jackets and pants designed for runners that would be sold under the Boulder River brand name. Not that good quality ones weren't already available, but with the constant evolution of high-tech fabrics, he thought they could do better while keeping the price tag reasonable. A minute ago, he'd been focused on wind and water resistance and whether the line ought to include a jacket that converted to a vest, something he generally thought was stupid but did sell.

"Excuse me," he said. "I need to take this call." He walked a few feet away from the two people showing him around the factory. They politely strolled toward the manufacturing floor to make it obvious they weren't trying to eavesdrop.

He didn't even get a "hello" out.

"I talked to Michelle this morning" was Dad's opening lob.

"You called her?"

Josef snorted. "You think she'd ever talk to me if she didn't have to? Hell yes, I called her."

Jakob could hear heavy machinery in the background. Dad must be out on a construction site. He was a major enough contractor to usually have half a dozen projects going.

"You couldn't have waited to let me know until tonight?"

"Did I interrupt something?"

"I'm in a meeting."

"Sorry." He didn't sound it. "She got me steamed. Acted like none of it was any of my business. I had to wring an apology out of her. 'It was wrong of me to use you,' she finally said. 'But I was desperate.'"

"She *was* desperate."

"Goddamn it, why didn't she tell me?" his father bellowed.

Jakob held the phone a little way from his ear. There had to be irony in him discovering he actually *did* understand and, yeah, even sympathize some with why Michelle had trapped his father into marriage. "From things she's said to Amy, I doubt she ever had anyone she could depend on. It probably never occurred to her it was possible."

Well, crap, he thought. Was he describing Amy, too? He had no doubt in the world that she would be a rock for anyone she loved, but he'd been able to tell that the concept of being the one doing the leaning was foreign to her. One minute she was grateful he was there, the next she swung out somewhere on the continuum between dismayed and panicky. Maybe she even resented feeling as if she needed someone?

His dad was quiet for a minute. "Maybe. Goddamn," he said again. "Amy's ignoring me, too." He was clearly disgruntled.

"She's going through a lot right now."

"With no one but that cold fish of a mother at her back," Josef grumbled.

"She's got me."

This silence sizzled with suspicion. "I don't get it."

"Dad, I have people waiting on me. This is not the moment for an extended discussion about my relationship with Amy."

His father ignored his effort to duck this entire conversation. "Does she know your thinking isn't all that brotherly anymore?"

Jakob looked over his shoulder to be sure he couldn't be overheard. "I'm not her brother."

"You're as good as."

That raised his ire. "No. I've seen her exactly twice in the last ten years, and we barely bothered with 'How are you, I'm fine' when we were both in your house. You're right. I don't feel brotherly." *And never did.* He made sure his voice was undiluted steel. "Stay out of it, Dad. This is none of your business." He ended the call and then muted the ringtone. His old man could stew if he wanted to; Jakob had a job to do.

And he sure as hell wasn't going to talk about his feelings for Amy with his father.

Then why did you hint?

Didn't.

Did.

Because he was tired of denying what he felt. Pretending had become dishonest.

Man, he hoped she was getting the idea. He hoped even more she wasn't appalled.

Swearing under his breath, he stowed his phone and started back toward the waiting pair. He was having trouble remembering where they'd left off. What he was thinking was that he missed Amy, all because he'd neither seen her nor called yesterday.

Tonight, he comforted himself. Or maybe sooner, if he got a break.

AMY WAITED FOR the doorbell. Inside, she was giddy. *He called to ask me out.* Her. Only her.

Pity, she told herself. Kindness.

But maybe not.

When she heard footsteps behind her, she turned.

"Are you sure you wouldn't like to come with us?" she asked, for at least the third time even though Jakob had not included her mother in his invitation and Amy really, really hoped Mom continued to say no.

Her mother had aged these past few days. Fine

crinkles in her skin seemed to be deepening into outright wrinkles. She couldn't be sleeping well. She still held her head high, though, and maintained a brittle composure. "Thank you, but no. Going out seems like too much effort. I'd like to call Ken a little later, too."

"Okay, Mom." Amy hadn't asked how much she'd told her husband about the rape. This wasn't the time, assuming her mother's relationship with her husband was any of Amy's business, anyway. *Not.*

"I looked something up today." Michelle's lips tightened. "Apparently in Washington State, the statute of limitations has long since expired for the crime of rape."

Not much could have made Amy forget Jakob's imminent arrival, but this definitely did. Amy stared at her mother. "It didn't even occur to me he could still be arrested. Although it should have," she continued, "given that you preserved DNA evidence."

"Not intentionally. I really have no idea why I put that pair of underwear in the envelope. They repulsed me so much."

"If a conviction were still possible, would you seriously consider going to the police?" Amy asked, as she groped to imagine her dignified and very repressed mother starting that kind of public spectacle.

She was slow answering. "I don't know. It crossed my mind, that's all."

"Do you regret not going to the police when it happened?"

"I never even considered doing so." Her mouth twisted in a painful smile. "That may be the saddest thing of all to say about the episode." She tilted her head. "It sounds like Jakob is here. Have a good time."

"Thanks." Still bemused, she grabbed her wool peacoat and went out the door. She wished she didn't feel as if she was abandoning her mother.

Jakob had gotten out of his SUV but she met him on the sidewalk. Handsome in a dark blue business suit, he opened the passenger side door for her. "Glad to see you're so eager."

"I'm desperate to get out of the house." Truth. Just not the whole truth. "After I left for college, I never went home for more than a Christmas break. It's been a long time since we spent any significant amount of time alone together. Ken cuts the tension. These last few days have been difficult." She reached for the seat belt.

"How could they be anything but, given the circumstances?" Jakob slammed the door then went around and got in behind the wheel. After pulling his own seat belt around himself, he made a sound she couldn't quite decipher. Exasperation? "I heard from Dad today, midmorning when we both should have been working." He shook his head. "Did you know he called your mother?"

"Yes. She implied it was my fault." Amy made a face. "I guess it *is* my fault."

"We can just as well blame the earthquake or the fact that some incompetent architect made a mistake figuring out the weight-bearing capability of the foundation for the building at the college."

His theory cheered her up. "Let's not forget that Ken was offered the chance to teach abroad for a couple of years, thus leaving Mom's mail in my hands."

"Which ensured you saw what your mother put in the time capsule. See? Not your fault. It was meant."

He was making a joke out of it, but not entirely, she thought. And he was right. If not for the earthquake and the damaged building, the time capsule wouldn't have been opened for another fifteen-plus years. And if the invitation had come a few months ago, Amy would never even have known her mother had ever attended Wakefield College, far less that she had tried literally to bury all the painful emotions about what happened to her there.

I would also never have known how bitter her feelings were for her own parents. Or that she might, conceivably, be at least a little bit proud of me.

"You're right." She smiled at Jakob. "I'm a leaf, sent spinning by a gust of wind."

He grinned back as the engine roared to life. "That's the spirit."

"Why did Dad call my mother?"

"I have no idea." He accelerated away from the curb. "But here's what I think. You need a break. Let's talk about something else."

Her mind, of course, went completely blank.

He glanced at her and laughed. "You definitely need a break."

"I guess so. Isn't it funny? I can go months at a time without giving so much as a passing thought to Mom or Dad. Right now, I'm like a…a teetotaler who is getting drunk and doesn't understand why the world's spinning around and her feet don't want to obey commands." She loved the concept. "I'm smashed."

"And tomorrow you'll have a hangover," Jakob said drily.

"Right. But if you don't let me touch a drop tonight, maybe it'll clear my system."

He chuckled. "One question before the topic becomes verboten. Do you know when she's planning to go back?"

"No. I figured this would be a flying visit, but it's turned into more." Amy frowned, thinking about it. "She's working through her own stuff. Maybe she came home only because she needed to, I don't know, shut me up, but that's not what's happening. Do you know what she told me right before I went out the door?" She didn't wait for his response. "She'd looked into whether it was still possible to file a rape charge against him."

Jakob only nodded. "I checked right away. You know an irony? I wasn't thinking and looked up Oregon first. If the rape had happened in this state, given that DNA evidence has become available, he could still be arrested and charged. It would be a 'he said, she said' thing, but her diary was pretty powerful. It's too bad that's not possible in Washington State."

"I was surprised she was even thinking about it. Given who he is, can you imagine the uproar? Mom's so…private."

"Yeah." Jakob was quiet for a minute. "Okay," he said then. "Topic of parents is officially banned."

The theory was good, but she had an uneasy feeling that was all they really had to talk about. Well, and their own dysfunctional relationship as kids. And how could they talk about that without the subject of parents intruding?

"Work." Amy was embarrassed to realize she'd said it out loud.

He only laughed again. "We can start there."

He talked about the outerwear line in the planning stage until they reached the restaurant. "I like Nostrana," he said, parking a block away, "but I should have asked if you have a preference. I know you haven't been in town long, and I got the feeling you haven't eaten out much."

"I can't afford to eat out much," she admitted ruefully.

"Not dating?"

She almost said, *What's that?* but restrained herself. "I mostly meet people when I interview them, and it just hasn't happened." Sad to say, she hadn't even been all that interested. Moving to Portland had been a big break for her. She hadn't missed anything she left behind.

The interior of the restaurant was warm and elegant, mirrors on the walls adding sparkle above wood paneling. Jakob laid a hand on her back as the maître d' led them between tables to one in a corner that allowed them extra privacy. Not until the waiter called him "Mr. Nilsson" did she realize he must be a regular.

When she asked, he admitted to preferring traditional food, and a somewhat traditional atmosphere. "I'm not big on places built around the chef as artist. I want to eat, I want to talk to my companions, not watch some celebrity chef in action. Just say so if you want sushi or something one of these times, though."

One of the many things she liked about Jakob, it occurred to Amy, was that he did focus on her when they were together. As they ate their way from primi, amazing onion soup for both of them, to formaggi, a buttery sweet cheese-and-ricotta cheesecake accompanied by espresso, Jakob barely looked away from her. He actually seemed interested in hearing how she got ideas for articles, found appropriate people to interview, made contacts at a wide variety of magazines. They talked

about the move away from print publishing and
how that would impact her livelihood. He greeted
a couple of people who stopped at the table to say
hello, but made no effort to expand those conversations. Only with one did he grin suddenly.

"Amy, here's a guy you should talk to." He introduced his friend, an architect who regularly do-
nated his services to nonprofits when they reached
the point of being able to build. Bryan Engel was
currently designing a theater space that would be
shared by a couple of organizations working with
children.

"I usually try to fly under the radar," he admitted
with a charming smile, "but in this case I wouldn't
mind drawing some publicity for what we're trying to do."

He was a good-looking guy, shorter and more
wiry than Jakob and dark-haired and dark-eyed.
The twinkle in those eyes and the compassion that
motivated him to give so much of his time made
him appealing. She mentally framed a few photos
of him that would certainly help sell the story. He
gave her his card and she promised to call once
she'd determined what kind of interest local magazines had. The best part was that he also tattled on
Jakob, who, it turned out, was heavily involved in
providing opportunities for underprivileged youth
to spend time in the wilderness—and his company
outfitted the kids besides.

When they were alone again, Amy narrowed her

eyes at him. "You would make *such* a great subject. I could use a pseudoynm."

He only smiled.

"See?" he said, as they walked out. "We made it through four courses without the words *Mom* or *Dad* crossing our lips."

"Maybe because our mouths were fully occupied eating."

"Maybe."

She was glad when he cranked up the heat once they were in his Outback.

"You in a hurry to get home?" he asked, looking over his shoulder as he signaled to pull out of the parking place. "You haven't seen my home turf yet. I can give you a tour."

Amy ignored the way her heartbeat fluttered despite the casual nature of his invitation. "Sure, that sounds good. Maybe if I stay out long enough, Mom will already have gone to bed by the time I get home."

Jakob laughed. "I have to admit, I was really glad Dad could only stay the one night. Not that I don't love him."

"I'm not even sure I..." Amy caught herself. "Oh, God. What am I saying? Of course I love my mother even if there have been stretches in my life when I didn't want to. And here we are, violating our agreement."

"You said *Mom* first."

She rolled her eyes. "Sure, blame me."

The childish exchange settled something in her. Inviting her to his place was friendly, that's all. Both of them were quieter than usual during the drive, though. Dumb to be nervous, but she was. She had no idea why he'd suddenly clammed up. It might have nothing to do with her, Amy told herself. He might have started brooding about those zip-off sleeves that converted a jacket to vest. Who knew? Given the length of the silence, she convinced herself to think about the architect, whose smile had seemed more than friendly. She tried to figure out why she wasn't more interested. He was her usual type of guy, smart, involved in the world around him, not seeming too full of himself.

The answer was within touching distance. Bryan Engel had been standing next to Jakob, who had spent the previous hour flattering her with the intensity of his complete attention. And compared to Jakob...well, there was no comparison.

On a surge of panic, she knew she *should* start seeing some other guy.

"Your friend, Bryan Engel," she said quickly, before she could change her mind. "Do you think he meant it when he said he'd be willing to talk to me?"

"Sure, why not?"

"Is he a nice guy?"

It took him a minute to answer. "Warning here—he's coming off a divorce." Jakob's voice was too deliberately neutral.

"And this has something to do with me doing an article about him?"

"He won't be able to track you down, but I'm betting he asks you out the minute you call him."

"I was with you. Won't he assume...?" She immediately felt foolish. "Oh. You did introduce me. He knows we're related."

Jakob shot a glance at her. "I may have told him I have a sister."

Deflated, she realized he was being protective. And to think she'd always wanted him to *be* her brother. Went to show you should be careful what you wished for.

"Are all men who just went through a divorce dangerous?" She had to say *something*.

"They tend to want to live wild for a while."

He braked, touched a remote control she hadn't noticed and turned into a parking garage as the iron gate rolled up.

It would be a mistake to ask, she knew it would. "You, too?" came out of her mouth, anyway.

The garage was well lit enough for her to see his face. "Yeah, I think I did. I was pissed at the world and feeling anticommitment. Maybe a little angry at women in general, too." His voice was harsh. "Is that what you want?"

"I've never been sure I was meant for commitment, anyway. I don't know anything about the happy family thing."

He steered into a parking slot, set the emergency

brake and killed the engine before he turned to look at her. "Does it change anything now that you know what was going on with your mother?" He sounded gentler now.

That allowed her to focus fiercely on his question.

"I still don't know if she couldn't love me because of how I was conceived, or whether she was so screwed up by her parents she wouldn't have done any better no matter what. I don't hate her, the way she did them, but I don't really know *how* a loving parent acts, either." It all poured out of her, this fear she'd held all her life. "Which sort of makes me think all I'd do is screw up another generation if I had kids."

"I don't buy that." Abruptly, he was mad. "At least until the divorce, Dad loved you completely."

"And then he ditched me!" she yelled.

Jakob reached for her. Shocked by her sudden turmoil, Amy shrank away from him.

He went very still. For a long moment, they only looked at each other. There were lines in his forehead she'd never seen before. Then, with a nod, he sat back in his seat. It was a minute before he spoke.

"He didn't ditch you. He drew back a little."

"I know that," she said tightly.

"But when you were six years old, that's not how it felt."

"No." She should have asked him to take her home. They'd had fun and should have ended the

evening on a better note. She didn't want to talk
about how she felt anymore. She was all grown
up, and it was past time to get over the "poor me"
syndrome. "Can we quit talking about this?" she
begged.

"Yeah. Can I say one thing first?"

"Can I stop you?"

He smiled, just a little. "Probably not."

"Then get it over with."

"I think you'd be a great mother. After your own
childhood, once you commit, you'll be in it one
hundred percent. Unshakable. And I've said this
before. You're nothing like Michelle. She's icy,
you're fiery. A little shy, too, which is an intriguing combination. You'd listen to your kids, really
listen. Defend them, and make sure they never had
a moment's doubt about how much their mom loves
them."

Amy was left speechless, shaken by the certainty
in his voice. He really did believe what he'd said.

He smiled again then reached over and unfas-
tened her seat belt. "Okay, I'm done. Let's go upstairs and I'll show off my view."

She gave herself a little shake but failed to restore her sense of reality. "Um…sure."

Fine. Great. She could admire his view, make
conversation, pretend she wasn't having an out-
of-body experience for reasons she didn't even understand. And so help her, she would not say one

more word about her mother, her father, her *other* father, not tonight.

They rode the elevator up in silence.

His was one of only two condos on the top floor. When he ushered Amy in, her heart sank a little because his place was so exactly what she'd expected, and because she loved it. The last thing she needed was another reason to like him.

Walls were either exposed brick or plastered in a thick texture and painted a creamy white. What must be original floorboards, wide and scarred, were now finished to a gleaming, warm chestnut color, the wear and tear part of the beauty. Artisan-made wood tables and bookcases accompanied a leather sofa and a couple of chairs upholstered in rich colors. A huge photograph of Mt. Hood reflected in a lake hung over the sofa; other photos were smaller and mostly caught the details nature did so exquisitely, like a few raindrops glistening on a newly unfurled fern frond. Overhead, ancient cracked beams were exposed along with the vaulted ceiling above. Kitchen and dining areas were part of the great room; only what was presumably bedroom and bathroom were partially walled off.

And beyond a wall of windows she could see a balcony and cityscape.

"It's perfect," she said. "Is this Susan's influence?"

Jakob lifted his eyebrows. "No. She kept our

condo. I bought this place after the divorce. This is all me."

Oh, no.

"I'm glad you like it."

Amy dropped her bag on an end table and began wandering, looking more closely at the art quality photos and a few paintings, which she suspected were all originals. They were more modern than she might have expected, lines and jewel colors rather than pictorial. She lightly ran her fingertips over the stained-glass shade of a tall lamp and then along the nubby back of one of the chairs. She became aware Jakob had leaned against a kitchen island that looked as if it had been rescued from a 19th century country store. He was watching her.

"What are you thinking?"

"I'm green with envy," she admitted.

He smiled. "Not all women would like it."

"No, it's not feminine. But it's peaceful."

"Yeah." He looked around. "Home feels like a refuge."

He showed off his amazing view from a wide balcony, but it was too chilly to stay outside, so they settled in the living room. The sofa was big enough, her feet might not have touched the floor, so Amy kicked off her shoes and sat cross-legged.

"You interested in Bryan?" Jakob asked.

She hesitated, knowing if she were smart she'd say, *Sure, why not?* "No" was what came out. "Well, I'd like to interview him. And he did seem nice enough." She frowned at him. "It sounds like he's a friend of yours. I'd think you'd be encouraging me. What's he doing, going through a woman a night?" she asked.

He looked at her for long enough to make her uneasy. She couldn't figure out what that pensive expression meant. "You and I have been spending a lot of time together," he said finally.

Amy nodded, inexplicably wary. Her pulse raced.

"I'm having a good time." Jakob seemed to be picking and choosing his words. "I don't like the idea of you suddenly being busy every night."

What did *that* mean? They were such good buddies, he was hoping she didn't find a boyfriend for a while? Frustrated, bewildered and flattered all at the same time, she nodded again, as if she understood.

His eyes had narrowed slightly. "You said I scare you."

She did her best to hide an involuntary flinch. "*Scare* wasn't a good choice of words. You confuse me. Unsettle me." Her voice was rising, the tension in it making her sound mad. "I don't understand why you've gone from despising me to wanting to be such good friends that I'm supposed to save all my evenings for you."

"But you also said you like what's happening with us."

"I do!" Her hands had begun to tremble a little. She balled them into fists. "But it doesn't make *sense*." That came out sounding more like a wail than she wanted to admit.

He made a sound that was too rough to be a laugh. "I've...taken myself by surprise, too," he admitted.

She wanted to beg him to tell her that he really liked her, that he wasn't pretending. But if he said yes, if he convinced her he meant it, well, that was confusing, too, because why now and not all those years ago?

"I've never despised you," he said, his voice deep and low. "It was...more complicated than that."

What if this was something she didn't want to hear? That would ruin everything? She said it, anyway. "You had issues."

His laugh—well, it *was* a laugh, but not a very happy one. "Oh, yeah."

Amy sucked in a breath. They were staring at each other across the living room, and how could she stay silent? "You said I had to ask. Well, now I am. What did you mean?"

A muscle spasmed in his jaw. He hesitated for so long she wasn't sure he was going to answer after all, even though she had the sense he'd spent the past week consciously herding her into a corner where she had no choice *but* to ask.

"Are you sure you want to know?" he said finally.

"No." She scowled at him. Irritation was a good

fallback for her. "But you keep hinting, so I know you want to tell me."

He was still sprawled in a loose-limbed way, but Amy was pretty sure he wasn't relaxed at all. His eyes were dark with some kind of emotion and his mouth had a grim line.

Jakob sighed and sat up, his gaze never leaving her. "I was jealous as hell when you were little."

"I know that," she said, puzzled.

"But then we moved to Arizona and there were longer stretches between us seeing each other."

"Partly because you did your best to have someplace else to be when I was coming," she couldn't resist reminding him.

His mouth twitched in self-mockery. "That's because somewhere about the time you were twelve or thirteen, I got to noticing you were a girl."

A wrecking ball hitting the side of the building wouldn't have torn her gaze from his. *Oh, my God, oh, my God.* Was he saying what she thought he was?

"True confessions. I may not scare you, but you scare me." His voice had gotten even deeper. The vibration sent tingles through her. "Noticing you that way scared the crap out of me."

"You…were *attracted* to me?" came out squeaky.

"Yeah." He ran a hand over his face. There was a faint rasping sound. "I did my damndest not to admit it to myself. The safest thing was just not to see you at all. If I couldn't manage that—" there was a hint of apology in his stormy eyes "—then next best was making sure you hated my guts and thought I hated yours."

"That's…" Amy shook her head, dazed. "I can't believe…I was so sure…"

"I worked hard at it."

She kept shaking her head as if she couldn't get it to stop. She was as stunned, if in a different way, as she'd been when she understood from her mother's diary that her father wasn't the man she called Dad. It was as if somebody had spun her round and round and now she was left staggering and trying to orient herself. *Up, down. Left, right.* "But…"

"But what?"

"If you knew I wasn't really your sister…"

"I didn't know. I guessed. Probably if I hadn't overheard as much as I did, I never would have thought of you that way. Trouble was, once the concept that you weren't my sister at all got introduced in my head, I didn't look at you the same. When we were younger, it translated to 'If she's not my sister how come she has to spend weekends and why do I have to be nice?'"

She huffed. "Nice."

He shrugged. "I guess I decided I didn't have to be."

"I noticed."

"Have I said how sorry I am?"

Amy gave a little laugh, although so many emotions were churning inside she couldn't have named one. "I think you've apologized for a few of your meaner escapades."

"Once a guy's hormones kick in, all he can see are tits and asses and the way a girl walks and purses her lips and smells." He shrugged. "But one thing I knew was that I should never, *never*—" and he sounded deadly serious "—have noticed any of those things related to my sister. It freaked me out, big-time."

"Yes." Her voice croaked. "I can see why."

"So—I convinced even myself that I wasn't noticing. I hated having you around and you were a stupid girl who Dad was too nice to, which was why I got hot and bothered when you wandered into the kitchen in the morning in your pajamas. It couldn't possibly be because the fabric was really thin and I could make out the shadow of your nipples."

In automatic self-defense, her arms crossed in front of her to cover her breasts.

Jakob's laugh was choppy. "I dreaded your visits."

She was still staring at him, that mongoose-to-a-snake thing. "I had no idea."

"I made real sure you didn't."

"I don't even know what to say." So true. "You just turned my world on end." It made her realize that he had loomed way larger in her life than was reasonable, considering how little they'd actually seen of each other. And now this.

"In a good or bad way?" His voice was husky, his gaze...searching?

Suddenly Amy knew how she felt. Blistering, steam-coming-out-of-the-ears furious. And yes, she *hurt* underneath, but she wouldn't think about that until later.

She scooted forward so her feet were on the floor. In the worst way, she wanted to launch herself at him and punch and kick and scratch.

His expression changed.

"I needed somebody to love me." It came out low and shaking with intensity. "Anybody at all. Instead, I grew up knowing I wasn't worth anybody's love. My own mother didn't want to touch me. My father was polite and pleasant, when he was stuck having me for a weekend. And my brother? Every time I saw him he did something vile to me to make sure I knew I wasn't welcome. I should have hated your guts, but I didn't. I kept hoping..." Her voice broke. Even angrier at having exposed her own naked vulnerability, she jumped to her feet. "If I'd had *you,* it would have made a difference. And now I'm supposed to say, 'Oh, cool, you really liked me after all'? Well, it's not cool!" She was screaming—like a fishwife, Mom would have said. And shaking all over now.

Jakob sat silent and seemingly stunned.

She fumbled her way back into her shoes and

looked around for her bag. "I want to go home. I can catch a taxi."

He stood, moving more stiffly than usual. "You know I'll take you."

"Fine." She stomped over to the door and waited, not willing to look at him.

He let them out; they rode the elevator down to the garage in silence. Amy felt like crying by the time they reached his SUV. But she wouldn't do it, not in front of him, not when he was the *cause* of this caustic grief that was eating its way through the lining of her stomach and taking a bite out of her heart muscle.

Jakob started the engine while she was still fastening the seat belt. He didn't put it in gear. "I suppose it's too little, too late to say I'm sorry." He looked straight ahead.

The anger was still there, but beneath it, beneath even the hurt that could have been grief, something else stirred. She was in too much turmoil to even try to identify what it was.

"This isn't funny."

"No." He still wasn't moving. His face looked harsh in the artificial lighting that cast stark shadows. "I never thought it was funny."

Why wasn't he backing the Subaru out, pushing the button to operate the parking garage gate?

"I have to think about this," she said.

After a moment he nodded. "Will you tell me one thing?"

His tone was so strange she couldn't help but look at him. He kept staring straight ahead, but not as if he actually *saw* the silent depths of the garage or the couple dozen parked vehicles.

"It depends," Amy said tightly.

"Did I shock you?"

Was he stupid? He thought she'd gone off the deep end because she was mildly surprised at this revision of their history? "Yes!"

He finally turned his head. His face was colorless. She wanted to believe the unnatural pallor was from the lighting down here. His eyes burned into hers, even though she wouldn't have been able to make out that they were blue if she hadn't already known.

"Does it repulse you to know your brother looked at you that way?" He sounded as raw as she felt.

She had to tear her gaze away. "You're not my brother." Oh, damn. Her voice was shaking again.

"No. But if I'd found out I was, do you know how I'd have felt?"

"No." She closed her eyes. "Yes." Drew a shaky breath. "This is why you wanted to go to the opening of the time capsule with me."

"I suppose it is," he said after a moment.

Her sinuses burned and she wished she understood what she felt.

Jakob waited for what had to be a minute. When

she didn't say anything else, he finally nodded, put the Outback into Reverse and released the emergency brake.

They didn't talk during the short drive.

CHAPTER TEN

AMY LET HERSELF into the house as quietly as she could. She was desperately hoping she could sneak up to her bedroom and avoid conversation. When she saw that her mother was waiting for her, all she could think was *Please, no. Not now.*

Michelle sat on the living room sofa in a pool of lamplight. A magazine lay beside her as if she'd set it aside as soon as she heard the key in the lock.

"Did you have a nice time?" she asked.

A nice time. Amy could quite easily have become hysterical.

"Yes, we had a good dinner. Jakob showed me his condo. It's gorgeous, riverfront, in what was an old brick warehouse."

Mom nodded. "I wanted to talk to you before you went to bed."

What could she do but force a smile, drop her purse on a side table and take a seat in one of the not-so-comfortable armchairs in the living room. "That sounds serious."

"I'm leaving in the morning."

The rush of relief and hope made Amy ashamed.

Nonetheless, she couldn't squelch it. She *needed* to be alone.

"Ken must be missing you."

Michelle's head bowed. "Yes, he says he is. But I'm not going back to Australia, not yet."

What? "Then…where *are* you going tomorrow?"

Her mother lifted her chin again and met her eyes. "I plan to visit Wakefield College. I've never been back, you know."

Amy felt stricken, which was astonishing given how much anger toward her mother she had hoarded. *No, not only Mom—I'm mad at everyone,* she realized.

Even through all of that, worry rose to the surface. "Are you sure this is a good idea?"

Michelle ignored her. "And then I plan to turn around and go to the coast. Go home." A ripple of some emotion passed over her face. "When my father passed away, I was in such a hurry to sell the house, I moved all of their nicer furniture and anything personal to a storage unit and…left it. I've been paying on that unit all these years."

"I…didn't know that." One more thing she didn't know about her mother. Apparently evidence of the rape wasn't the only thing Mom had tried real hard to bury.

She had never seen an expression so fragile on her mother's face.

"It has become apparent to me that there is quite a lot I haven't dealt with. You were right when you said I never talked about my childhood or young adult life. What I need you to know is that most of that wasn't a conscious decision. The only secret I knowingly kept from you was the circumstances of your conception. I couldn't see how that would do anything but hurt you. I wasn't aware that I was managing to hurt you every day anyway."

Her chest was being painfully squeezed, boa-constrictor tight and tighter. "Mom…"

Her mother shook her head firmly. "You've been honest. Please don't deny what you really feel."

Amy subsided, although she was having trouble drawing a breath.

"If nothing else, it's ridiculous to waste so much money to keep a storage unit forever. Particularly since I doubt there's much in it I want to keep. I may simply give it all to a local thrift store, or—who knows?—perhaps I'll hold a sale, if the storage facility permits that."

Her mother, putting little price stickers on everything, smiling and accepting a dollar for this, ten dollars for that. Holding a garage sale. Not possible.

"I'd like to come with you," Amy said, not sure if she meant it but knowing this was something she had to do.

Michelle shook her head. "Thank you for offering." She even smiled, so tentatively it was nothing Amy recognized. "If this trip was purely practical, to clean out the unit, I would accept. But I want to drive around town, perhaps take walks, go through the things my parents left and think. It's past time, I'm sure you'll agree."

"Will anything change?" Amy couldn't help asking.

The strain on her mother's face aged her. "I don't know. I hope it will. I have always held a great deal of myself back. Intimacy of any kind has been very difficult for me. I fooled myself into thinking that was my business and only mine. Clearly, that's not the case. I do love you, and I love Ken. He's been very patient, but I need to open myself to…" She hesitated. "*Feeling,* I suppose, even when that isn't comfortable."

"Oh, Mom." Amy's voice cracked.

"I intend to get an early start. You needn't get up with me unless you're already awake."

"Are you sure you don't want company? I'd like to come if you'll let me." Saying it this time felt sincere. *Yes. This is something I want to do for her.*

Michelle's smile was softer than any Amy remembered, either, but she was also shaking her head. "This needs to be a personal journey." She actually laughed. "I sound as if I've started reading self-help books, which I promise I haven't."

Amy laughed, too, if shakily. "I'll hold you to that."

"I'm off to bed, then." Her mother rose to her feet. "Good night, Amy."

She stood, too. "Good night. Um…if you change your mind…"

"I won't, but thank you." Mom nodded with her normal briskness and started for the staircase. Hand on the banister, she paused. "I'm guessing I'll be gone at least a week, perhaps as much as two. I'll keep you informed."

"Please."

Amy was left standing near the foot of the stairs after her mother had disappeared above. The click of the bedroom door closing was as decisive as ever.

She felt very strange. Adrift. Nobody's motives were what she'd thought them to be.

I do love you.

Was it true? Had her mother always loved her and simply been unable to show her emotions?

And Jakob… A bolt of lightning seemed to flash in her peripheral vision, followed by the crash of thunder. She shivered at the power. *Nope, not ready to think about him.*

Of course, there was no way she could avoid it. All of this was so…intertwined. It *shouldn't* be. He and Mom had only the most distant and long-ago relationship. But they were her life, two of the three people she'd needed most. And now all three were claiming what she saw, what she experienced, wasn't really the way it had been at all.

Would believing any or all of them heal her, or

tear her apart? she wondered, and kept standing there for a long, long time.

I NEEDED SOMEBODY to love me.

Slumped on his couch, Jakob groaned and buried his face in his hands. Damn it, damn it, damn it. He'd *known* how she felt. How poorly her tough-girl persona guarded her underlying vulnerability. And still, he hadn't fully understood how completely he had devastated her. Even though his own feelings for Amy were huge and entirely subterranean, somehow he'd still managed to deceive himself and believe that his little sister really did dislike him. That his unrelenting cruelty had done nothing but infuriate her.

I should have hated your guts, but I didn't. I kept hoping... Remembering the expression on her face when her voice cracked, Jakob yanked painfully at his hair. In his head, he heard her finish, softer, more tremulous. *If I'd had you, it would have made a difference.*

Protecting himself, he'd never considered the cost to her. Even these past weeks, getting to know her again, letting himself begin to hope that the impossible might actually *be* possible, he hadn't had a clue how much he'd hurt her, or how she'd react to his upbeat news that, *Oh, by the way, really I always liked you just fine—in fact, I had the hots for you.*

And he was surprised she hadn't reacted with delight? Flung herself in his arms?

More like, once and for all hated his guts, and who could blame her? Not him.

He didn't know if she'd answer the phone if he called her tomorrow or the next day. Whether she'd ever want to see him again, talk to him.

I have to think about this, she'd said.

Like she needed one more thing to think about. One more betrayal to try to understand.

Why hadn't he waited? Given her a chance to deal with the shock of finding out who her father was, of the lies her mother had told? Offered the uncomplicated, loving support she needed?

Because he was selfish, Jakob concluded. One hundred percent. It had always been about him. *His* torment, *his* guilt, because he'd felt something he knew he shouldn't. Thank God he hadn't labeled it love, because love wasn't selfish.

Shock hit him with all the cold, brutal force of an avalanche. No, it wasn't love then. Only…the potential. A seed he'd recognized and had to kill by salting the field. Staring at the wall of windows, seeing neither the reflection of his condo and of him, nor the lights beyond, Jakob realized he'd failed. A seed had sprouted anyway.

He loved Amy, fierce and vulnerable—*not my sister, thank God not my sister*—as he'd never loved anyone.

And the only grain of hope he could hold on to was one of the last things she'd said.

You're not my brother.

He had to accept whatever she decided. If what she needed was an affectionate, supportive step-brother, by God that's what he'd be, although he didn't like to think what that would do to him long-term.

Didn't matter. *She* did.

HER MOTHER WAS trying to be quiet, as Amy had tried the night before when she crept into the house. But what snatches of sleep Amy had gotten weren't deep enough to allow her to miss hearing the bed-room door across the hall opening.

She dragged herself up, made a face at herself in the mirror and went downstairs. She'd shower later—if she didn't go back to bed.

Her mother, already dressed, had just poured herself a cup of coffee. "I tried not to wake you."

"I know. It's okay. I wanted to say again that if you change your mind at anytime, I'll be glad to join you. I've helped friends with garage sales and I've bought half of what I own at them. I'm a whiz at pricing."

"I'll keep that in mind." Her mother was shaking her head in faint disapproval. "You know Ken and I together make an excellent living. I don't under-stand why you've been so stubborn about accepting help."

"Because I'm stubborn?" She grinned, although the stretching of her facial muscles reminded her of the yoga class a friend had once persuaded her to take. The body did not like being asked to contort in unexpected ways.

"I'm afraid you came by that naturally," Mom said, shaking her head.

"You can say that again." Amy crossed the kitchen and gave her mother a hug, which did *not* feel natural, but did feel right. She wasn't stupid enough to give her time to reject or return the brief embrace, though. Rejection was too good a possibility.

Mom looked startled and the faintest of flushes touched her cheeks. "We do have some things in common."

"Probably more than I've wanted to admit." Another unsettling thought in a succession of them.

Ten minutes later, Mom was gone. She'd already packed the night before. She had decided to take Ken's SUV rather than her own sporty Volvo, in case she decided to keep more from her parents' house than she expected. In parting, she gave Amy's car a disdainful look, but said, "If you'd like to park in the garage while I'm gone, you're welcome to. You know where the spare remote control is."

Yes, Amy knew. Mom had made sure she knew where *everything* was. In case she forgot, there were lists. They had their own binder. Every name and phone number she could possibly need, from carpet cleaner to window washer. Where to find hidden keys, a credit card she could use for home repairs, emergency numbers.

Amy's car would probably be scared if she parked it in the garage. After a lifetime as an out-door car, it might get claustrophobia. Plus, she was pretty sure a week or two protected from sun and rain wasn't going to magically restore the shine to the paint job.

She had a sudden image of Jakob studying her car, then reaching out to finger a spot of rust. His expression, come to think of it, had looked a lot like Mom's.

What if he called today?

Don't have to answer.

What if he came hammering on the door?

He won't, she thought.

She'd told him she needed to think, and she did. She was entitled. But today, she had other things to do. Gardening was not among them. Her mother, Amy had noticed, hadn't been able to resist dead-heading and watering her roses. Amy had braced herself for a lecture afterward and been surprised when there were no accusations of neglect. She wanted to think that was because she'd actually been doing a good job taking care of the garden.

But, heck, maybe the real truth was that Mom had been shaken out of her usual behavioral patterns, too. They were both feeling their way.

Maybe, Amy thought with a new stirring of unease and hope, things could be different.

She tried to imagine her mother turning to return the hug, and failed.

A PICTURE OF her father appeared right above the fold on the front page of the local section in the morning newspaper.

Amy stared at it in shock. It looked as if he'd been waylaid by the press on the front steps of the courthouse. Microphones bristled along the bottom of the photograph. His intensity was visible even via black-and-white newsprint. He had been looking directly into the camera, which made her feel as if he was looking at *her*. She scanned the article, which mostly summarized the testimony of defense witnesses, concluding with statements both from the defense attorney and from Steven Hardy, who expressed confidence in the case he'd presented and the jurors' ability to see the truth.

She hastily turned the page so she couldn't see him anymore. Thank goodness Mom was in eastern Washington by now and reading some other morning newspaper.

At which point it occurred to Amy that Hardy must often be quoted, at least, in the paper, and this was unlikely to be the first time a picture of him had appeared, either. Her mother must have learned to hide any discomfort, which she wouldn't have wanted Ken to notice.

Amy rolled her eyes. As if Mom wasn't a champion at hiding what she felt.

Still, it had to be pretty awful for her to discover, first, that the man who raped her lived right here in Portland, and worse yet was a prominent citizen who often appeared on local news broadcasts and in the daily newspaper. Amy didn't like seeing his face. How much more horrible it had to be for Mom.

Yesterday Amy had finally managed to email the article about motorized bikes off to the publication at the top of her list. While she was at it, she resubmitted a couple of others that hadn't yet found a home. This morning, she'd received email acceptance of yet another article, a long, reflective interview with an eighty-six-year-old man who'd spent fifty years employed first as a sanitation worker and later for the city public works driving a street sweeper. He knew full well most people looked down on "garbagemen," but he had touching pride in having done a job that was important if most often unnoticed. There were funny stories about oddball things people left at the curb for disposal, a dark story about a dismembered body he had discovered in his load, the time he'd slowly pursued a purse snatcher in his street sweeper vehicle. He'd chuckled over how often his wife had to wash their sheets, especially in hot summers when he could never seem to get clean enough in the shower. Amy was really proud of the article, although it had been risky to write, not suitable for most publications. Now it had found a home. This time her pleasure wasn't all financial.

Mom would still be in Frenchman Lake, unless she'd gotten there, felt nothing but horror and turned around and left. It was probably a good thing that so much had changed. Not the campus, though; the presence of a few new buildings wouldn't overshadow how much the college must still look like it had thirty-five years ago.

Mom hadn't said where the rape had taken place. Steven Hardy's dorm room? An off-campus apartment? Surely not outside—spring would barely have been a hint in March, in eastern Washington.

Amy made herself finish the newspaper and then dropped it in the recycling bin. Out of sight, out of mind.

Her thoughts roiled anyway. All it took was the unexpected sight of *him* to stir up weird and conflicting emotions. He repulsed her, and fascinated her. She hated being fascinated, or any sense that she was drawn to him.

I want to talk to Jakob.

How could she, when she was still operating in avoidance mode?

He hadn't called, and she was glad. Mostly glad. She missed him, which was disturbing in itself. Had she ever missed anyone in her life? Amy didn't think so. Friends came and went. Guys were around for a while and then weren't. She might have felt a pang a few times, but nothing any stronger than that, which was probably why none of them had stuck around.

This huge desire for one person's company, to talk to that one person, was new.

After wandering aimlessly around, she ended up in the living room, where she curled up in relative comfort on her mother's too-stiff sofa. She gave fleeting thought to the big, deep leather sofa in Jakob's condo. Designed to lounge.

She was still mad, she decided, and had good reason to be. But also… Oh, face it. Thrilled. He had lusted after her. How amazing was that? A lifetime of feeling inadequate, certainly not wildly desirable to men, and it turned out that Jakob had had a major thing for her all that time. So major, it had scared him.

No, a voice seemed to whisper—*not past tense. He said you* scare *him.*

That didn't mean he was hinting at the possibility of anything happening between them now. He might only have wanted to clear his conscience. It had been a long time since either of them had been a teenager.

But then she remembered scattered moments, a few things he'd said. *I kind of like what's happening with us.* And him asking whether she had come to terms with the fact that they weren't related.

Why would he care if he didn't have something in mind that wasn't brotherly?

The way he'd touched her that night in the kitchen, when he came to dinner, a brush of his knuckles against her cheek and then bending his head so that his mouth couldn't have been an inch from hers.

Why don't you sleep on that?

Even then excitement had zinged through her. It was just…mixed with so much else.

He scared her, too.

She did want him in her life. Amy knew that for sure. But a sexual relationship? Her body leaped to life at the mere idea, but she was still confused in her head. Even thinking about it took a major readjustment.

Would he be patient? Or was this a now-or-never decision?

"I could ask."

Way to go—start talking to herself. Unlike friends who also lived alone, that was one thing she never did. She was too *used* to being alone. Holding conversations had never been necessary to her. People who talked to themselves, Amy believed, were only filling in until they had someone to talk to.

And now she yearned to talk to Jakob, who seemed to understand why she was so confused and upset, who seemed able to untangle some of the knot inside her.

With a sigh, she knew she had to call him.

Maybe even forgive him for all the misery he had put her through.

She might have to forgive Dad, too, and even Mom.

Because nothing was as it seemed.

She could almost hear Jakob ask, *Is that so bad?*

No, of course it wasn't. Only—she couldn't help feeling like that English building on the Wakefield College campus. It looked fine, plenty solid, built as it was of stately brick. But really it was having to be torn down. The flaw in its foundation that doomed it had been there from the beginning.

That's me, she thought dismally. Secrets exposed, damage irreparable. Definitely no solid foundation.

So…if nothing was as it seemed, that meant she wasn't, either, didn't it?

Stupid to be dazed by the obvious. Upside? At least she knew what was wrong with her. Wryly, she thought, *I guess I'm a tear-down, too.*

BROODING OVER FINANCIALS, Jakob frowned at his computer. He'd gone into his office on Saturday to make up for some of the time he'd missed lately.

The first few weeks at the new store in Flagstaff were looking good. Really good. He was less pleased with the obvious downward trend at the Santa Fe location. He was most disturbed because he still thought it was an ideal location for a Boulder River store. The manager who had shepherded the store through its opening and first year had left, though, lured away by a chain that sold women's apparel, and been replaced six months ago. On his recommendation, the assistant manager had been promoted.

Past time Jakob flew down there and spent some time analyzing the problems himself.

He grunted. He'd had the same thought last week…and the week before. Unfortunately, he was no more eager to head out of town now than he'd been then.

His personal phone rang, and his heartbeat gave a sharp kick as he reached for it. The jolt was all but painful when he saw Amy's phone number.

"Hey," he said, answering.

"Hi."

The little pool of silence was not peaceful. His apprehension was too acute to allow him to endure it long. "What's up?" he asked.

"Mom's gone out of town. I just thought we could get together." She paused. "If you want to, that is."

If he *wanted?* "I do," he said hastily. "Ah… where's she gone? Not back to Sydney, I take it?"

"No." She gave a little laugh. "She's taking a 'personal journey.'" Jakob could hear the quotes. "She's going to Frenchman Lake, and then to Florence, on the Oregon coast. Did I tell you that's where she grew up?"

"Yeah, I knew that." He felt reluctant sympathy

for a woman he'd never liked. "Did she want to do this alone?"

"Apparently. I offered, she refused."

"Why don't you tell me about it over dinner?"

"Okay. I can cook if you want to come here. I mean, we don't have to always go out."

Always. He rejoiced at the word. It implied a future, didn't it?

"Sounds good," he said. "Six o'clock work for you?"

It did. A moment later, she was gone and he laid down his phone. He stared at the computer monitor, comprehension slow to click in.

When it did, he had no trouble deciding Santa Fe would have to wait. The downturn was subtle and didn't qualify as an emergency.

A man who loved his job and what he'd created, he wished like hell it was time to leave for Amy's.

OF COURSE, HE had no idea what to expect when he got there. At least he felt reasonably confident she wasn't going to tell him she was still so pissed, she'd be glad not to see him for another five years.

After all, she'd said "always."

He parked at the curb and bounded up the front steps with all the eagerness of a teenage boy going to see his girlfriend with the full knowledge that *her parents weren't home.* Jakob was a little amused at himself.

Amy had the phone to her ear when she let him in, though. She grimaced an apology and mouthed, "Mom."

He nodded his understanding as he followed her inside and closed the door behind him. Mostly tuning out what she was saying, he appraised her as the conversation continued.

She looked really good. Her hair was shiny and bundled into a careless knot at the back of her hair. A strand had already escaped to curl on her neck. As she often did, she wore black tights or leggings, he wasn't sure which. Today they were topped by a teeny tiny, very short, stretchy skirt with broad stripes of red and black that hugged a shapely butt. He completely approved. The fire-engine-red knit top had the slouchy neckline she seemed to like. Trailing her into the kitchen, Jakob couldn't decide if he liked the sight of her ass better, or her nape and the shoulder that was mostly bared. The bare feet were cute, too.

God help him if she told him what he'd said freaked her out and the deal was friends or nothing.

But—wouldn't she have worn something more gender-neutral if that was the message she wanted to send? Or maybe she didn't know how provocative that stretchy bit of fabric over her ass was.

Puzzling over that one, his attention was still caught by the smell of something really good when they reached the kitchen. Definitely Italian. When he heard her say, "Drive carefully, okay?" Jakob tuned back in.

Amy listened for a moment. "I'll expect to hear from you then," she concluded, and closed her old-style phone before setting it down.

"Mom's heading for the coast in the morning. I pointed out that it would totally make sense for her to stop here—it's halfway, right?—and spend the night at home on her way, but she was vague and I could tell she didn't want to."

"Is it you she doesn't want to see?"

Quirky little lines formed between Amy's brows. He could tell she was really thinking about it, but she didn't appear all that bothered.

"I don't think that's it," she said after a minute. "I mean, she called. She just seemed...like maybe she doesn't want a dose of the here-and-now in the midst of her past life regression. If that makes sense."

Yeah. It did.

While she pulled a salad from the fridge and then a pan of lasagna, followed by garlic bread from the oven, she told him about her mother's decision to visit old haunts.

"How long ago did her parents die?" he asked, surprised.

Amy had to pause to think, her small hands still encased in padded oven mitts. "Oh, boy. Her mother back when I was in college. She had cancer, I know. With my grandfather, it was his heart.

I think he died not that long after Mom married Ken. Which would make it something like eight or nine years ago."

"Did you go to the funeral? Either funeral?"

She shook her head. "I'm pretty sure there was one for my grandmother, but I'm not sure Mom even had one for my granddad. I mean, she saw to his burial, but... Obviously, she didn't have a lot of fond feelings. Ken was with her that time."

Her tone told him she hadn't been invited on either occasion. Not that anybody *wanted* to go to a funeral, but when you didn't have a lot of relatives, it would hurt not to be included. That set Jakob to wondering how much it hurt to have her mother insist on making this journey into her past alone.

"I didn't know them that well," Amy said. From the jut of her chin he could tell she was defying any pity he might dare to feel.

"You didn't have any fond feelings, either." He didn't know who he felt sorriest for, Michelle, Amy or the grandfather who, in the end, hadn't had a single member of the family who truly mourned his passing.

"No." Amy handed him the basket holding the garlic bread. "Help yourself. Did you see the picture of Steven Hardy in the paper this morning?"

Her last sentence came out of left field, but he only nodded. "I hoped you didn't."

"Poor Mom."

Jakob could only nod. He finished dishing up

and was quiet for the next few minutes mostly because the lasagna was so good. The sandwich he'd
eaten at his desk for lunch was a distant memory,
and pretty dry and unsatisfactory at that.

"I'm sorry I got so mad the other night," Amy
said abruptly.

His head came up.

"I wasn't fair. I do understand why you were so
freaked out. And even why...well." Her eyes slid
away from his. Was her face coloring? "I mean,
there I was, a teenage girl and a stranger, showing
up to stay in your house and share your bathroom.
Like you said, boys that age think about sex all the
time, so..." Oh, yeah, her cheeks were definitely
pink now. "Although really, I was so skinny and
freckled and...I don't quite get why you'd do anything but vaguely notice."

"You know you've got some serious self-esteem
issues?" he asked, in lieu of getting mad.

Her gaze, showing both alarm and surprise,
touched his briefly. "That's not true! Shouldn't we
be realistic about ourselves? I'm a good writer. I'm
not a raving beauty." Her bare shoulder lifted in a
careless shrug. "I wouldn't trade one for the other."

"I thought you were beautiful." His voice was
thick. "Still think. You can't tell me no one else
has ever said that to you."

"No-o. Not exactly." In full-fledged blush now,
Amy looked so shy, he was more reminded than
ever of her younger self. "One guy said I had a

pretty smile." She seemed to be offering that up as…he didn't know. A way to say, *I haven't been totally deprived?*

"You do have a pretty smile," Jakob said as gently as he could. "But it's more than that. You've always made me think of catching a glimpse of a wild creature while hiking. You go home feeling deeply privileged and awed to have been so lucky, and, hell, maybe sad, too, because you might never have a chance like that again." And what was he doing, waxing poetic? If being compared to wild-life would seem flattering in any way to a woman. He braced himself for her reaction.

She was staring at him now, her eyes so beautiful he couldn't look away. "If you liked skinny and brown-haired, why did you marry a Nordic goddess?"

"I don't know," he admitted. "I never let myself think about you. I never met anyone else like you. And your hair isn't brown."

"Mostly."

He shook his head. "Chestnut, maybe."

"So." Her voice had sunk to almost nothingness. "When you told me, were you just clearing your conscience?"

Trust Amy to go for the jugular.

"No," he said huskily. "I guess I did want you to know I didn't treat you the way I did because I de-spised you. You do have really crappy self-esteem, and I don't like it. I hate knowing some of that's my fault. But the truth is, seeing you and knowing for sure that we're not related…" He felt like squirming. This was a lot harder than he'd envisioned, when he'd let himself imagine getting to this point with her.

"Means you want to act on your teenage fantasies?" She might be trying to sound amused, so either of them could retreat from this whole idea at anytime.

If so, Jakob didn't like it. "I didn't let myself have fantasies. There were a few dreams…." *Don't go there*, he warned himself. Those dreams had seriously disturbed him when he was a teenager. "No." Guttural, he didn't sound like himself. "This is about here and now."

Anxiety and maybe even desperation filled her eyes, making the color even more extraordinary. He thought she would have liked to bolt, but wasn't letting herself.

Instead she kept her head high and her gaze meeting his. "So you want…?"

Incredulous at the question, he tried to get a better read on her. Hard when all he had to do was look at her face and he felt a flicker of the wonder he'd tried to describe to her. Maybe *beautiful* wasn't the right word. *Wild* was closer, with a forehead that was almost too high, wide, delicate cheekbones and the sharp chin, the whole forming a triangle dominated by eyes the color of a fox's or a wolf's.

Did she really not understand what he was saying?

"You," he said. "I want you."

Was that a small flinch?

And then, belatedly, he got what she was asking. "Not...just to take to bed. If you feel anything the same, I want us to find out where it can go. I... really like spending time with you." When she didn't say anything right away, he had to clear his throat. "If...all you want is a stepbrother or, I don't know, a friend, say so. I can dial it back. I don't want to lose you, to make you so uncomfortable you don't want to see me." Oh, man, he sounded like a crazy. Why wouldn't she crave a brotherly relationship with a guy who'd just confessed to having lusted after her for something like twenty years?

It was all he could do not to groan. He should have taken it slower. Way slower. Said something like, *Let's be friends. And, yeah, I've noticed you're a woman so that might be something we can explore someday if it doesn't make you too uncomfortable.*

Amy seemed frozen. Paralyzed by shock.

"God," he said explosively, pushing his chair back. "I should have kept my mouth shut. You're dealing with too much already. I'm such an idiot. I..."

"I do." It was barely above a whisper. Her expression was almost…stricken. "I mean, feel the same." She kept looking at him, searching his face.

For understanding? For reassurance that he wasn't putting her through this on a whim?

It took a few seconds for the sense of what she'd said to hit. When it did, jubilation slammed into him. She felt the same. He could have fallen to his knees in celebration and the most profound relief he had ever felt.

"Amy." He blundered to his feet.

After the tiniest of pauses, she stood, too. He took a step toward her and with a shaky hand smoothed a wayward curl from her face, the way he'd imagined a thousand times.

Then, very slowly, giving her time for second thoughts, he bent his head.

CHAPTER ELEVEN

THE BRUSH OF Jakob's lips against hers was so soft, Amy almost thought she was imagining it. With her eyes closed, she could be dreaming. She stood with her weight shifted forward as if she was about to rise to tiptoe. She had the astonishing feeling of lifting her face to the sun, waiting for the heat to soak in deep and reach the place where she was always cold.

His hand slid around to cup the back of her head. Still blind, she lifted her hands to his shoulders and flexed her fingers experimentally. A ragged sound escaped him. His mouth came back to hers, still gentle. He nibbled at her lower lip, suckled it, then soothed it with a stroke of his tongue.

Amy wasn't sure she could move. Was this really happening? Was his touch as tender as it felt?

She touched his tongue with hers and whispered, "Garlic."

His tongue stroked inside her lips. "Balsamic dressing." The smile could be heard in his husky voice.

He nuzzled her, kissed her more deeply, then

lifted his head. Amy had to open her eyes to see him. What was he thinking? The blue of his eyes had darkened to near navy, and from his expression he was completely absorbed in *her*. Everything she saw on his face stunned her. *He* looked stunned, too, and awed—that was the word he'd used. As if he couldn't believe this was happening any more than she could. As if he'd never in his life wanted anything more. With his free hand, he caressed her cheek, and she felt him tremble.

With a moan, she surged up onto tiptoe and kissed *him*. Hard, and probably ineptly, but with everything she had in her.

He broke. The hand that had been on her face was suddenly gripping her butt and lifting her hard against him. The fingers on the back of her head clenched in her hair. He devoured her, his tongue thrusting now instead of tempting. She strained against him, and he pulled her tighter than she'd known she could go. She lost all sense of him and her. There was only *them,* pleasure and need underlaid by sharp disbelief.

They turned in a half circle, a slow dance, and crashed into something.

"Ow!" she cried.

"What?" He lifted his head.

It was the windowsill that had hit the small of her back. "I…we…"

He swore and abruptly stepped back, his hands sliding to loosely grip her upper arms. "I lost it."

His voice came out guttural. "I don't know what I was doing. Amy...I'm sorry."

Chilled, even though she could see the fierce need he was trying to bank in the slash of dark color across his cheeks and the glitter in his eyes, Amy shook her head. "It wasn't only you."

"Man." He squeezed her arms once, then let her go and backed up another step. "I was about to..." He looked dazed now.

She wanted him to do whatever he had been about to do. Amy was a little shocked to realize how much she did want it, and him. Her knees were wobbling, an ache between her legs was sharper than she'd ever felt before, and she was still breathing hard.

"Nobody has ever..." Oh, my God. Had she said that out loud?

His eyes became more intense. "Has ever?"

Polite lie, or make a fool of herself? But he'd given her honesty, and how could she do anything else?

"Wanted me like that."

Jakob half groaned, half laughed. "Fallen on you like a starving animal?"

This was beyond embarrassing, but she said it, anyway. "It sort of felt good."

He stared at her for a long moment. After what she'd said, Amy couldn't quite bring herself to meet his eyes.

"Yeah," he said slowly. "It felt so good, I'm

thinking maybe it's better we bumped into something. Until a few weeks ago, we hadn't seen each other in years. You thought I was your brother. Two days ago, you were shocked when I told you I wanted you when we were teenagers. I'm really pushing. You need to be sure."

Was she sure? Amy stood there feeling bemused and stupid even as she wanted nothing more in the world than to cast herself back against that tall, hard body, have his mouth descend again on hers, feel the vibration of his deep groans. Her gaze lowered to an erection there was no way he could hide, and she had to tighten her thighs to quell a vicious cramp of longing.

But I had to ask myself whether I'm ready. That means something, doesn't it?

"Mom and Dad..." she heard herself say.

His lashes veiled some of his intensity. "You're thinking it's going to be awkward."

"Isn't it?"

A nerve jumped in his cheek. "Probably."

She hated that he sounded so grim. She had hurt him, she suspected. What would he do if she said, *Who cares about them?*

"Maybe we should...well, finish dinner," she said instead. Speaking of awkward.

He moved his head as if his neck was painfully stiff. "Okay. Sure."

They retreated back to their seats. Amy stared at her plate as if it was something unfamiliar—a

Nordic ski binding, and she had to figure out how to wedge her foot into it.

After a minute he took a bite.

She did the same. She knew how to chew after all.

Garlic.

Balsamic dressing.

They'd tasted each other. She stole a look at him to find he was watching her. She had a feeling he was thinking the same.

"Dad suspects," he said.

"What?" Amy set down her fork.

"I guess I've said enough, or gave off the wrong vibes when he was here. He, uh, isn't all that happy."

"Oh." *Say something else.* "If he was telling the truth and really does think of me as his kid, then, well, this would take some adjustment for him."

"It's taking adjustment for us."

"Is it, for you?"

He shook his head in negation, then nodded, too. "I can't lie. Of course it is. I spent a lot of years denying what I felt. Even when I found out what happened to your mom and knew for sure that the two of us aren't actually related, I didn't immediately jump to thinking I'd do anything about it." His mouth quirked, relaxing his face to something closer to the Jakob she knew. "I took a whole week to admit I was kidding myself. I had to find out if there was any possibility."

"It should feel weirder than it does," she blurted.

He gaped at her for a moment, then shook his head and laughed, a low, rough sound. "Well, that's the last thing I expected you to say."

"Because of the way I blew up at you the other night?"

"No, because…" He frowned. "You never had any reason to suspect we weren't brother and sister."

"That's true, but we never *acted* like brother and sister. And what relationship we had was so many years ago…." She shrugged. That said it all.

"Still." He didn't look satisfied.

She knew, then, that she had to tell him some more of the truth, even if doing so made her feel naked. And not naked in the middle-of-a-passionate-scene way. More like if she'd walked out of the dressing room at the swimming pool without remembering to put her bathing suit on first, and now everyone was staring and she was trying desperately to cover her body.

"The way you acted hurt my feelings more than I let you see," she confessed. "And that was because I idolized you. You were big and strong and smart and handsome. Partly I was envious because you looked like Dad and even a little like Mom. You know?"

Jakob nodded, his expression… Well, she wasn't sure. Pitying? No, more troubled, Amy thought. The lines in his face had deepened.

"But partly…" She tried to sound nonchalant; this wasn't any big deal, she'd been a kid, and kids had these big, extravagant emotions. "Well, I thought you were cuter than any of the other guys. More…everything. It wasn't, you know, romantic or anything, but the boys in middle school and high school never measured up."

She had one hundred percent of his attention. "If you'd known I wasn't your brother…?"

His voice made her think of the scratchy texture of his jaw when he was kissing her. Heat moved through her. "I'd have had a huge crush on you," she admitted.

His eyes had darkened. "Damn. I want to grab you again."

She wanted him to, too. So much she quit breathing, only yearned. And he was right—until two days ago she hadn't even dreamed that she *could* feel this way about him.

"Man." He bowed his head. "Give me a minute."

This was surreal. The most handsome man she'd ever met was so hungry for her—her!—he looked as if he'd give up eating and drinking and *breathing* to have her. She wanted to believe in what she was seeing, what he had said, but it was hard. It seemed to violate everything she'd ever known about herself.

The poor sad girl no one loved. The misfit in her own family. Smart but freckled and skinny as a young teen, so not cool.

Stunned at how completely negative and even pathetic that all sounded, she cringed inwardly, but made herself continue.

Later, once she'd reached adulthood—sure, guys had liked her, but...

The *but* brought her to a stop. A listening sort of stillness. She thought things like that a lot and never examined them. Because of Jakob, she'd started to.

So...about those guys. Had she never been totally convinced they really wanted her? Was it possible there were a few along the way who did?

Had she always doubted them, the way she was doubting Jakob right now?

Yes.

"Maybe we should call it an evening." Jakob's voice jolted her from her self-absorption.

She tuned back in to see that he was studying her, those troubled lines apparent again.

"No!" Amy was startled by her own vehemence. "Please," she said, more softly. "Will you stay and...and talk to me?" She glanced ruefully at her plate and then his. "We never do very well with the meals I cook, do we?"

He gave a grunt of almost amusement. "Food's never at the top of my mind when we're alone. Restaurants are safer."

She shivered with longing again, but still felt that unease. "If you'd rather go..."

"No." His smile might be crooked, but it felt real. "I'd like it if we could talk. Maybe cuddle, too."

And so that's what they did. Jakob helped her clear the table and put away the leftovers. He eyed the pie she'd set out on the counter with interest and said, "Maybe in a little while."

He settled with a sigh at one end of her mother's sofa and lifted an arm in invitation. Amy plopped down on the middle cushion and leaned tentatively against him. His arm wrapped her shoulders and drew her closer. After a stiff moment, she surrendered. He felt so good.

He started talking about work in a way he hadn't before, even admitting to some mixed feelings about further expansion.

"Opening the store in Flagstaff ate up most of my summer. And now there are problems in Santa Fe…. I got into this because I love the outdoors and I want to equip people right so they have the best possible experience when they put that pack on their back or go sea kayaking or whatever. The result is, I have less and less time to get away myself."

Amy twisted a little to see his face. "And then I came along right when you had a break and instead of heading for the mountains you've been taking care of me."

His shoulders moved and he rubbed his cheek against the top of her head. "I can't think of anything I'd rather do than get to know you. Give you support when you need it. And hey, you had good timing."

She made a face, even though he couldn't see it. "For my breakdown, you mean? Just think of the fun things you could have been doing instead of coaxing me to eat and take a shower."

"I've had fun." His chuckle was a rumble against her cheek. "Maybe not that part, but...otherwise. Haven't you?" He sounded a little more careful.

Amy smiled, remembering the hike and the day in Astoria and even the weekend in Frenchman Lake, before she saw what her mother had left in the time capsule. "Yes, I have. These few weeks have been...weird. You probably won't believe me, but I'm usually on a pretty even keel." Too even, she thought in sudden perturbation; she never let the loneliness overwhelm her, but she had also blocked any real happiness. "I can't remember ever being so down or so up before."

"Carnival ride?"

Amy made a soft sound of agreement. "A dozen, at least. So many I'm dizzy and maybe ready to puke after all that cotton candy, but also feeling..." Alive. Aware. Deeply happy. Should she admit all that? Or to the underlying apprehension that soon the rides would go silent and the carnies would turn out the flashing lights and it would all be over?

How was it possible to be so happy and so unhappy all at the same time?

Jakob was waiting.

"…good," she finally said.

His arm tightened in a hug. Somehow he knew how confused she was. Usually she didn't like having anyone try to look deeper, but for the first time in her life she was grateful he could.

"Let's make a date," he suggested. "You ever been in Portland during the Rose Festival?"

"No." Of course he knew she'd gotten her degree at Reed College here in Portland. The famous Rose Festival was held in June. "School let out in May and I always got jobs elsewhere."

"Every year there's a fancy carnival at Tom McCall Waterfront Park. Fireworks, too, and dragon boat races, and parades."

"A parade of ships." She'd seen pictures and thought it looked cool.

"Right." He was smiling, she could tell. "What do you say?"

"I'm short. You'll have to find me a good spot to watch any parade."

He laughed. "Deal."

"Then it's definitely a date." Amy was proud of her breezy tone, when really her strange mood had her feeling melancholic. June was eight months away. What were the odds they'd still be spending time together that far into the future? Would he think of her when the Rose Festival did roll around, maybe with a pang for something that didn't quite happen?

I could try believing, she thought, but wistfully, because of course it wasn't that easy.

"You working on anything?" he asked after a minute, and she told him about how she'd discovered the Willamette Valley farm that was producing olive oil.

"Olive trees thriving in a wet, cold climate?" She shook her head. "They planted the orchard…oh, almost ten years ago now, and they mill the oil themselves. Yesterday I talked to a chef who raves about it. I don't usually write about food or restaurants or wineries. This, though, struck me as…quixotic."

He got that right away. "Tilting at windmills."

Amy laughed, taking satisfaction in the article that had been taking shape in her mind yesterday and today despite all her personal turmoil. "Right."

"You called Bryan yet?"

She'd done that today, too. "Yes. We're having lunch next week."

Jakob didn't move so much as a muscle. "Date lunch?"

"Business lunch."

His chest rose and fell with a breath, and she realized that's what had been missing. "He ask you out?"

"No, and I would have said no if he had."

"You're not interested, huh?"

She shrugged.

Of course he couldn't just accept that. "Because of what I told you about him?"

Amy straightened away from him. His arm fell back to his side and there was surprise on his face. "No. I think you made it all up anyway because you were jealous."

"Uh…" His grin had to be sheepish. Humor crinkled the tiny lines fanning from his eyes. "I might have exaggerated."

Amy sniffed.

"Well, then?"

"Well then what?"

"Tell me," he coaxed. "I want to know why Engel doesn't do it for you."

His charm was on full display, but she also realized he was a steamroller. Well, duh. Nobody built a business the size of his without a more than healthy quantity of determination and sheer doggedness and probably a good dose of inquisitiveness, too.

"You know why," she said grumpily. "I told you."

Heat seemed to flare in his eyes. "Tell me again," he said, voice a little huskier.

"You were there."

He took her hand in his and used it to tug her forward. "And no guy ever measures up."

Oh, so true. "Humph" was her commentary.

He laughed, low and triumphant, and then kissed her.

Completely unable to resist, Amy rose to her knees so she could lean in and kiss him back, with all the fervor she had never known she could feel.

THE WEEK THAT followed was so amazing, Jakob kept having this sense of unreality. That was Amy's small hand gripping his. Amy sternly correcting whatever wrongful political opinion he had just expressed. And, yeah, when he kissed her, sometimes he had to lift his head just to look down at that pixie face and believe it was her melting in his arms.

A teenage crush hadn't been a lot to base a relationship on, however powerful and lingering it had been. What he was finding was how much he liked the here-and-now Amy, who was one of the strongest personalities he'd ever known.

Volatile, too. Pugnacious, quick to take offense, fiery in defense of any underdog, all of which reminded him of the five-year-old who'd slugged it out with a *boy*. Hiding his amusement was sometimes a challenge. He was tempted to ask how often she ended up with a black eye.

She was quick to laugh at herself, too, though, and nothing gave him greater pleasure than her two versions of a laugh—one a surprisingly uninhibited guffaw, the other a giggle that sounded so young and always left her looking surprised.

Her happiest moments always seemed to end up shadowed, as though happiness could never be uncomplicated for her. The momentary dimming of her expression had a way of tangling him up inside, because he was partly to blame for some of what haunted her.

He loved her willingness to try anything, from

different foods to offbeat movies to whatever outing he suggested. With Halloween upon them, they went to a pumpkin farm and got lost in the corn maze, then carved two jack-o'-lanterns for the front steps of her mother's house. He came over for dinner and helped her dispense candy to the neighborhood children allowed to trick-or-treat. They went on an art gallery walk one night, ending up at a brewpub, where she wrinkled her nose and admitted she didn't like beer but drank a bottle of the dark, yeasty ale, anyway. A couple of early evenings after work, they ran together, making use of parts of Portland's extensive trail system.

And they made out, like a pair of fourteen-year-olds wary of the real thing but really, really horny. She made him laugh even when he wanted her so desperately he didn't know how he could wait. Her vulnerability had him tender despite the fact that he was spending more time aroused and unfulfilled than he had since…hell, since he was sixteen and she was staying in the bedroom across the hall from him.

He frequently found himself remembering those hot summer weeks when she'd come to visit, the most miserable of his life, but he kept trying to slam the door on the memories. She was here, this was now. He'd lie in bed at night—alone—confirming to himself that he'd have asked her out the minute he met her, even if they had no history. He didn't want their relationship to be about times he couldn't go back and change, about the way he'd hurt them both with his cruel efforts to make her hate him.

All the common sense in the world failed to shut down the memories, though. He had a couple of shockingly vivid and erotic dreams in which they were teenagers and he'd slipped into the guest room—which, in the way of dreams, looked nothing like the extra bedroom as he recalled it, but he knew that's where he was, anyway. After the second one, he woke up so aroused he groaned and flung an arm over his eyes. Why wasn't he dreaming about the Amy he'd kissed good-night only a few hours ago? What was his subconscious trying to tell him?

On Friday she had lunch with Bryan Engel. Jakob was restless and irritable as he brown-bagged it at his desk. He had no reason to be jealous, but was, anyway.

He knew what the trouble was. A few days ago he'd suggested he talk to his father, be upfront. He'd seen her shock.

"We don't have to do that yet, do we?" she asked. No, be honest—begged.

What could he say? "Of course not. But sooner or later, we do."

She had nodded, but doubtfully, and he filled in the blanks.

They had to tell their parents only if the relationship was still ongoing.

Any and all doubts were on her side, and *that's* why he was irrationally, stupidly jealous.

Didn't it figure that was the one evening they hadn't made any arrangement to get together.

Amy called him midafternoon, though. "Your friend Bryan has done some of the coolest projects!" Her delight obvious, she enumerated those projects at some length while Jakob seethed. "And since he's been trying to fly below the radar—his words, remember?—he's saved himself for me. All for me!" she crowed.

Despite himself, her pleasure in the lunch smoothed the rough edges of his mood.

"And I know he never would have talked to me if it weren't for you," she concluded. "So thank you, thank you, thank you!"

"Glad I could be useful." Smiling now, if reluctantly, he even meant it.

"Just think how amazing articles about you *and* him would be. Bookends. No, Portland's sexiest and most compassionate bachelors! Damn it. If only I could interview you."

"You can interview me anytime, babe," he drawled. "Seems to me you did some…interviewing last night."

She blew a raspberry that made him laugh. "If only we didn't have the same last name."

That wiped the smile off his face. She was quiet a little longer than was natural, too.

"I take that back," she said, sounding more subdued. "But you know what I mean."

"I know."

"I should let you go," Amy said, brisk again. "I taped the interview, and I need to type it up and start thinking about who else I need to talk to."

He gritted his teeth. Would he sound desperate if he asked her to dinner?

"I know I've been monopolizing your time. You might be busy tonight. But I'd be glad to try cooking again if you want to come over. Although I may not forgive you if you spurn my food again," she joked.

"I don't know. Us alone again." His blood heated even as he tried to respond in the same spirit. *Alone again.* Accompanied by a deep, primitive drumbeat, the words sang to him. "But I'm tough. I guess I can handle it."

"Any requests?"

You. He cleared his throat. "We could just order in since you've had a busy day."

"No, I don't mind cooking."

They agreed on a time, and she was gone. Jakob's bad mood was erased as if it had never been. No carving tools and slimy pumpkin innards heaped on the table between them this time. Alone together!

Don't rush her, he warned himself.

Even so, he was as blasted eager when he bounded up the steps to Michelle's front porch as he'd been that other, ill-fated time. Didn't care that it was pouring rain and he was getting soaked. There were no more secrets between them, they'd been having fun together, she hadn't said much in days about her mother or her biological father. She seemed to be okay. If she was still as disturbed as she'd been, she would say something to him, wouldn't she?

She was on the phone again when she opened the door. She peered past him at the rainy night and mouthed, "Bryan."

"You were fantastic," she said, heading for the half bath under the staircase. When she returned with a towel, she was still talking. "Yes, I'm sure I'll have more questions for you once I talk to people at the nonprofits you've helped." She thrust the towel at Jakob, who ran it over his wet hair. "Uh-huh."

Jakob kissed her forehead and she made a cute face for him. He took off his shoes and left them by the door, then padded after her to the kitchen. Spicy smells greeted him. Chicken tacos, he diagnosed, seeing the corn tortillas and small bowls of salsa, sour cream and chopped cilantro.

Sudden silence behind him made Jakob turn. Amy's gaze was on him as she listened to whatever his friend was saying.

"That's very flattering," she said, then was apparently interrupted.

A wave of raw possessiveness had Jakob's body going rigid.

"No, I do mean it, but I'm involved with some-one already."

He relaxed slightly, but the adrenaline was still doing a number on him. He was really glad Engel couldn't see Amy right this minute, wearing knee-high boots over snug, thin pants topped with a drapey, thigh-length sweater. Then it occurred to him that Bryan probably *had* seen her like this; no reason she'd have changed since lunchtime. No wonder the bastard had asked her out—and was still talking.

"Actually," she said after a minute, "he's here right now."

Jakob held out his hand. She shook her head ve-hemently and backed away. He held her stare and waggled his fingers. After a moment Amy gave an-other huge, exasperated eye roll and handed over the phone.

"Hey, Engel," he said. "It's Jakob."

He knew flabbergasted silence when he heard it.

"I thought she was your sister!" his friend choked out.

"Stepsister, and our parents divorced when she was six and I was nine. We hadn't seen much of each other in years when we discovered we both lived in Portland."

"I could have sworn you said…"

"You heard wrong."

"Well, damn."

Jakob laughed. "Sorry," he said insincerely.

Bryan grumbled some more and was still at it when Jakob gave the phone back to her. She didn't say much, but laughed a couple of times and finally closed the phone and laid it on the counter.

"Satisfied?" she asked with raised eyebrows.

"Yeah." Jakob was embarrassed to realize how smug he felt. This desire to claim a woman was new to him.

"It might have been better if I could have strung him along until I'd finished the article."

"You'd have gone out with him for no other reason?" he asked incredulously.

Her look was indignant. "Of course not, but if you weren't around I probably *would* have gone out with him. He's good-looking, he's nice, he has a sense of humor, he's giving lots of time to good causes…. What's not to like?"

"Nothing," Jakob admitted. "Wild behavior aside," he added belatedly.

"Right. Sure." She headed for the fridge. "Beer?"

When he agreed, she grabbed one for him and poured herself milk.

"You bought the beer for me," he said, pleased.

"For guests," she agreed, then laughed at his expression. "Of course for you. You're the only guest I've had."

That required a kiss, which held back dinner for a couple of minutes. She wrestled out of his arms eventually, though. "Oh, no, you don't! We're eating dinner no matter what."

"Alone," he reminded her, feeling aroused but good. "Dangerous."

They kept it light for much of the meal. Her tacos were seriously spicy, which he liked. There was nothing bland about Amy; he'd have been shocked if her favorite foods were mashed potatoes and macaroni and cheese out of the box.

"For someone who isn't that interested in eating, you're a fantastic cook," he said.

"My checkered career. I waitressed one summer and swore never again, but a friend who runs her own catering business hired and trained me. I worked for her for...oh, probably five years. We were a perfect match, because she only needed help part-time and intermittently. I could drop everything and work ten-hour days when a big shindig came along, and was fine if she didn't need me at all for two weeks."

"Ah. Makes sense. Was that when you lived in Seattle?"

"San Francisco."

He'd forgotten she lived in the city by the bay for a few years. One place Jakob had never lived, but he had spent time there.

They talked about why he didn't yet have any California stores, although he currently had someone researching possibilities.

Eventually, Amy served a dessert of key lime pie that she admitted had come from a neighborhood bakery. She got a little quieter then.

"You heard from your mother?" Jakob asked.

Her eyes flashed surprise when she looked at him. "How do you read my mind?"

"Sometimes I think you read mine, too."

She frowned at him, then shrugged acknowledgement. "She called today."

Jakob waited.

It took her a minute, and she started slow, but it came out that Michelle had let sadness seep through her usual reserve, and Amy had begged to be allowed to join her in Florence and help go through the grandparents' stuff.

"No surprise she refused." Amy gave a twisted smile, the one that always gave him an uncomfortable bump in his chest. "She might have to actually talk to me. Share some memories. So not her style."

"It sounds as if she is talking to you more than she ever has." He wouldn't let her see how angry he was at Michelle. Whether she was indifferent to her daughter's pain or just plain insensitive, he had quit seeing a rape that had happened thirty-five years ago as an adequate excuse.

"Yes." She used her fork to squish a bite of her pie. "No, you're right. I'm expecting too much. Did I tell you?" The glint of gold was absent in her big, caramel-brown eyes. "Right before she left, I hugged her. I can't remember how long it's been since I did that. Just for a second, I thought..." She pressed her lips together. "I wondered if the time would ever come when she'd hug me back. But I know how dumb that is as a fantasy." She was really good at sounding uncaring, amused at herself. "A few times I've seen Ken put his arm around her, but she never leans against him the way women do. Honestly—I have a really hard time picturing them in bed together." She laughed, her body language easing. "I'll concede, who does want to picture any parent having sex?"

"Not me," he said fervently. "Oh, man, that was the worst part when Dad was dating Martina. There I was—what? fifteen?—thinking about nothing but girls' tits and asses...."

"And the way she walks and smells." She scrunched up her nose again. "I remember."

"Right. And what's my father doing but having sleepovers down the hall. I'm sure he thought they were quiet, but a couple of times I heard the headboard banging the wall. It was all I could do not to race for the bathroom and puke."

"It didn't turn you on?" She looked brightly interested.

"God, no! They were *old*."

The next second, they were both laughing.

He didn't know about her, but he felt a lot better after that. He was able to go back to enjoying the tart lime pie and the coffee Amy had served with it. She even finished her slice, half the size of his.

"Mom did talk about some things she might bring back with her," Amy said suddenly. "A couple of family quilts. Apparently my grandfather's grandmother was a quilter. Mom says she'd forgotten, because they were kept rolled in pillowcases in a cedar chest. The good news is that according to her they're in pristine condition. She says I can pick whichever one I want to keep."

"No bad memories attached to them for her."

"No." There were some other things, too. Her grandmother had a glass-fronted case of porcelain collectibles that Amy, on the rare visits to their house, had been strictly forbidden to open. "Mom says she was, too. Once her dad whipped her because he caught her looking and he didn't believe she hadn't opened it so she could touch, too. What a creep. No wonder she hated him. Anyway—she says she thinks some of the figurines are actually pretty valuable. Meissen, Spode, I don't know what else. They're more Mom's style than mine, but she says she's bringing all of them home, too, and we can look at them and decide what we want to keep and how to sell the rest."

"She is talking to you, then."

Tiny creases formed between Amy's eyebrows. "I guess so." After a minute she shrugged. "That's the story. Enough said about Mom."

"Good." Watching her as closely as he had been, Jakob had seen the signs of nerves she couldn't quite hide. He was feeling some tension himself. They'd both finished dinner. Even coffee. They were alone. Last night's kiss had come close to getting out of control.

He cleared his throat. "Is there any chance at all you plan to invite me to stay tonight?"

She eyed him warily. "What if I don't?"

Don't push.

He offered what he hoped was a reassuring smile, when the truth was his body had already hardened at the very thought of going upstairs with Amy, turning into her bedroom instead of her mother's.

"Then I politely kiss you good-night at the front door and go back out in the rain." Which hadn't let up; he could hear it on the roof and it ran down the small-paned windows, obscuring any view beyond the glass.

"Oh." She was fiddling with something, as she often did, in this case the unused bread knife that was getting rolled between her fingers. She looked down at what she was doing. "I suppose you're impatient."

At her small voice, he grabbed for what patience he did have left. "Amy…" He waited until she lifted her eyes to meet his. "I want you, but I can wait." Too bad his voice, river-rock rough, belied the words.

Her gaze momentarily flitted away, shy. But Amy was too direct for much evasion. After a moment she looked squarely at him. Her chin was high and defiant. "Actually…" She sounded gruff. "I'd like it if you did stay."

He'd braced himself for anything but. It took a minute for dreams to become belief. There was a fleeting moment of remembering what he'd told her, about how he'd always seen her as shy and wild, and how awed he felt just to see her, touch her.

That awe was part of the most powerful tangle of emotions he'd ever felt. "Amy," he said, raw.

Her smile was shy, but brazen, too, and so sweet he was lucky he could stagger to his feet.

"Amy."

She came out of her chair and into his arms with a rush.

He was ready for her. He thought he'd been ready his whole damn life.

CHAPTER TWELVE

ALL THROUGH DINNER, Amy had known what was coming. She'd *planned* it. She might even have been insulted or hurt if Jakob hadn't asked whether he could stay.

But a part of her still wished he hadn't. These weeks with him had been magic, the best of her life. And sex… Well, that was something she wasn't very good at.

Not that she didn't go through the motions. Guys mostly seemed satisfied, and sometimes she even enjoyed herself. But she knew she walled the most essential part of herself off as soon as things got intense.

She'd realized a long time ago that she had a problem with being touched and held. She and her mother were two of a kind.

Maybe it was inevitable when you grew up in a home where everyone was very, extremely careful *not* to touch. She wouldn't even want to try if it weren't for her dad and those first few years. Prekindergarten memories were scattered and not always clear, but they were there: her running to

Daddy when he came in the door and him laughing and swooping her up, swinging her in a circle, dangling her over his shoulder and ignoring her giggling protests. She could see the world from the perspective of sitting on her daddy's shoulders, her small fingers gripping his hair for security. Story times, encircled by his big arm.

So she wasn't like those babies raised in orphanages who had passed the point where it would ever be possible for them to enjoy physical intimacy. But sometime after her daddy moved out, taking Jakob with him, Amy had frozen inside. Now, even when she was turned on, getting naked with someone, having full body contact, letting a man be all over her and inside her, always had her feeling... She couldn't even name it. Like she wanted to shrink away and protect herself.

Kissing was okay, sex not so much.

So far, she hadn't had any of her usual squeamishness with Jakob, but they hadn't taken their clothes off, either. She'd been able to hope. This was Jakob, who had always been perfect in her eyes. Amy wanted to see him unclothed, tall and strong and golden. She just had this really bad feeling that sex would go wrong somehow and ruin everything.

That *she* would ruin everything.

Now the moment had come and, despite all her fears, she threw herself into his arms, closed her eyes and pressed her face to his chest. Breathing in his scent—male, woodsy and uniquely him—both calmed and excited her.

One of his big hands cradled the back of her head, the other roved restlessly up and down her back. It was a moment before she realized his hands both were shaking.

"Jakob?" She looked up.

She didn't know that expression on his face.

"It seems like I've wanted you all my life."

Oh, boy—if anything was calculated to scare her, that was it. Talk about expectations.

Amy tried to smile. "Now you get me."

"Yeah." His voice was hoarse, his eyes searching hers. "You look scared to death."

"No." Honesty seemed to be important. "Well, nervous. Um…I know you don't like it when I say this, but I'm not that…"

"What?"

"Beautiful!" she blurted. "I'm skinny. I don't *know* why you want me, okay? And I don't know how I can possibly measure up to what you seem to feel."

During her speech, she felt him stiffen. Frustration tightened his mouth and darkened his eyes.

"You're right. I don't like it. To me, you are beautiful. Why can't you accept that?"

"Because I know I'm not!"

His hand dropped from her back. The one on her head moved in a rough caress, as if he couldn't help himself, then dropped to his side, too. "We don't have to do this."

She stepped back, pride keeping her head high even though her eyes burned. "That's not what I was trying to say."

"Then what was your point? You think I'm taking pity on you? Or maybe just getting it where I can, and—hey!—we're spending a lot of time together?"

"No!" She balled her hand into a fist and punched his chest. "You know it's not that! You asked if I was scared, and I am, that's all. Because you… you're…" Her voice cracked.

Suddenly his arms were around her again, his face close, his tenderness giving her goose bumps. "What am I, Amy?"

"You're…" She forced it past the lump in her throat. "Special. I don't want to disappoint you, that's all."

"How could I be disappointed?" His lips moved softly over her face, forehead, temples, cheeks. He nuzzled her, his breath warm on her skin. "Making love isn't a competitive sport. There's no scoring system. If we're awkward, then we'll be less so the next time. It's okay to laugh at ourselves, you know."

Her knees were melting wax. "Okay," she managed to respond.

"If this still feels too weird, we can wait, you know. I meant it."

A fireball in her chest made her push away. "You're really hung up on that."

She'd known why he was being so patient. What she couldn't decide was whether he really thought she was freaked out because she'd believed he was her brother—or whether *he* was the one who couldn't get past it. He didn't seem to understand that her problems didn't have anything to do with him, except for him being...oh, her dream. Her Mr. Perfect.

"Me?" he said, looking startled. "No, I just want to make sure you're not."

"Fine." She took a deep breath, laid her hands open on his chest and rose on tiptoe to kiss his jaw. "Are we going to do this, or not?" she murmured.

Jakob gave a gruff laugh. "You kidding?" He wrapped his hands around her hips and brought them flush against him. His erection was thick and hard, pressed into her belly. "Can we go upstairs?"

"Yes, we can."

"The kitchen..."

Her rude response made him laugh. Joy and hope seemed to rise in her, so that she wasn't sure her feet were actually touching the stairs. Mostly what she felt was his hand holding hers tightly. She felt it when he squeezed her butt partway up, too.

"The things you wear," he said. Or she thought he said.

He crowded her against the wall when they reached the top of the stairs and kissed her. She felt that and nothing else. She'd have sworn her blood had become thick and slow and syrupy.

A few more steps and they stumbled into her bedroom. Jakob peeled off her sweater before they reached the bed. She'd worn a bra tonight, her lacy best, even though she didn't really need one. She watched carefully for any disappointment when he looked at her, and saw only heat in eyes that blazed blue. He cupped her breasts and moved his hands in a gentle, circular motion that made her moan and let her head fall back. The next moment, he'd swooped her up and deposited her on the bed.

Her bra fell away.

"You're delicate." His voice had gone as thick as her blood. "So pretty." He bent her back and licked her nipple, then drew it into his mouth.

Amy made incoherent sounds and grabbed onto his powerful shoulders for purchase. After a minute she tugged at his shirt and he half cooperated in her effort to strip it over his head, even though he was reluctant to let her go long enough.

After that he kissed his way down her belly and finally planted a knee on the bed as he reached for the zip inside the calf of her right boot. "Do you know how sexy these are?" He pulled the zip down really slowly, as though he was unwrapping her.

"I hoped," she said, knowing she was flushed and trembling, wishing he'd hurry.

He tugged the first boot off then went faster on the second one. He chuckled at the sight of her bright, striped toe-socks before sending them fly-ing, too. An openmouthed kiss on the arch of one foot made her toes curl. With a groan, he sat up straight and peeled off her leggings as if she were a banana and all he wanted to do was bite into the soft flesh.

After that, he tried to slow things down and she taunted him into speeding up. Oh, she wanted to see him—all of him—but wasn't as good at peel-ing as he was. She forgot the athletic shoes and bunched his jeans and knit boxer shorts up at his ankles before he laughed and finished undressing himself.

Nothing in her life had ever felt as good as full body contact with Jakob did. Stunned, she went still just for a moment to savor. His muscles were so smooth and hard, so warm and eager to flex at the slightest touch from her fingertips. The hair on his chest was dark gold. She wanted to explore, but even more she wanted to get closer yet. To be part of him.

He kissed and stroked and licked while she did the same, and then he was between her legs before he rumbled and rolled off her.

"Condom."

She'd kept using the birth control patch because it was habit and you never knew when you'd be glad, even though she'd had no reason to be glad in a long time. He must have felt it on her hip, but she'd always insisted on a condom, too. This was the first time ever she was tempted to say, *You don't have to use one*.

He came back down on her, his mouth voracious, his tongue stroking hers in a rhythm that made her body ache and her hips rise. And then he was in her, pushing deep, and she whispered, "Jakob." Nothing else.

Magic.

He was saying her name, too, as their bodies rose and fell, missed a beat, struggled and came together in harder, faster plunges. He lifted his head and watched her, his eyes shockingly blue, his lips drawn back from his teeth, the skin stretched taut over angular cheekbones.

When she fell over the edge of the world, she couldn't have stopped the keening cry if she'd tried. His eyes closed, as if in bliss, and she felt him throbbing inside her as he thrust deep and held himself there.

Then his head dropped, his forehead touching hers, his weight on his elbows. With a groan, he flipped them both, so she was on top of that long, strong body, her head on his shoulder.

Amy lay there, loving the sound of his heartbeat, the way his broad chest lifted with each breath, not sure she *could* move. Dazed, she thought, *What was that?*

"And you thought I'd be disappointed," he whispered.

This was the first time ever *she* hadn't been disappointed, either. And—wow—she discovered that scared her, too.

A memory flitted through her mind, about that time he'd compared her to a wild creature he had been lucky enough to encounter. He'd talked about being awed, but it was the rest of what he said that she felt like a chill on her overheated skin.

You were a little sad, too, he'd said, *because you might never have a chance like that again.*

What if *this*—what she'd felt tonight—was her one chance. Something she'd spend the rest of her life dreaming about?

Because, no matter what he said, she couldn't believe she could possibly be enough for Jakob. This might, in some kinky way, have been a fulfillment of his forbidden teenage fantasy. And if so...well, he'd get restless soon, wouldn't he?

"I'D LIKE YOU to meet more of my friends," Jakob said simply. He couldn't figure out why Amy was resisting his invitation.

"I'm not really good at parties." She twirled the straw in her chocolate milk shake and refused to look at him.

They'd had a fantastic day—at least, he thought they had. Snow in the mountains was scant so far this year; November was usually too late for most hiking, but he and Amy had been able to enjoy a short trail along the Salmon River in Mt. Hood National Forest. This time, he had insisted on outfitting her with good quality hiking boots, which he thought were cute on her small feet. Once again, he'd had the impression she loved the silence, the deep forest and glimpses of icy river. The air was crisp and cold enough to turn her nose and cheeks red—hell, probably his, too. The chipmunks made her laugh, and she was dazzled by a distant glimpse of a black bear that hadn't yet hibernated. He'd have loved to spot a marten, whose clever, triangular faces reminded him of Amy's, but those were rare in the middle of the day, as the member of the weasel family was mostly nocturnal.

Amy had been chattering happily during their stop halfway back to Portland for burgers and fries until he'd mentioned the afternoon party a couple of his friends were holding tomorrow.

"They're actually barbecuing," he'd told her. "They have a covered patio with one of those ridiculous grills that looks like it should belong to NASA. Big house, though. If it's cold or raining, we don't have to step outside. Doug's the one who loves that damn grill. He can freeze out there by himself."

The first words out of her mouth had been "Oh, I won't know anyone."

To which he'd said, "You'll like them."

The problem, he was coming to believe, was that *she* didn't think they'd like *her*. He couldn't figure it out. She wasn't shy—she sure as hell hadn't been when he introduced her to Bryan that night at Nostrana. She was constantly interviewing complete strangers and apparently winning their confidence to an extraordinary degree.

"Wait," he said, something that felt like anger but wasn't quite rising in his gorge. "Is this like you not wanting to tell Dad and your mom that we're involved?"

She lifted her chin at last and her eyes flashed defiance. "What are you talking about?"

"You're embarrassed to be with me."

The color stung into her skin by the cold deepened as he watched.

"I just don't want to be flung into the deep end, okay? I can deal with one person at a time. But a whole group staring and wondering…" She stopped so suddenly, he could see the skid marks.

"Wondering what you see in me."

She snorted.

Goddamn it. "Wondering what I see in you," he said slowly. "That's it, isn't it?"

"Don't be ridiculous."

Oh, that convinced him. "Why can't you get past this?"

The defiance deserted her, leaving her looking pinched and forlorn. "I'm trying," she said, softly enough he had to tilt his head toward her to hear.

"Damn it, Amy." His throat felt clogged. As usual, she messed him up—one minute he was pissed, the next sad, then happier than he'd ever been in his life. Sometimes, like now, it all got mixed together. He wasn't sure if he was more patient with her lack of self-esteem because of the share of guilt he carried, or less.

He almost grunted, as if he'd taken a blow. What a self-centered bastard he was being. If she'd only blossom into a sunny state of complete self-confidence in their relationship, he wouldn't have to feel guilty anymore, right?

"Okay." The word came out gruff and small. "I'll come."

He reached across the table for her hand, which for once didn't return his clasp. "No. I don't know why I made an issue out of this. If it doesn't sound fun, we won't go."

"You could go, anyway."

He shook his head and retrieved his hand, not liking the cold, unresponsive feel of hers under it. "Everything we've been doing is to please me. The first time you balk, I sulk."

"No, that's not true. Everything we've done together has been fun. I always thought of hiking as sweat and hard work to see a view you could admire from your car, but it's not. I loved today. I've never been in a corn maze, or gotten a pumpkin at a farm instead of the bin at the grocery store. You're sharing your world, and I love that."

"But you'd rather we stick to it just being the two of us when we go out."

She shook her head, determined. "No, I mean it. I'd like to go. I was being twelve years old again.

'Dad's making Jakob take me and he'll ditch me the minute we get there.' Stupid."

After a minute he nodded. What else could he do? Refuse to take her? "I think you'll like everyone."

"I'm sure I will. Maybe Bryan will be there."

"Not if he knows what's good for him."

She grinned at him, and he hoped the confidence that let her taunt him was real.

AMY WAS "ON" from the minute he picked her up Sunday. She'd worn another of those sassy little skirts over tights and the knee-high boots. The belted knit shirt was more like sweatshirt thickness than what she usually wore; Portland weather had taken a turn for winter at last. They'd been lucky yesterday. Today was gray, dark and cold enough he knew snow was falling at only slightly higher elevations. She added a wool peacoat and gloves before they went out the door.

During the drive, when he asked if she skied, she made a face.

"Alpine. And that was a lo-o-ong time ago. Do you know how expensive it is? It was fun, though, except for the frost-bitten-toes part."

He laughed. "See, the thing about cross-country skiing is that you're working hard enough to keep you warm."

"Oh, sure. I've watched the Olympic games. I

remember this guy crossing the finish line with a beard frosted white so he looked like Santa Claus."

He nipped her chin between his thumb and forefinger. "By the hair of your chinny, chin, chin. We'll put you in a fleece mask. Promise."

"Oh, God. You're trying to turn me into an outdoors girl."

She said it gaily, as she'd said everything so far, but he gave her a sidelong look, trying to read how serious she was.

"Say no anytime." He made sure she could tell he meant it. "We don't have to share all our hobbies."

He'd braked for a red light and was able to turn his head to meet her eyes.

"If you ask me to go mountain biking, I'll say no. I'd say no to the Portland to Seattle bike ride, too. Or is it the other way around? This other stuff, I'm willing to try. I'm not an outdoors girl because I never had the chance. Can you see Mom hefting a pack? Even Dad likes luxury when he isn't tromping around in the baking sun on a job site. I never actually understood how you got hooked."

"Boy Scout leader. Most of the jamborees—you know, mass camping—those I didn't like. But I was lucky and had a leader who took our troop hiking, backpacking, birding, some minor rock scrambles. He was a good guy."

"Was?" Amy asked.

His fingers flexed on the steering wheel. "He

had a brain tumor. A couple of surgeries, but it got him. His son and I are still friends."

"I'm sorry." She laid a hand on his thigh, squeezed and then let go. His flesh preened at her every touch. To him, her hand felt red-hot, branding him through the heavy denim. His dick stirred.

Not now, he told it. *Later.*

Doug and Cheryl Leveck lived in a minimansion on a sloping lot above Lake Oswego. Cheryl was management at Intel, Doug an orthopedic surgeon. They were loaded.

Amy made some admiring sounds as they circled the lake, which was beautiful even on a bleak day. The town proper reflected the income of residents—most of the shops were trendy and expensive, with hardly a chain store to be seen.

"Ugly house," he commented as he pulled to the curb in front of it. Half a dozen other vehicles had gotten here before them and clogged the long, curving driveway.

Amy studied it. "Not ugly. Ostentatious."

"Yeah. I like Doug especially, though. I think the house may be more Cheryl's taste."

"Maybe not," Amy pointed out, "considering that Doug's the one who revels in his monster barbecue grill. Would *you* want one?"

"Hell, no!" He grinned at her. "You might be right. And those are words I don't often say."

He locked up. Driven by freezing rain, she scampered down the driveway fast enough he had to take long strides to be close enough to catch her if she slipped in those boots and went down. They were shaking rain—or was it sleet?—from their hair when Cheryl let them in, enveloping Jakob in a big hug. Other voices rose in greeting. Amy kept smiling.

Not a shy bone in her body, he tried to believe, but failed. Good at faking was more like it.

It occurred to him belatedly that almost everyone here was financially successful. That's not why they were his friends—mostly these were people who loved the mountains the way he did. But maybe that wasn't enough; maybe he looked for friends who also shared the drive that made him ambitious. Or was it a passion for something, that made them successful?

He introduced Amy around. Almost immediately, a face lit. Erica and Tom Riehl were winemakers who in only ten years were building a major reputation. "You're a writer!" Erica exclaimed. "That piece you did for *1859* on the old fisherman was amazing."

He had his hand on Amy's back, casual but proprietary. He would swear he felt a subtle relaxation.

"Thanks. I've sold a couple of things to them. Even though they're heavy on promoting Oregon and tourism, they're open to interesting microcosms. I write all kinds of articles, including the five ways to make your wardrobe sexier ones, but my favorites are the in-depth portraits of people who have lived extraordinary lives."

Doug brought them glasses of wine. Pretty soon, she was ensconced on the sofa holding court. As the only new face, she was under heavy scrutiny. He was relieved to have Alicia Cuddy grab the seat next to her. She was one of the few here who *didn't* make big money. The director of a wildlife sanctuary, she was more into the outdoors than her significant other, Ray, whom he didn't see here today.

Even when he left Amy for a few minutes at a time, he could hear her laugh, mostly the giggle. The guffaw required letting go, and no matter how relaxed she appeared he knew she wasn't doing that. He wanted to think she was having a good time, but couldn't be sure.

"Stepsister, huh?" Doug said, having asked Jakob to carry some of the steaks and burgers out to the patio.

"Damn it's cold." Jakob hunched his shoulders. "My friend, you're supposed to have barbecues in July."

Doug, who'd begun to bald, gave the grin that made him look like an aging cherub. "I fire the thing up at least once a week year-round."

Jakob just shook his head.

Doug nodded toward the living room. "What's the story?"

He gave the edited version.

"She's hot," his friend observed, "but not your usual fare."

Jakob felt his facial muscles tighten. He didn't even like the word *fare*. "Didn't know I had a usual."

"Blonde goddesses."

"Bullshit!" Thank God Amy wasn't hearing this.

Doug had paused with a platter of steaks in his hand. His gaze was sharp. "Susan. Jenna. Emily. I know there were a couple of others."

"I was trying to punish Susan." In dismay, he thought, Is *that what I was doing?*

"You're in love."

He let out a long breath. "Yeah. I guess I am." How long he'd been in love with Amy was something he didn't like to think about.

"She know?"

"We haven't used that word yet."

Expression softening, Doug slapped him on the back. "She's cute."

He almost reacted in outrage. Cute? She was a hell of a lot more than that. But then he smiled wryly. He liked Cheryl, but she was a rack of bones coupled with one of those overly pillowy mouths that gave him the creeps. To each his own.

He and Amy stayed until the end. She hugged Cheryl, and then Alicia, who left at the same time they did, staying animated until they were well up the driveway. Then she went silent. Jakob discovered he wasn't in as good a mood as he'd thought he was.

"No Bryan," he said, touching the button to un-lock his SUV.

"Sad to say." She hunched inside her coat. "Brrr."

It was already dark. There was currently no pre-cipitation, but he had a feeling the mercury was de-scending into freezing tonight. Wet roads might be treacherous in the morning.

Not until they had their seat belts on and he had cranked the heat up did he ask if she'd had a good time.

"Sure," she said, sounding surprised. "You're right. They were all nice." Pause. "Mostly."

In the act of releasing the emergency brake, he looked at her. "Mostly?"

"Oh, one guy hit on me." He couldn't see her face well in the dark, but heard distaste in her voice.

"Who?" he asked.

"Not saying. They're your friends."

"Everyone came as part of a couple except Ali-cia."

She shrugged.

"That the worst that happened?"

"One of the women…uh, Sydney, I think. Or Cindy?"

"Sydney," he said tersely.

"She expressed surprise at me and you. Thought maybe we were just friends."

"Because?" He was trying to see her face even though he couldn't. His foot remained on the brake, one hand gripping the steering wheel so hard it creaked.

"You and I both know I'm not your type."

Man, he hated her shrugs, careless and self-deprecating.

"Bullshit," he said for the second time today.

"They all seem to know you pretty well."

"What did they say about me?"

"Nice things." At last, Amy turned her face toward him and he was able to make out her features in the light from the dashboard. Her mouth had a curve that might have been a smile, but her eyes were deeply shadowed. "They're your friends, Jakob."

"Apparently not the asshole who hit on you."

"Well, maybe not him so much. I kind of had the feeling it wasn't me so much as getting in a jab at you."

"Spence," he said softly.

Her surprise wasn't hidden quite fast enough. "Why the enmity?" she asked, after a significant pause.

"We're in the same business, more or less. He's vice president of a company that makes paddleboards, skateboards, that kind of thing. We carry a limited number. He keeps pressing for a bigger commitment using the friend card, I'm not that happy about how his products do for us. We've had some fiberglass separation, that kind of thing. The bigger problem is that his wife and I are good friends. Have been since college. He sees that as a threat."

Amy was quiet for a minute. In the interval he finally put the Outback in gear and pulled away from the curb. The headlights picked out shiny pavement in a very dark night.

"How good?" she asked.

"Not sexual, if that's what you want to know."

"Does *he* know that?"

"He would if he'd ever asked Fay."

"Asking and believing are too different things."

His neck felt stiff. In a futile effort to loosen it, he rotated his shoulders. Right this minute, he thought it might take a chiropractor.

"You must run into people all the time who've read your writing."

"More often lately." She paused. "I thought maybe you'd primed...who was it? Erica? Sarah?"

"Erica. I wouldn't do that to you, Amy."

She had to hear that she'd offended him. She lifted a hand as though she was going to touch him, but her fingers curled into her palm and she tucked it against her stomach.

"I'd like to stay tonight," he said after a minute, quietly, trying to keep the humming tension out of his voice.

She glanced his way, but they were on the freeway now and he couldn't afford to let himself be distracted from the traffic. "Sure," she said. "But won't you have to race home in the morning to change?"

"I brought a duffel bag."

"He's taking me for granted," she told any unseen listeners.

Serious? Teasing him? Damn, he hated this uncertainty.

"I want enough trust between us that we *can* take each other for granted."

It was a long time before she answered. "I want that, too," she said, in a voice that made him think of old bruises, yellow under the skin. "I do, Jakob."

"Okay." Despite the road conditions, he reached out and took her hand. He held on until he had to shift down to leave the freeway.

CHAPTER THIRTEEN

WAS EVERYTHING GOING wrong her fault?

Amy's gloomy conclusion: probably.

But in this case, she didn't think it was her imagination that Jakob was really, really quick to pounce on her whenever she said anything wrong.

Every time they'd seen each other the past few days, a high tension wire ran through every word they said. He was careful, she was careful, and then they ended up sniping, anyway.

She wanted tonight to be different.

Dinner at his loft condo, which she'd dreaded all day since they did better in public than when they were alone.

He'd picked her up, since parking in this part of town was a bitch to find and there were no slots for visitors downstairs in the garage.

He started on dinner as she wandered, checking out his selection of books. One whole case held titles on preservation of old growth forests, rivers, wildlife, along with huge glossy books full of glorious nature photography. Otherwise, he had the same mishmash most people did: some mysteries, sci-fi, biographies, stuff likely left from college courses, half a shelf of books on digital photography and editing, a small library having to do with smart business.

"How did your day go?" he asked from the kitchen.

"So-so," she said, her back to him. "I got a couple of rejections. I swear, they always come in bursts."

"Idiots."

Amy laughed. "I'd agree, except it's the nature of the business. An editor might like my writing and topic, but the article doesn't meet their current needs. That's their favorite line, by the way. All it means is I shoot out queries to other publications. Usually, though not always, I find a taker. Maybe not my first choice, but once in a while it turns out better. There's always a sting to the rejections, though."

"I can imagine."

She kept talking, and he listened, something he did well. She found herself editing what she said, though, because if she even hinted at self-doubt, he would jump on her. And yes, he had reason, but *she* had reason, too. And anyway, didn't everyone doubt him or herself some of the time? Feel unworthy or incompetent, fat, ugly, stupid? So why wasn't she entitled?

Because without noticing I've spent my whole life feeling sorry for myself?

She heaved a sigh.

"What's wrong?" Jakob asked, from so close behind her she leaped six inches.

"Oh! I didn't hear you coming."

"Why are you concentrating so hard on my bookcase?"

"Don't you know how much you can tell about someone by what he reads?"

"Hmm," he said. "I don't know what *you* read. I've only seen a few books in the house."

She made a face at him. "That would be because mine are mostly in boxes and Mom doesn't care if she owns books. All they do is collect dust, she says. She gets hers from the library. She can't imagine why anyone would reread a book, especially a novel."

He chuckled. "Sounds like an old argument."

"Mom and I have spent thirty-four years either being icy polite or arguing. The arguing was icy polite on her side, too."

There was definite amusement in his eyes. "Yeah, you weren't icy polite when I lived with you. Not to anyone." The beginning of a frown drew his eyebrows together. "Well, that's not true. You always were different with Michelle. A little standoffish, I guess."

Conscious of a familiar hollow beneath her breastbone, Amy shrugged and turned back to the bookcase. "Chicken or the egg."

"Why do you always do that?"

She went still at his edgy tone. "Do what?"

"Shrug, just so everyone knows whatever should have hurt doesn't. And, in this case, turn your back on me."

She faced him, keeping her head high. Here we go. "I didn't know I did."

His jaw was tight. "Nobody has ever pointed it out before?"

"Nobody has ever felt compelled to criticize everything I do or say, if that's what you mean."

"It wasn't criticism. It was a question."

"Oh, bull!" She got mad like a spark leaping into flame. "You know, I'm getting the feeling you don't actually like me very much. Not *me*." She pointed her thumb at herself. "You know, our relationship hasn't changed as much as you think it has from when we were teenagers. You're still quick to attack."

"What the hell are you talking about?" His eyes narrowed; his jaw jutted. "I ask you a question, and it's an assault?"

"Yes!" Amy cried. God, she was overreacting, and she couldn't seem to help herself. She struggled to calm herself. "Can we not do this?"

"This?"

"Analyzing each other?" *You analyzing me?*

"It was a simple question. Aren't we supposed to be getting to know each other?" The words were okay; the hint of aggression in his voice and body language wasn't.

"You know me." She was almost begging. "You

know why I shrug and pretend I don't care when sometimes I do. You're not asking a question, you're jumping on behavior you don't like."

"That's bullshit," he snapped.

All she did was look at him and fail to see any chagrin or even softening. After a minute, she shook her head. "You know what, I'm not in the mood for this." She spun away and crossed the open space to where she'd tossed her coat over a chair. "Let's just say I'm in a bad mood. I'm going home."

"Running away."

The sneer in his voice made her want to throw something.

She kept going instead, slamming his door behind her. She was waiting for the freight elevator, hearing the creaks and groans as it rose, when he caught up with her.

"I'll drive you."

"I'd rather catch a cab." She was perilously close to crying and could not make nice with him for the twenty minutes a crosstown trip would take.

"Not many of them come by out here."

"I can walk two blocks. It's not late."

The doors opened. She refused to look at him or acknowledge him when he got on with her. She pushed the button for the lobby floor. He pushed the one for the parking garage.

"Amy." His voice was rough, his confusion apparent. "I don't understand."

"I don't want to do this right now."

"When are we going to do it?"

She closed her eyes, sucked in a deep breath and tried to regain some control. Thank God, the doors opened to an empty lobby and the sight of the rainy street beyond. She managed a step before they silently slid closed again and she saw his hand pressing the button.

In a fury, she finally turned on him. "What are you *doing?*"

"I'm not letting you get away like this. Amy, I don't know what happened."

She knew suddenly that she couldn't stand going on like this. Why had she ever imagined this would work?

"We both know something's wrong with me." She didn't let herself react to the shock on his face. "I have this feeling you're trying to fix me, and getting frustrated it isn't happening quicker. Well, I'm sorry. I happen to like myself the way I am. Do *not* interrupt," she snapped, when he started to do just that. "And yes, that means stumbling around a lot and not always feeling sure of myself, but that makes me a better writer. Arrogant people can't get under anyone else's skin, feel what they do. I can."

He pulled his head back. "I take it I'm the arrogant one."

"If the shoe fits." Oh, childish.

"I'm not trying to fix you."

"Yeah," she said slowly, really thinking it through for the first time. "I'm pretty sure you are.

It has to be guilt. All of a sudden, you're my best friend in the world, you think I'm sexier than any woman you've ever met, even though your friends were clearly stunned at what you'd dragged to their house."

A storm cloud rolled over his face. Amy didn't let it stop her.

"Exotic." She huffed. "I can't believe I bought that for a second. Sure. That's me."

"You're determined not to let anyone love you, aren't you?"

"Why would anyone?" she yelled. "Look where I came from!"

They stared at each other. Even she was taken aback.

She retreated a step, fumbling behind her for the panel that would allow her to escape.

"You're so hung up on the past, you can't let yourself believe what's right in front of you." He sounded sad and angry both.

Amy shrugged, then cringed at the expression on his face and the startled realization. *That's what I always do. He's right.*

Could she make him understand? She had to try.

"That was a stupid thing to say. You were right— obviously, my biological father is not a monster whose genes infected me with something horrible. I'm still coming to terms with what the rape does mean, with finding out why I'm different. When I said something is wrong with me, I didn't mean it the way you took it. I mean, *in your eyes* I'm flawed."

"I don't think you're flawed. I'm in love with you, Amy."

She shook her head hard. "Don't say that. Not now. Listen. Please."

He bowed his head and ran his hand over his face. "I'm listening."

"If we'd met out of the blue—say, I came to interview you—and you'd asked me out, would you think of me as exotic or different?"

He stared at her, his eyes intense. "Why wouldn't I?"

"Because I'm not. Because it's only in the context of our family that I'm different."

His breath rasped out. "You ever heard that saying about the eye of the beholder?"

"Okay, forget that. I have self-esteem issues." In a different mood, she would have laughed at her use of that word. *Issues.* It seemed they both had them. "You wouldn't have reacted the same if we didn't have the past hovering. You'd have asked, you'd have listened, you'd have understood or gotten irritated and ditched me. Whatever. You wouldn't secretly be blaming yourself. Everything I said wouldn't stab you with guilt."

If his jaw got any tighter, he was going to crack a molar. Eventually he managed to talk. "I have listened. I've understood. You're the one who keeps thinking everything about us has to do with having grown up together."

"No." She hugged herself. "That's you, Jakob. Yes, I have trouble believing the golden boy I idolized would ever look at me, but it's you who still remembers lusting after his sister, and how he treated her to keep himself safe." She reached out and pushed the open button. "Now I'm going home."

"We can get past this," he said to her back.

She hadn't moved yet. "I don't know if we can."

"Please let me drive you home."

Tears were so close she didn't know if she could hold them back that long, but after a moment she nodded.

Once again, they made the entire drive without talking. He pulled to the curb and braked. She reached for the door handle.

"I love you," he said, his voice low, gritty. "The woman you are. Maybe I'm still mixed up about those years. I don't know. The thing is, I'm pretty sure I loved you then, too. Separating then from now isn't easy."

"I know that," she said. Whispered. "I'm sorry, Jakob. I guess I really do better by myself."

She got out and fled before he could say anything else.

JAKOB WENT HOME to a burned dinner, the squawk of the fire alarm and emptiness that felt like a black hole.

When the phone rang an hour later, he lunged at it, but the caller was his father, not Amy. He muted the ring and went back to staring into a future so empty, he didn't know how to face it.

He went to work the next day, made himself go through the motions and came home to an emptiness as profound. This time when his father called, he answered.

"Yeah, Dad."

"Thought you could tell me how Amy is. She's worse than her mother. Neither of them will return a call."

He hadn't known anything could hurt like this.

"I don't know," he said after a minute. "We had a fight last night. She, uh, told me to get lost."

The silence was so long, he began to think the call had been dropped. "Dad?"

"What did you do?" his father asked.

"Good to know it has to be my fault." Here he'd worried Amy blamed herself for everything wrong up to the kitchen sink not draining, but what do you know? *He* was the one who screwed up the most wondrous thing that had ever happened to him.

"That's not what I meant."

"Sure it is. And you're right. I told her I love her. And yeah, I slept with her. That's what you do when you fall in love with a woman. But, turns out, she doesn't believe anyone *can* love her. And me, I gave her reason to think…" His voice cracked like a fourteen-year-old boy's. He couldn't finish.

"I really didn't mean it," his father said, his voice gentle the way it had been for Amy. "I guess I always knew there was something."

"I don't know what to do," he told his father, who gave him what he could—sympathy—but didn't have any answers.

A SCRATCHING SOUND had Amy stiffening. She lay in bed, eyes shut, trying to convince herself that she could sleep. She *had* to sleep. Human beings couldn't live without sleep, could they?

Thump.

Primitive fear slid up her spine. Human beings didn't always live after an intruder stole into their house late at night, either.

The next sound she recognized as the back door being carefully closed. Oh, God. Someone was in the house. She hadn't been imagining things.

She inched to the edge of the bed and found the floor with her bare feet. Did she have *anything* that could serve as a weapon?

Flashlight. The one she had was army surplus. She slid open the drawer on the bedside stand and found it by touch. Then, heart thudding, she tiptoed through the darkness, peeking cautiously into the hall.

A light came on downstairs. Not moving, not breathing, she stared. Did burglars or—oh, God—rapists turn on a *light* when they broke into a house?

Of course they didn't.

She heard footsteps.

"Mom?" she called, still clutching her heavy flashlight.

"Oh, dear. I was hoping I wouldn't wake you."

Amy advanced to the top of the stairs. "You scared me to death!"

At the bottom, her mother looked up at her. "I'm later than I told you, but surely you knew I'd call if I wasn't going to make it tonight."

She'd been vaguely aware Mom was among the callers she had ignored last night and today. She hadn't checked voice mail, either.

"I'm sorry. I must have been asleep," she lied. "What time is it?"

"It's only a little after ten."

"Why didn't you drive over from the coast in daylight?"

"I took a last look around."

"Florence isn't that big."

"No," Michelle said wearily. "It was a goodbye. I never intend to go back."

Amy finally noticed how haggard her mother looked. She'd aged some more while she was gone.

"Are you all right?" Amy asked tentatively.

"Of course I am. If I take a shower, will that keep you awake?"

"I can't sleep, anyway." Oh, boy. Had she actually said that aloud?

"What's wrong? You've sounded happy when I called."

"Wow, you noticed?" Immediately she regretted the bitterness that lent sharpness to her automatic comeback. Was she turning into a bitch? Recent experience said yes.

Or—new and more unpleasant thought—had she *always* been one, and that was why nobody ever seemed to stick long? She wasn't disappointing them with her inadequacies, she was driving them away.

"I'm sorry. I didn't mean that."

Her mother kept standing at the foot of the stairs, as if she was too tired to mount them. "I think you did. I'm certain I deserved it."

"We can't go back," Amy heard herself say. "Let's…concentrate on moving forward." Because she was so good at it. "You'd think *I'd* taken up reading self-help books. Or maybe I should switch to writing greeting cards."

To her astonishment, Michelle laughed. Then she kept laughing, sinking onto one of the bottom steps and bending over until her head almost touched her knees.

Amy half fell down the steps, sliding on her butt the last few, until she reached her mother, who was now both laughing and crying in horrible gulps.

"Mom?"

Her shoulders kept heaving. Amy hesitated, thought, *I'm used to rejection,* and put an arm around her mother.

Who abruptly went still.

Instinct learned from a lifetime had Amy wanting to snatch her arm back and retreat. She saw Jakob sneering, heard him say, *Running away?* And hugged her mother tighter.

Michelle lifted an astonished, distraught face, then leaned against her. After a moment, her arms crept around Amy, too, and they sat there holding each other close. Her mother's tears wet the T-shirt Amy slept in.

No moment like that was going to last long. Mom collected herself and her pride, straightened until her back was very straight and looked ahead. In profile, that blotchy, puffy, wet face was almost that of a stranger.

"I apologize. That wasn't like me."

What was she supposed to say? Good? Nothing seemed like a better choice.

"Thank you," her mother whispered.

"Everyone cries." Oh, sure, state the obvious.

"I have not for a very long time." Michelle sighed. "I need to blow my nose."

Amy heard herself giggle. "Yeah, you do."

Astonishingly, her mother laughed again. "Oh, lord. I'm glad Ken can't see me."

"Maybe it wouldn't be such a bad thing if he could." Crying on Jakob, it occurred to her, had been better than crying alone.

She didn't always do better alone. Maybe, she thought, it's just less scary to be alone. Safer. *I am an island.* Except she wasn't.

Her mother stood in stages, as if her joints hurt. She disappeared to the half bath under the stairs. Amy heard the toilet flush, water running, and sat waiting until Mom reappeared.

Her face was ravaged, but after a moment Amy realized that wasn't why she was so nearly unrecognizable. There was something else. Not the recovered dignity, but some emotion or inner alteration that seemed to soften her features.

"I've decided I'm going to confront him." She said it quietly, calmly, with resolution. "I understand the trial has ended."

Amy nodded. The arsonist had been convicted. Steven Hardy had emerged triumphant, and with his photo once more in the *Oregonian*.

"It might be possible to catch him in his office. Or perhaps I can make an appointment using an alias."

"Unless he's followed you." Seeing her mother blanch, Amy regretted what she'd said. "Not literally. Online. Knowing you're out there must scare him, wouldn't you think?"

"Perhaps initially, but after this many years? I doubt it."

"Why don't I make the appointment. He wouldn't have any reason to recognize my name."

"Unless, as you said, he knows that I married a man named Nilsson."

"Okay, I'll use a pseudonym." She almost felt

her own spine straightening. "I want to go with you, Mom."

"I was hoping you would," her mother said, completely astonishing her.

JAKOB WANTED TO be angry as well as devastated, to convince himself she wouldn't give him a chance, that *she* was the one with a problem. Two things stopped him.

The first was something his father said. Not in their last conversation, but years ago. Jakob couldn't even remember the context.

"You can lie to other people, but not to yourself." The moment had been totally serious. Jakob still saw the expression on Dad's face. "Somebody accuses you of something, go home, cool off, and accept responsibility for the part that's yours. No more. No less."

The second thing that hit him was a passing thought of his own, one of the pissed ones. *All I wanted to do was help her heal…*.

He hadn't gotten any further than that. Instead he'd thought, *Shit*. He'd said he wasn't trying to fix her. But *fix* and *heal,* they could be synonymous, couldn't they?

Struggling for complete honesty with himself wasn't easy. He thought he'd faced everything when he had admitted first to himself and then to Amy how he felt about her when he'd been a teenage boy and what he'd done about it. But what else was hiding under there?

Yeah, he asked himself that night, lying in bed, light from the window that looked out on the Willamette River filtering through the blinds, what about her insistence that her looks were completely ordinary and he was the one with the skewed perspective? Poor self-esteem on her part, purely eye of the beholder on his...or something else going on?

It was true that he had mostly dated tall, athletic, classically beautiful blondes. Not exclusively—a few brunettes had crept in, though never a redhead. Freckles he'd steered clear of. Otherwise—blondes. He couldn't deny it. More uncomfortable yet was the realization that those women had more closely resembled Amy's mother as a young woman than they did Amy. Not the athletic part, of course, but she was the classic, elegant blonde, and a good four inches taller than her daughter.

Because she was emotionally inaccessible to him, had she set up some kind of challenge in his psyche? He was a man who thrived on challenges, who *looked* for them.

Maybe.

In the back of his mind, he'd always suspected what he was doing was seeking out women who *didn't* look like Amy. Every time he'd seen even the faintest resemblance in a woman he met, he'd made sure she saw the "not interested" signals. No way in hell was he going to deal with the idea that he was in bed with a woman subbing for his maybe sister. That was creepy. So he went for completely, safely different.

Either/or, he thought. Could be both.

None of that answered a more basic question. What was it about Amy that had made him as a teenager lust so desperately for her? So, okay, he'd always had the voice in his head that said, *You know she's not your sister.* Which, coupled with the fact that she arrived one day with breasts when she'd been flat as a board the last time he saw her, pretty well guaranteed that he did look.

So...would I have been looking no matter what, as long as she was reasonably pretty?

He couldn't imagine. Boys with stepsisters probably did have occasional, sexual thoughts about them. This was different. He had craved her, and it wasn't only sexual. It was...he still didn't know. The sadness and hope in her big brown eyes. The fire and the vulnerability. Her determination to hide her hurt.

And now I'm pissed off when she's still doing the same thing?

He groaned and hammered his pillow into a new shape. Sleep wasn't a lot closer.

The next day, he had to work hard to hide his general state of testiness from his staff. He made an excuse to avoid lunching with a couple of people he liked, and had his P.A. send out for lunch. When it came, he swiveled his chair away from his desk, propped his heels on a windowsill. Looking at the not-so-fabulous view, he took in a row of now leafless trees and the parking lot beyond, and slowly unwrapped the chipotle chicken sandwich.

This dragging sense of grief was making him the next thing to useless here in the office. No matter who he was talking to, what he was thinking about or studying, a significant portion of his attention was focused on his phone, which had remained stubbornly silent. Even friends weren't calling.

Ring, he would will it, which only went to show he had no superpowers at all.

Call her? Not yet.

The sandwich should have been spicy; he hardly tasted it. He kept thinking back.

Why Amy?

As he ate, mechanically and with no real appetite, he found himself recalling his earliest memories, many of which involved her. He'd been so intensely curious. Some of that was jealousy, of course. Why was *his* daddy cooing and cuddling her all the time?

But it wasn't only that. He'd plain been fascinated. Dad had sometimes let him hold her—supervised, of course—but Michelle seemed to see his interest as a threat. Either that, or she couldn't be bothered indulging the little boy he was.

Something else came to him when he remembered those years. Maybe because Dad worked such long hours, Jakob had been lonely. Once he understood he had a sister, once she smiled at him with open delight, those intriguing colored eyes sparkling, he had wanted to *be* her brother. Maybe to bond with another person.

Michelle had kept it from happening. Possibly with malice aforethought, although probably not. Most likely he'd only been an inconvenience, something she had to accept to acquire a father for the baby she had already carried.

But her keeping him at a distance like that had increased his fascination with his little sister while leaving him unsatisfied. Then came the divorce, the visits he'd both resented and wanted, the puzzlement because Amy wasn't like him. Even then he'd thought of her as somehow magical.

Staring out at yet another rainy day—this was Portland, after all—Jakob felt as if puzzle pieces were slotting into place. It all made sense.

The complex, baffling feelings he'd had for the girl who might or might not be his half sister made sense. He heard again her accusation: *You wouldn't have reacted the same if we didn't have the past hovering.*

Honesty compelled him to admit that she was right. A lot of what he felt for her had roots in their shared childhoods. Should he be bothered by that?

No. Asking him to pretend she was a new girl-friend, a woman he had no history with, was ridiculous. He'd loved and hated the little girl who threatened his place with his daddy, loved and hated the teenage girl who awakened such frightening feelings in him—and he loved the woman she'd become.

He did feel guilty. She was right again. He'd been letting that ride him.

The feeling that stole over him was familiar, but it took him a minute to identify it. Sometimes he'd find himself in an alpine meadow, or tucked out of the wind in a rock chimney with a thousand-foot drop below to an impossibly blue lake, the air so clear and pure, his vision sharpened, and this same feeling would grab him by the throat.

It was complete and utter peace, letting go of frustration and day-to-day striving, accepting a perfect place, a perfect moment with joy.

He was okay with the past. He didn't care how he'd come to love Amy. For the first time in his life, he wasn't bothered by the fact that he'd wanted her when he shouldn't have. And he couldn't imagine why he had thought he had to heal her. He loved everything about her that made her complicated and vulnerable.

Always had. Always would.

He wadded his lunch wrappings in a ball and deposited it in the trash container beneath his desk. He looked at his phone, black and silent, and willed it to ring.

He'd give her a couple more days, then call her. He couldn't believe she wouldn't listen.

AMY WAS SURPRISED at how easy it was to make an appointment to see Deputy District Attorney Steven Hardy. She'd decided to take a chance and use her own name. Unless he really had been keeping an eye on her mother online or via a P.I., there was no reason he'd recognize it. If he did...well, she'd try again, and use subterfuge the next time.

Her credentials were evidently sufficient. A couple hours after her initial phone call, his gatekeeper called her back to offer her an appointment two days later.

Mom nodded at the news, expression cool and serene, but her eyes looking oddly blind for a moment. "Thank you," she said.

She had a book about roses open on the table before her. When Amy's phone rang, Mom had been about to show her pictures that theoretically demonstrated the proper techniques for pruning roses. They went on with their lesson as if nothing had happened. After studying the pictures, Amy accompanied her mother into the garden despite the drizzle, and Mom told her where she'd make cuts. Both were wet when they went back inside.

"I'm sure Mr. Cherpeski would be glad to do the pruning if you'd prefer," her mother was saying.

Amy shook herself like a wet dog, earning a reproving look from her mother.

"And waste the lesson? Don't be silly. How much damage can I do?"

Mom's frown dissolved into an unexpected laugh.

"Quite a lot, but there's only one way to learn. I suppose at worst, it's like a bad haircut. Your hair grows back."

Amy grinned at her, astonished to be laughing with her mother, of all people. "Good deal." She headed for the coffeemaker. Mom agreed that she, too, could use something hot.

Not until they sat down did Amy nerve herself to raise a subject that was part of what had kept her awake the past two nights.

"I've been thinking."

Mom's expression was pleasantly inquiring.

"It's about Jakob."

Pleasantly inquiring became guarded. "He doesn't seem to be around."

"No, we had a…well, a fight, I guess. I think some of what he said is true, which means I have to eat my pride, which is taking me a while."

Her mother understood pride. She nodded.

"The thing is…I'd like to ask him to come with us. To our meeting with Steven Hardy."

Instead of reacting with indignation or even surprise, Michelle considered her. "Why?"

"Before you came home, I was trying to go off by myself to investigate who the guy is. That's always been my way, you know? I'd have probably holed up in the house, quit eating—" Again. "Jakob wouldn't let me. He said we were in this thing together. That if we need answers, we'd find them together."

He'd said one other thing, too. *Don't try to get rid of me, because I guarantee you'll fail.* She *had* succeeded in getting rid of him, and that gave her a hollow feeling inside.

"I think both of us could use his support," she said finally.

Michelle turned her head and gazed out the window for what had to be a minute or two. Long enough, Amy chickened out enough to hasten into speech again.

"If you'd rather not, I understand, though. I'll respect whatever you want."

Her mother met Amy's eyes, and hers had that look again, as if she wasn't really seeing. "If you'd like to ask him, I have no objection. Perhaps we've both been too determined to do everything by ourselves."

Amy had expected a no. A little dazed, she thought, *The times they were a-changin'.*

Oh, wow. Now all she had to do was call Jakob and hope he wasn't mad at her enough to say, *Yeah, you know what? You're on your own.*

Only, she found she had this rather startling faith that he would never do anything like that to her. That, in fact, she really, truly could trust him.

Once, she would have called herself naive, an idiot for thinking any such thing.

Mom wasn't the only person who seemed to be changing.

CHAPTER FOURTEEN

JAKOB THOUGHT ABOUT going out. Maybe just to a bar, maybe see if any friends wanted to meet up. Another evening of pretending he was interested in a television show or book held no appeal.

Trouble was, getting shit-faced while being surrounded by sweaty bodies and loud voices didn't strike him as an improvement. And he couldn't think of anyone he actually wanted to hang out with.

He poured himself a bourbon and water, turned on the TV, watched for five minutes, turned it back off. Finally he put on a coat and went out on the balcony, where he could smell the wet air and watch for stars or glimpses of the half moon when clouds shredded.

His phone sat on the small table next to him.

Man, he was a sad case.

He was sagging low in the chair and a second drink was starting to take the edge off when the phone actually rang. He grunted, reaching for it. What were the odds it was Amy calling?

He blinked, staring at her name. Removing his

feet from the railing, he sat upright, hesitated, then answered.

"Amy?"

"Jakob. Hi." Her voice was really soft, even timid.

Some acid words surfaced, but he held them back. "What's up?"

"I made an appointment with Steven Hardy. Mom wants to confront him and I said I'd go. We figured he'd recognize her name, so…"

"Probably, although it's been a lot of years."

"Would you ever forget?"

"Depends whether he shocked himself and it was a defining event in his life. I'm guessing some guys who commit date rape and get away with it become repeat offenders."

The silence hummed.

He cleared his throat. "I'm sorry."

"No, you're right," she said. "I didn't think."

Neither of them said anything else for a minute.

"I wanted to let you know. And, well, ask whether you'd come with us."

Jakob had to rerun what she'd said before he was convinced he'd heard right. She wanted him with her.

Hallelujah.

"I can't believe you called."

"Why?" She sounded defensive.

"Because before I had to coerce you to let me in." He rubbed his forehead. "Because of the way we left off. The last thing you said was that you'd rather do things alone."

In the ensuing silence, Jakob realized how much he would give to be able to see her face, to have any clues at all to what she was thinking.

"I was wrong," she said, in a small, husky voice.

He was desperate to ask how much she'd been wrong about, but no way would he jeopardize this small opening she'd given him.

"You were," he agreed, but…gently. Agreeing, that's all. "You and your mom want to go to lunch first?"

"I don't think so. I can't imagine either of us will be hungry or feel like, I don't know, socializing."

With him, a mere acquaintance? But that was him being sensitive. Chances were, she hadn't meant it that way.

Was it possible she was straining to interpret his pauses, too?

"I don't blame you," he said. "All right, I'll pick you up at one-thirty."

"We could meet you there."

"Neither of you should be driving."

"Oh. Okay," she said softly. "Thank you, Jakob."

Incredibly, he was smiling when he told her she was welcome and ended the call.

AMY LURKED IN the living room to one side of the window watching for Jakob's arrival as if she was sixteen and he was her first date. Her relief was as huge, too, when she saw his Outback pull to the curb.

"He's here, Mom!" she called.

"Coming." Michelle descended the stairs with the aloof dignity of Queen Elizabeth. She had dressed as carefully as if she expected to appear on the evening news, too.

Armor, Amy thought, having donned her own, although a rather different style than her mother's. Mom had gone for slacks and a jacket over a silk shell, her hair drawn into a smooth chignon. She always went for pale neutrals—pale blue and gray today. Amy had thought of wearing her best suit again, but the voice of defiance rang out. She'd chosen a *very* short sweater dress in a vivid plum color instead, over black leggings and black knee-high boots with three-inch heels. A scarf in a dozen shades of purple with a few streaks of scarlet wrapped her neck and trailed over her shoulder. Her hair, she'd finally clipped away from her face and otherwise left loose and wild.

She braced herself when her mother saw her, but Mom only nodded as if she understood. Both had put on coats by the time Jakob rang the doorbell. Amy's was red wool, her mother's knee-length and pale gray.

Amy opened the door, chin up. Jakob smiled at her, a glint in his eyes. "Nice," he murmured, then nodded at her mother. "Michelle. You ladies look outstanding."

He, of course, looked the executive he was in a well-cut, charcoal-gray suit. No, what he really looked was fabulous. Big, solid, broad-shouldered, dark gold hair curling at the crisp collar of his blue shirt, which accentuated the blue of his eyes.

He briefly laid a hand on Amy's back as she closed and locked the door, then turned to pass him. The touch was light, barely felt through the heavy wool of her coat. *I'm here,* was all he seemed to be saying.

Her throat seized up.

She didn't contribute to what conversation there was during the drive. She couldn't seem to track anything that was said. Her mother's composure impressed her. Mom was the one who had to be really freaked.

They had been instructed to come to the district attorney's office at the courthouse, semifamiliar territory to her. The halls were no less busy today, their ride up in the elevator silent. Michelle expressionlessly gazed at the numbers above the doors, although the hand gripping her purse showed white knuckles. Amy kept flashing back to the brief encounter in the courtroom below, the intense stare from eyes so much like hers.

After a glance at her, Jakob handled the brief explanation to the receptionist and once again placed his hand on her back as they were led to Deputy D.A. Hardy's office. Amy was rather astonished to see that his other hand rested on her mother's back.

With a funny little bubble of amusement, she wondered whether he was offering silent support, or propelling them inexorably forward.

Then she was walking into the office, her eyes locked on the man who rose to his feet behind his desk.

This light brought out the red in his hair, increasing the resemblance to a fox.

To me?

It was her he looked at first, the same shock on his face she'd seen that day in the courtroom without quite realizing that's what it was. And then his gaze skimmed past Jake and settled on Michelle.

For a moment no one moved. The man staring at her mother didn't so much as blink. Amy was only vaguely aware of the click of the door closing behind them.

"Michelle Cooper." He sank heavily into his chair. "I hoped…" He closed his eyes momentarily and shook his head. "I always knew this day would come."

Without a word, Jakob guided first Amy's mother and then Amy to the two chairs that faced the desk. He took up a station behind her, one hand resting on her shoulder. It might be the single most comforting touch Amy had ever felt in her life.

"You hoped?" Michelle said, voice cold enough to freeze marrow.

"That it was a nightmare. That you'd left school for some other reason."

"That you'd never hear my name again."

He dipped his head. After a moment his gaze turned again to Amy. "That day when I saw you, I knew. I told myself it couldn't be, but I knew."

"We don't look that much alike." Yes, they did, but she wanted to acknowledge it now more than ever.

After a moment he reached for a picture frame on his desk she hadn't noticed and held it out to her. "My daughter and son."

Jakob was the one to step forward and take it. He tilted it so that she could see the photograph of a woman and a man, both looking to be in their early twenties. The guy didn't have a face Amy would have noticed in a crowd. The young woman was another story. She riveted Amy, who stared in shock. She heard herself make a sound.

Jakob's fingers massaged the ball of her shoulder.

"Your sister," Steven Hardy said.

She would have known they were related if they'd come face-to-face on the street. She had more freckles than Amy did, and her eyes were more hazel than brown, but the hair, cropped short, was the same, and the shape of her face and the chin, Amy saw every day in the mirror. Even her build, slight and petite.

Jakob carefully laid the framed photograph on the desk. Michelle's gaze flicked to it, then returned to Hardy.

"Do you have any idea what you did to my life?" she said in a hard voice.

He shook his head, pinched the bridge of his nose, then nodded.

"You try rape cases," Amy said.

"Yes." His voice was hoarse. "I do." There was pain in his eyes when he looked at Amy's mother. "Every time I talk to a victim, I see you."

"Giving them justice, when I didn't get it."

"Yes."

Amy wished, suddenly, that they had a recorder. He wasn't denying anything. Would he, if they went to the press? Had it occurred to him they *could* be secretly taping?

"I was drunk," he said after a minute. "That's not an excuse, only…" He trailed off as if forgetting what he had meant to say. "I woke up in the morning, puked my guts out and tried to remember what happened. No." He breathed heavily for a minute, his jaw working. "I didn't want to remember. I was scared to death. I kept waiting for the cops to come for me."

"I wish I'd called them."

He nodded. "You can still ruin me."

"I want to," Michelle told him, and it was clear she meant it. The very fact this man lived in the same city had terrified her not so long ago, and now she showed only anger and resolve.

"I hope you won't," he said, sounding tired.

His eyes dropped to the photo of his two children and anguish made his face spasm. "I want you to know I never did anything like that again. I'm still ashamed to know I was capable of being that kind of animal. I have…tried since to redeem myself." It was the first time he'd done anything like beg.

Michelle's hard stare didn't soften. His shoulders twitched, not quite a shrug. Silence settled.

Against her will, Amy was transfixed by how much he looked like her. How much *she* looked like him.

I don't want to.

She wanted to feel no connection at all. But…oh God, her sister. She couldn't stop herself from dropping a hungry gaze to the face of the very young woman with whom she felt an undeniable connection, even if this sister never knew.

He must have noticed. "Emma. Her name's Emma. Her brother…" The hesitation was almost infinitesimal. "Your brother's name is David."

"Not *my* anything," Amy said fiercely. "They have nothing to do with me."

Her comment clearly caused him more pain and she didn't care.

He looked at her mother again. "What did you do when you left Wakefield? If you don't mind telling me."

She wrenched her gaze from his, bowed her head and seemed to contemplate her hands, marble-white

FROM THIS DAY ON

and unmoving. "I knew I was pregnant. My parents would have blamed me. I was fortunate enough to meet Amy's father."

"My father," Jakob said, speaking for the first time. His eyes were cool and direct. "He's a good man."

Steven Hardy flinched.

"Amy did not know until recently that Josef was not her biological father. I'm sorry she ever had to find out."

He was the one to bow his head now and fight for control. "You have no idea how sorry I am."

"I don't care." Moving swiftly, Michelle snatched up her purse and rose to her feet. "Then, I was so afraid I hid from you. I couldn't go to class. I could barely make myself scuttle to the dining hall. Just once, I wanted to look you in the eye and make sure you knew you did much worse than push me into sex before I was ready. Probably all *you* worried about was that it was unprotected. Let's have one honest moment. You raped me. You are no better than the men you prosecute." She turned and started for the door.

Amy rose hastily. Jakob's arm curled protectively around her.

"What are you going to do?" Hardy asked.

Amy's mother paused only briefly. "I haven't decided," she said, and kept going.

Jakob opened the door and ushered the two women out. They left silence behind them.

As SHE HAD on the trip downtown, Amy sat up front beside Jakob, her mother in the backseat. Mom had insisted. Amy mostly gazed out the side window without really seeing anything, although she was aware of his occasional glances. Once she caught him watching her mother in the rearview mirror. As little reason as he had to like his one-time stepmother, he looked worried.

When they reached the house, he parked at the curb and got out. Both of them were slower to move, so he was able to make it around, open their doors and even put a hand under Michelle's elbow to help her out. Then without a word he walked them to the front porch.

Amy unlocked. She wanted to ask him in—and she didn't. She'd be sorry she hadn't if Mom went straight to shut herself into her bedroom, but Amy felt like she needed to make herself available. Plus…she wasn't sure yet what to say to Jakob.

It seemed rude, though, not to say anything.

"If you'd like to come in…"

He shook his head before she could finish. "I need to get back to work and you'll both feel like you have to make conversation if I stay."

Her mother held out her hand. Her dignity was unimpaired, but the ice had melted and she was once again the woman Amy hardly knew, older, somehow more vulnerable and yet approachable in a way she never had been.

"Thank you," she told him. "I suspect you came

today for Amy's sake, not mine, but having you present steadied both of us, I think. I'm sure you had plenty of important things you should have been doing instead. This was kind of you, Jakob."

He shook his head. "We haven't had the best relationship, but I haven't forgotten the couple hundred school lunches you packed for me, the times you drove me to school when I missed the bus, or to Little League or a friend's house. We're still family."

Tears sprang into her eyes. "Oh, dear."

He laughed, a chuckle low in his throat, and leaned over to kiss her cheek.

The astonishing rush of emotion on her mother's face stunned Amy. Mom managed a nod at him then fled inside. Amy had to blink back tears of her own.

"Thank you." She dredged up a smile for him. "Really."

He smiled again, kissed Amy, too, but on the lips, and turned to go. Dread filled her.

"Are you…" Oh, no. She was really going to cry. "Are you still mad?"

"Mad?" He raised his eyebrows. "I was never mad, Amy. More shocked."

She nodded. Her fingertips crept up to touch her lips, still warmed by his.

"See you," he said, took the porch steps two at a time and crossed the small front yard in a few strides.

Amy was still standing in the same place when

the Outback pulled away from the curb and turned at the corner, disappearing from her sight.

JAKOB'S PHONE RANG when he was only a couple of blocks from Amy's. On a leap of hope, he fantasized that she would beg him to turn around and come back.

Not Amy. Bryan the compassionate architect. Amy had described him that way, to Jakob's irritation. Usually he didn't like to talk when he was on the road, but for some reason he answered and put his phone on speaker.

"So, you gotten bored with your stepsister yet?" his friend asked hopefully.

He laughed. "Sorry, no. And you can forget the stepsister part. It's ancient history."

"You do share a last name."

"She's Amy. I don't think about her last name."

"Well, damn. I was hoping for a rebound effect."

"Not happening." He hoped like hell Bryan didn't call Amy. And that, if he did, she didn't happen to mention she wasn't seeing Jakob anymore.

Except that wasn't true. They'd not only just seen each other, but he also thought it was a major breakthrough. He still remembered his frustration back when she admitted to having gone alone to slip into the courtroom to see her father the first time. After having encouraged Jakob to go back to work so she could be sure he wouldn't interfere—or be at her side.

Now she had admitted she'd been wrong, she didn't have to do every hard thing in her life alone. He was willing to bet those were words she'd never spoken before in her life.

Bryan suggested they get together soon without getting specific. Jakob agreed in the tone that said, *Yeah, sure, someday,* without any suggestion he wanted it to be soon.

Making the decision to work from home, Jakob called to inform his P.A., who had a couple of messages for him.

A minute later, he couldn't have said what they were.

Maybe he should have been pushy and accepted Amy's not-all-that-sincere invitation. But he knew he had been right not to intrude. If Amy had been alone, that would have been different. He thought she and her mother needed to talk. He was still blown away that Michelle had been willing to let him accompany them this afternoon. Asking for more would have been a mistake.

The question was, should he make the next move? Or did Amy need more time?

He pulled into his parking garage and sat for a minute before he got out. He couldn't help wondering what Amy and Michelle were saying to each other. The whole scene with Hardy had been difficult and painful all around. He felt no sympathy for the man; he had committed an unforgivable sin. The sad part was that, by all reports, he was a committed public servant. The tormented glance he'd given the picture of his children made Jakob think he was a loving father, too. There'd been a second photo displayed on his desk, too, that Jakob hadn't seen but assumed was the wife. She and Hardy's kids would be devastated if Michelle decided to level any kind of public accusation. Them, he felt sympathy for. Michelle had barely glanced at that picture. She had burned with her own outrage, her own devastation.

A decisive man who rarely second-guessed his choices, Jakob wouldn't have wanted to make the one that faced a woman who had suffered in silence for thirty-five long years and finally had summoned the courage to alter the balance of power. Yeah, she would be hurting other people if she did decide to ruin him. But what would continued silence do to Michelle?

Jakob shook his head, got out and locked. Despite everything, he felt lighter as he walked to the old freight elevator. Today, Amy had raised him from the depths. She'd have never asked him to stand by her today if she didn't trust him, at least. He had to believe that.

"YOU DIDN'T EAT anything," Amy said tentatively to her mother's back. She finished hanging her coat and closed the door to the closet. "I could heat some soup or make sandwiches."

Her mother hesitated. "I don't know if I can eat."

"You should, you know."

A faint smile curved Michelle's lips and her eyes focused on her daughter. "People who live in glass houses."

Amy managed a small laugh. "I will eat if you will."

"Very well."

She put on a can of black bean soup, deciding a hot meal might do them both good. Her mother drifted over to the small paned windows and gazed out at her garden. Amy would have thought it dreary, but for once the symmetry and rigid lines worked better than a looser cottage style that would have been nothing but soggy brown stubble and random, arching canes at this time of year. Was this what it meant to give a garden "good bones"?

Taking sour cream and a block of cheddar out of the refrigerator, she kept an eye on her mother.

"Did we accomplish anything?" she asked, after a minute.

Mom turned. "I don't know. I think I'll have to process it."

Amy nodded.

"Your resemblance to his daughter is quite remarkable," Michelle observed.

Trying to hide her flinch, Amy reached for the grater.

"And to him. I knew, and I didn't." She moved restlessly, her gaze fastened on something Amy couldn't see. "Your hair, of course, and the shape of your face."

Amy was concentrating on grating the cheese when she glanced up to see that her mother was now focused entirely on her.

"Whatever you may think to the contrary, I didn't see him every time I looked at you. You are very much your own person."

"Thank you." Inadequate, but Amy hoped her mother meant what she'd said. She'd have given a lot *not* to resemble a biological father she didn't want to acknowledge. Finding out how much she looked like him had increased her distress. It made her feel as if she was made up more of *him* than of her mother.

And considering the lifetime of resentment she had stored up against her mother, none of that filled her with a sense of goodness.

"Once in a while you'd have an expression, or turn a certain way, and I couldn't help seeing him," Michelle continued.

"Mom?" Michelle raised her elegantly shaped eyebrows. "You should have quit while you were ahead."

Her mother looked surprised, then apparently reviewed what she'd said. "It wasn't often."

Amy spooned the sour cream on top of the soup, then carried the bowls one at a time to the table. Her mother had poured them glasses of milk.

"Will you tell me about him?" Amy asked. "Not

the rape. Just…how you knew him. Whether you were friends."

Over lunch, Michelle did. Apparently Steven Hardy had been friendly from the minute he slid into a seat next to her the first day of a beginning economics class. She described a twenty-year-old guy who was funny and smart, but whose jokes sometimes had a cruel edge. There had been flashes of temper every time he asked her out and she made yet another excuse.

"He confronted me once at a frat party. I was with someone else and hadn't expected to see him. I don't think he was drunk when we talked, but he started putting away beer, and he watched me until I left. By that time, he was falling-down drunk. He apologized the next time I saw him and said he wasn't much of a drinker."

He was a politics major, on the debate team, a wunderkind even on a campus where the students were all above average in brains and academic ability.

"You're telling me I got smart genes?" Amy asked.

"I suppose I am." Her mother had finished her soup and now looked at the bowl as if she wasn't sure what it was doing in front of her.

"Okay," Amy said. "And a temper, too."

"I doubt temper is hereditary."

"Maybe not," she conceded. Nature versus nurture. Each human being started with a pool of built-in abilities and shortcomings, shaped then by parents and environment. She had the trickle of a thought: a man *could* change, if he was sufficiently motivated—say by shame.

"He startled me—almost scared me—a couple of times, not on purpose but because he had this way of moving that was so quick and silent. I'd think I was alone, and there he was."

Amy remembered, that day in the courtroom, the way he'd turned with a seemingly preternatural suddenness.

"Listening to myself," her mother said, "I'm realizing that there were things about him that made me uneasy. Then, I never stopped to analyze why he made me a little nervous."

"I've read that humans are the only species that disregards internal warnings. Any hint of danger and a rabbit bolts—"

Her mother's eyebrow quirked. "Or freezes."

Normally, she'd have been amused. This subject was too sensitive. "Panics, anyway. It doesn't stop and think, It's silly to worry just because that eagle is soaring low. I've seen it around a lot and it's never come after me before."

"That was me."

"We're better at hindsight than we are at foresight." Reassuring her mother, of all people, felt awkward.

They both fell quiet.

Her mother pushed the bowl away at last. "It's to his credit that he didn't try to deny what he did."

"Yes."

"I wonder why he didn't. I could never prove anything."

"He doesn't know you have DNA."

Michelle looked impatient. "That doesn't prove anything, even if it hasn't degraded. All he'd have had to do was argue consensual."

Amy conceded the point grudgingly.

"He seemed...different."

"It's been almost thirty-five years. I'll bet you've changed as much or more. From what you say, you weren't very confident."

"No, I wasn't." She sighed. "I think he might be genuinely remorseful."

Amy thought so, too, but... "Is that enough?"

"I don't know. I've been too angry today to be able to think reasonably yet."

"You were amazing."

Mom swung a surprised gaze to Amy. "Thank you."

"You were."

The connection was brief but real. A spark of true emotion with this woman who *looked* like her mother but was subtly altered.

Oh, well. She remembered her original quest when she'd moved in for this housesitting stint. She would uncover clues to her mother's true identity. She would somehow, magically, get to know the woman who had always been an enigma to her.

She'd succeeded beyond her wildest dreams.

Either that or an alien had taken over her mother's body.

"I'm going to leave in the morning," her mother said. "I haven't told Ken everything. It's time I did."

Not surprised, Amy nodded.

THE FLIGHT WAS an early morning one. Amy didn't envy her mother the grueling hours ahead. She couldn't imagine spending that long cramped in a coach seat on an airplane. Although wearing the same outfit she had on the outgoing trip, Mom already looked weary and rumpled in a way she hadn't when Amy had picked her up at Portland International so recently. Amy only hoped Ken recognized her at the other end.

Mom had recovered enough to suggest coolly that it would be fine if Amy wanted to drop her at the curb at Departures.

Amy's fingers tightened on the steering wheel. "I'll walk you in."

No argument, at least. Her mother didn't say anything when Amy drove into the parking garage, or when she insisted on pulling the suitcase into the terminal.

They stopped for Mom to check the bag, and then headed for security. Just short of the end of the line, Michelle stopped and faced her.

"This visit didn't turn out quite the way I expected."

"What did you intend?" Amy asked, although she suspected.

"To tell you it was none of your business."

"You did tell me."

Those perfect eyebrows arched. "Too late." The tiniest of frowns marred her forehead. "I was quite angry, you know."

Amy nodded.

"I'm beginning to think it has turned out for the best."

The grudging concession almost made Amy laugh. "Living with a secret that damaging can't have been healthy for you," she pointed out.

"I suppose it wasn't. Or, as it turned out, for you, either."

Wow, she'd noticed? Amy felt a little bad at the thought; she and Mom *had* made progress.

"I can never be the mother you want me to be," her mother said, as if her thoughts had paralleled Amy's.

Amy met her eyes. "How do you know what I want?"

"I see other women. I saw them then. I just..." She seemed to struggle for a moment. "I did my best."

If that didn't sound like an epitaph. For the first time, though, Amy didn't feel bitter. Probably her mother *had* coped the best she could.

And now...well, events had pushed her into changing. Amy was beginning to think they might actually be able to build a meaningful relationship, even if it was never filled with warm fuzzies.

She noticed the clock on the wall and felt regret. "You'd better go."

"Yes." Her mother hesitated, and for a suspended instant Amy thought she might hug her or kiss her cheek. But this was Mom. She simply nodded. "Please stay in touch. And if the pruning doesn't go well…"

"Beg Mr. C. for help. I will. Promise. Email me when you get there."

"Very well." Michelle joined the line, and although Amy watched for a while, she never turned her head.

CHAPTER FIFTEEN

JAKOB WAS RUNNING his electric shaver over his jaw when his phone rang. The phone he'd taken into the bathroom with him so he didn't suffer from separation anxiety.

"Hi," Amy said after he'd answered. "It's not raining today. I wondered if you'd like to go for a run after work."

"Yeah," he said, a huge smile growing on his face. "I can do that."

"Okay, well…" She sounded hesitant enough that interrupting was easy.

"I'll pick you up."

"I'll expect you," she said, and was gone.

He looked into the mirror and realized his jaw was only half-stubble-free. And he was going to draw blood if he didn't quite grinning.

"MOM'S GONE," AMY said.

Jakob braked at the stop sign a block from her house and glanced at her. "Already?"

"She said she hadn't told Ken everything and thought it was time she did."

He turned the corner and accelerated. "Did you two talk?"

Wearing no makeup and with her mass of hair in a ponytail high on her head, Amy looked barely legal age. She had on low-slung run pants and a snug-fitting, seamless, long-sleeved shirt he recognized as a Boulder River offering from a year ago. They'd touted it for the fabric's breathability and the shirt's comfort as a base layer. He hadn't seen it as sexy until now.

"Some."

He had to drag his mind from the way the fabric stretched over her small breasts, and back to the topic at hand.

"You know what she's going to do?"

Amy shook her head. The ponytail swung. "She did say she thought he might be genuinely remorseful."

"That was my impression, too."

"She talked about what he was like back then, too." She frowned ahead as he turned the Subaru into the small lot that offered access to one section of trail. "She said he was really smart and ambitious. Debate team. Biting wit."

"None of that's changed. From all reports, he can slice defendants off at the knees."

"He had a temper. He didn't like hearing no."

"If he still has a temper, he's gotten good at hiding it." Jakob had read everything he could find about the man. "He's controlled in front of juries and judges, and young attorneys in the office all talk about what a mentor he's been to them. I didn't get any undertones."

"No, and he's been married for twenty-six years."

He shrugged. That meant only so much. "Women tolerate abuse."

"That's true. Still…"

He parked and they got out. Jakob locked, then put his keys in a pocket he could zip closed. He put the temperature at about forty-five Fahrenheit, comfortable once they got moving. He began to stretch as Amy did the same.

Not until they began at a slow, easy pace did he say what he'd been thinking. "Part of me thinks the guy deserves whatever Michelle decides to dish out. The other part of me feels some regret. He's doing good."

She started to pick up the pace and he lengthened his stride.

"I told Mom whatever she decides I'll support."

"What about you? He looked as if…" He didn't finish, not sure how to put it.

"As if he thinks it would be great to incorporate me into his family? Never mind what kind of explanation for my existence he plans to come up with?" She gave a short, harsh laugh. "Any reaction I got from him is because I look like *her*."

It had stung, Jakob could tell, to find out she had a sister who, at least in looks, was like her. The discovery would make anyone uneasy, but Amy more than most. If she'd grown up with this sister, she wouldn't have been the odd one out. She would have had the sense of kinship, of family, she'd lacked.

"You do," he agreed, without any special emphasis.

"Would you be attracted to her?" Amy asked, her tone suddenly hostile.

For any guy with brains, the correct answer was a gimme. But he doubted Amy would believe any "no" that came too quick. He dredged up a memory of that photograph. His reaction to it had been a sharp sense of surprise and some anger, because he knew it would hurt Amy. Now he did his best to recall the young woman's face.

"If I'd never met you…I don't know," he said slowly. "Probably wouldn't have occurred to me. She's too young for me. As things stand—no."

"Why not? She looks like me."

"There's a resemblance. That's not the same thing. And she's not you. Looks are only a part of what I feel for you."

She speeded up again. He kept pace. Half a mile passed without either of them saying anything. Occasionally one or the other had to drop back to pass or let themselves be passed by bicyclists and other runners, including a couple of women pushing high-wheeled baby strollers.

"He's not my father," she said flatly. "My curiosity is satisfied. That's all I wanted. I have a dad."

"Who'd be mad if he heard you say anything else."

"I've figured out that I wouldn't be as normal as I am if it weren't for him."

"As normal as you are?" Maybe unfairly, that set him to steaming. "What's not normal about you? You think other people don't have self-doubt? Sexual hang-ups? Shitty relationships with their parents?"

"You know what I mean."

"No, I don't."

Their feet pounded in unison. If he hung back a little, he could watch her mass of curls bob and swing. Her stride was smooth and natural, her legs long for her height and her butt taut.

"You want to try cross-country skiing?" he asked.

Her cheeks and nose were red when she turned her head. "How can you be mad one minute and ask me something like that the next?"

He grinned. "I think I can convince you to like yourself better." He lengthened his stride again, issuing a challenge.

Amy shot him a look and passed him by. He glanced at his watch. "Let's turn around."

Without argument, she slowed and made a U-turn, then stepped on the afterburners. They didn't talk for a while after that. Even he was breathing hard by the time he estimated they were half a mile from the parking lot and began to slow down. When she realized she'd lost him, she looked over her shoulder, had to do a quick-step to avoid mowing down a white-haired jogger, and let herself relax into an easy pace, too.

Not until they were walking a cooldown did he say, "So?"

"So what?"

"Cross-country skiing?"

"As long as you guarantee no defective bindings."

He laughed. "That's a low blow."

Amy smirked, having obviously enjoyed delivering it.

"Is that a yes?"

"That's a yes, I'll try it. Emphasis on *try*. No promises here."

Was there a subtext? he wondered. Had she realized he'd been hinting for a future with her? He couldn't tell.

"If you like to run, you'll like Nordic skiing," he told her, keeping it light. "Gliding is better."

She wrinkled her nose at him. "But you have to be surrounded by snow and frigid air to do it. *I* like not seeing my breath."

"That's my Amy," he said without thinking.

She came to a stop and bent over, hands on her thighs. "What's that supposed to mean?"

"You're back to fighting weight."

He could tell she was thinking about it. Finally she straightened, rolled her shoulders a few times and then punched the air. Fighting, but definitely bantamweight.

No, he thought with amusement, flyweight.

One of her fists came to rest against his chest. "*My* Amy?" she asked, eyebrows arching high, but a hint of vulnerability in her eyes.

"Yeah," he said, voice scratchy. "If I get my way." He took her small fist in one of his hands, lifted it to his mouth and kissed her clenched knuckles. "You ready to go?"

She was dazed enough for it to take a minute for her to answer. "Oh. Sure. Anytime."

He let her hand go, took out his keys and asked, "Your place or mine?"

They went to his.

In the car, Jakob settled the brief argument by pointing out that they both needed showers, and she'd look better wearing one of his T-shirts than he would wearing one of hers.

He didn't say whether the shower would be taken together, and Amy wasn't quite confident enough to ask.

Conversation died shortly after that exchange. Sexual tension thickened the air and made it hard to breathe. She would have thought it was in her imagination, but then she saw the tightness of his grip on the steering wheel and the jerk of a muscle in his jaw when he glanced sidelong at her.

She hopped out as soon as he parked and started straight for the old freight elevator. His remote control beeped and his footsteps sounded on the concrete right behind her. Reaching past her, with one stab Jakob summoned the elevator. Amy stared straight ahead, waiting for the doors to open. He stood so close, she felt the heat of his body. A spasm of longing felt like a lightning bolt.

She was going to feel really dumb if he offered her the shower first and then wandered to the kitchen to see what he could put together for dinner.

The doors opened and a guy about Jakob's age stepped out. The two men exchanged a few words. Unable to parse what they were saying, Amy waited inside. She wanted him so desperately, she didn't know how she was going to wait.

If he wanted her the same way.

He stepped in beside her and pushed the button for the top floor. Still silence. They both stared straight ahead.

What if he doesn't...?

Amy didn't let herself finish the thought. It was her insecurity speaking, not the core certainty she was beginning to accept, the belief that Jakob meant what he said. And one of the things he'd said was, *I love you.*

She had come to believe that he *had* wanted her

as a teenager, that the attraction he'd spent two decades fighting was the reason for their distant relationship.

Why *couldn't* he be in love with her? She was worthy, wasn't she? She was trying very hard to convince herself that she was.

Please let what he said be true.

The elevator let them out and all they had to do was cross the wide hall. Jakob had his keys in his hand. He opened the door and let her enter ahead of him.

"Amy." He shouldered the door shut and turned her to face him. His eyes searched her face for one hungry moment, and then she rose on tiptoe and met his mouth when it crashed down on hers. He was shaking, she realized, and she might be, too. She sucked on his tongue and he groaned. After a minute she realized he was trying to peel off her shirt without breaking the kiss and she wriggled to help.

Finally he did lift his head long enough to get rid of the shirt. She tugged at his, too, and it also went flying.

Then he looked down at her. "You'll give me another chance? You mean it?"

"Yes. It wasn't all you. Or even mostly you."

"Yeah, I think it was," he said, "but I've figured things out." His thumb moved over her lips. His gaze was heavy-lidded but tender, too.

"Me, too," she managed to say, before he slid

both hands inside her stretchy pants and began to strip them down.

"Shoes."

"Damn," he muttered, and dropped to his knees to untie her Nikes.

Amy braced one hand on his broad shoulder and threaded the fingers of her other hand into his hair. A deep, rich gold, it felt heavy and smooth to the touch. She didn't care that it was a little sweaty; after all, she was, too.

He wrenched off one shoe and tossed it, then the other as she lifted each foot in turn. Two more clunks and his were gone, too. Then he surged to his feet and lifted her. She flung her arms around his neck and wrapped her legs around his hips as he carried her around the half wall to his big bed.

He laid her down and then stopped, knee planted between her thighs, to rake her with a gaze that sent heat shimmering through her. He made a guttural sound and bent to suckle her breast through the sports bra she still wore.

Amy arched up, moaning. Desperately wanting the wet heat of his mouth on her skin, she pulled the bra off over her head then clenched her fingers in his hair as he kissed and licked and suckled her again.

He said something against her breast.

"What?"

Jakob lifted his head. "These have been the worst few days of my life."

"I didn't mean anything I said."

"Yes, you did." The stubble on his jaw rasped against her belly as he moved his mouth downward. "But we'll talk about it later."

Thinking about how much she'd sweated on their run, she had a moment of panic when he nuzzled the hair at the junction of her thighs, but he started nibbling and kissing his way upward again. "I want you."

"Yes," she said fiercely. "Now, please."

He laughed, rough and triumphant. "Do you want me to use a condom?"

"No."

The heat in his eyes almost incinerated her. A guttural sound burst from his throat and he rose long enough to rip off his own pants. He was over her, the head of his penis pressing at her opening, in one swift move. "Now?" he asked hoarsely.

She couldn't form a word. She lifted her hips and he thrust, and the surge of pleasure was almost matched by relief. Buried deep inside her, he went still for a minute, his eyes locked on hers. Seeing that her depth of emotion was matched by his made this moment one she wanted to freeze-frame so that she could recall it forever. This was different than the first time they'd made love.

Because it was love. She did believe.

Almost.

And then he began to move, and she whimpered

and clutched at his shoulders and rocked to meet his every thrust.

Jakob was the only word she could manage when for one timeless moment their bodies fused and her entire world imploded.

HE LAY ON his back and thought of all the other nights he'd stared up at the dark beams above him. He'd always felt alone, even on the few occasions he'd had a woman here.

This was different. This was Amy.

Her head rested on his biceps and her arm stretched across his chest. Her hand kept smoothing his muscles, her fingers searching for his nipples, then tugging gently at chest hair. *Her* hair, of course, frothed out of control, covering his pillow and part of his chest and neck, one wild tendril tickling his nose. He smiled and blew, his eyes crossing as it briefly writhed in the slight breeze.

He could have stayed here forever, but he had a feeling the not-so-fresh scent rising to his nostrils was coming from his own underarms, and new sweat was drying atop old.

"Hey," he said. "Up for a shower?"

She made a humming noise and her head lifted. He could tell she was trying to see his face. With a grin, he rolled, pushed aside hair and kissed her, more of a big smack than a signal of intent.

"We do stink," she agreed with the crinkle of her

nose that he thought was unbelievably cute. Her favorite word related to herself.

"Shower, then eat, then back to bed," he suggested.

"As long as you cook." She sounded sassy. "I haven't managed one of your dinners yet."

It was true. They hadn't done well together at his place. That was one reason he'd wanted to bring her back here tonight instead of going to her mother's house. Then there was the fact that her current home *was* her mother's house. At least his condo was emotionally neutral.

They showered together, soaping each other, Jakob shampooing the hair that had fascinated him for his entire life. He loved rinsing it, watching the way it seemed to repel water so that the curls could regain their spring. The water ran hot against his back when he lifted her against the tile wall and made love to her again, her buttocks gripped in his hands. He felt as if he was going deeper than he ever had in his life, and when he came it was with shuddering power he could see echoed on her face.

He didn't want to admit his legs felt weak when they got out of the shower, but he staggered slightly.

"Okay, I will not go on a diet so you can take me up against walls," she declared, laughing at him. "Maybe it's looming middle age getting to you. I have to be the smallest woman you've ever done that with."

"Never have before." The admission actually

gave him pause. He and Susan had showered together, sure, but he'd never wanted to take her up against the wall.

"Never?" Amy eyed him, and he could tell she didn't believe him.

"Never," he repeated firmly.

"Oh." Her mouth curved in satisfaction. "It was fun."

"Yeah, it was." He smacked her butt. "I'm weak with hunger is what's wrong with me."

He pulled on a pair of jeans. Amy wore nothing but one of his T-shirts, as he'd envisioned. It hung to midthigh on her. Even as relaxed as he felt, knowing she wore nothing at all beneath it kicked him into being half-aroused.

He grilled sandwiches and produced a coffee cake he'd picked up at a bakery the other day. They sipped coffee and looked at each other across the table.

"You were right," he said abruptly. "I did feel guilty. There's nothing about you that needs fixing. I'm the one who wanted to feel better about myself."

But she was shaking her head before he finished. "No, I've been listening to myself. Even in my head, I put myself down a lot. It's habit, I guess. And it's weird, because I don't like it when anyone else puts me down. You'd think with low self-esteem, I'd be more...I don't know, downtrodden. Wearing a Kick Me sign."

Even though she was serious, Jakob laughed. "That's not you."

She made a face at him. "No. That's when I got in trouble at school, you know. Somebody would dismiss me, say something like 'you're too little to do that' and I would just explode. I thought I could do everything." Sadness shadowed her eyes. "Except make anyone love me. After you and Dad left, I quit believing anyone ever would."

Jakob unclenched his jaw. "God, I'm sorry. I have my share of the blame, but I was a kid. Why Dad and your mother couldn't see what was happening, I don't know."

She had dried and loosely braided her hair. Now the braid slipped over her shoulder and lay between her breasts. Her face was utterly serious. "People who live with chronic pain tend to mostly look inward, don't you think? Now I think that's what happened with Mom. She tried to bury what happened, but it kept hurting. Maybe that's why she couldn't see what the people around her felt."

If she was going to forgive him, Jakob knew it was reasonable that she also forgive his father and her mother, but he wasn't so sure Michelle had ever been capable of loving anyone else. For Amy's sake, he wanted to believe he was wrong, though.

He made a noncommittal sound that seemed to satisfy her.

"I never realized I was so negative." *Her* gaze was turned inward now.

Jakob hated what she was doing to herself. One more thing that was his fault, because he knew he was responsible for the fact that she felt compelled to examine her self-image.

"So—" She focused on him, the same vulnerability in her eyes he'd seen earlier. "I plan to work at it, but I need you to be patient, too. If, well, you plan to be around."

He clunked his coffee mug down on the table. "*If* I plan to be around? How often do you think I tell a woman I love her?"

Amy didn't flinch at his anger, but she looked wary. "How would I know?"

He held her gaze.

"Not very often?"

"Twice. Susan, and you. And with Susan—" Another regret, but one he'd have to let go of. "I think I said it because the time came in our relationship and she seemed right. Not because I felt anything for her like I do for you."

He watched her absorb his words. "Oh," she said softly.

"You're it for me, Amy." When she sat, seemingly stunned, he felt compelled to keep talking, to tell her some of what he'd understood about their past. "In the end," he said finally, "I realized that none of it matters. Do any of us ever really know why one person pushes the right buttons?"

The gold seemed to shimmer in her eyes, but he couldn't tell what she was thinking.

"Have I scared you now?" he asked.

She shook her head, then bit her lip. "Not exactly. Trust is hard for me." She frowned. "No, that's not right. I think it's you. You were always my...standard. My ideal. You know that. I always felt this sort of longing, wanting to be good enough for you."

He closed his eyes.

"No, listen." Her small hand touched his. When he turned his over and gripped her, she held on, too. "The thing is, it's happened. Everything I could ever have wanted. Taking it in is a little hard, that's all."

"Amy..." He *couldn't* let go of her. He had to have that connection. "I'm human. I'm sure as hell not perfect. I shouldn't be anyone's ideal. I can be a real bastard. Ask any of my business competitors. I'm driven, impatient, sometimes a workaholic. I can't measure up to whatever you're thinking."

Her eyes were somehow knowing, and he had that eerie sense again that she must have some fairy blood in her. Then a giggle cascaded from her, and she was his Amy again.

"Did I say you were perfect?" Her laughter made him happier than anything ever had.

"I might have come up with that word on my own." He wanted to share her amusement, but couldn't, not yet. *She'd* scared him. Sooner or later, he'd get irritated with her again, or impatient, or he wouldn't see that she needed something from him he wasn't giving. He needed her to love *him,* imperfect as he was.

"I haven't forgotten the blue boob, the monster coming out of my closet, the pigtail you cut off. In fact, you were such a jerk, I can't believe I'm here!"

"Uh…yeah."

She quit pretending to be indignant and became genuinely troubled. Small lines puckered between her eyebrows. "It hasn't even been a week since you were acting like a jerk all over again."

This time, she tugged at her hand. He wouldn't let her go.

"Did I say I'm sorry?"

"Not exactly."

"I am." He had to clear some grit from his throat. "Sorrier than I can ever tell you. I wanted you to trust me and lean on me and then I turned on you because you'd exposed behavior of mine I didn't want to remember."

"You're being hard on yourself."

"Am I? You don't think I deserve it?"

"I don't know. I did feel betrayed when you quit listening to me and got angry instead. But you've been pretty amazing, too. Getting through all this would have been a lot harder without you."

Okay, it was time to frame the big question, and, man, he didn't want to. But he knew he had to ask.

"Do we have too much history, Amy?"

"TOO MUCH…" THE words died on her lips.

He looked unexpectedly grim. "I love *you*. Can you separate the man I am now from your jackass big brother? Even from the man who helped you get through finding out the truth about your father? Let's not forget I had ulterior motives."

She blinked at that. "You wanted to know whether we were related."

"Yeah. Finding out was really important to me."

"Why?" she asked, some of the intensity she felt in her voice.

"Why?" Jakob stared at her as if she'd gone off her rocker. "You know why! I wanted to let go of some of the goddamn guilt."

"Oh, come on!" she scoffed, instinct driving her. "How often did you even *think* about those days? What difference does it make now that you felt some inappropriate sexual urges? You don't think the average teenage boy doesn't get a hard-on because he accidentally saw his mother or sister naked getting out of the shower? I'll bet you haven't given me a thought in years except when Dad said something about me."

He glared at her. "Your point?"

"My point is, I don't think you helped me out of guilt at all. I think we got together for dinner that night and you were attracted to me all over again. I think you wanted answers so you could come after me."

The glare might have singed the tips of her hair.

Except his expression slowly altered. He was thinking. Not thrilled about it, but doing what she asked. And, finally, his mouth curled ruefully.

"I guess you've nailed me." At whatever he saw on her face, the amusement became real. "And you're feeling smug about it."

"Yes, I am." She grinned, then got up and circled the table. By the time she reached him, Jakob had swiveled and was holding out one arm. She sat on his thighs, kissed his stubbly jaw and reveled in the feel of his arms enclosing her securely. She didn't lean against him, though, because she wanted to be able to see his face.

"Still means I was being selfish," he said after a moment.

"I don't mind selfish because you wanted to go after me." She cupped his jaw in one hand. "You worked really hard at it. And you didn't quit when I fell apart and became…well, not that appealing."

"You are always appealing." His eyes were warm, his voice husky. "You make me feel a lot of things I never have before. One of them is…protective, I guess. I want you to know that I'm here for you. Always."

Tears burned in her eyes. "I don't mind, as long as *you* know it goes both ways. I'm not usually as self-absorbed as I must have seemed lately."

"I know that," he said. He turned his head just enough to nip the soft flesh on her thumb.

She was melting down, and this time in a good way. "How?" she asked, voice shaky.

"Because I've read a lot of what you've written. Your empathy and insight and heart shine through." He kept on nibbling, then drew her thumb into his mouth and sucked.

A shock of sensation zinged through her. "Oh," she mumbled, then frowned. "All you said you'd read was a couple of my articles."

He smiled at her, his eyes as blue and clear as she'd ever seen them. "I did some research. I've found...probably twenty or so."

"Oh," she mumbled again. She squirmed on his lap.

He gripped her thigh and moved her closer to his body. His hips lifted slightly and she almost moaned.

"We're supposed to be talking," he growled.

Amy wriggled some more. "Aren't we?"

"You still haven't told me how you feel about me."

Hadn't she? "You know."

The big hand on her thigh trapped her and kept her from moving anymore. "I've been hoping." He sounded hoarse. "That's not the same thing."

"I'm crazy in love with you." Saying that felt like stepping out of an airplane. Beginning the plummet to earth. She'd never imagined she would have the courage. The faith. But this was Jakob.

He searched her face for a long moment, seeming stunned. Then he squeezed his eyes shut and drew a couple of hard breaths before pinning her again with those blue eyes.

"Are you, uh, tied to your mom's house for two years?"

It was hard to think. "Well, sort of. I mean, I should stay in Portland. I promised to take care of the garden. But I don't suppose it means I have to live there."

"If I have to, I'll move in there," he said. "But I'll keep feeling like a guest. Despite the recent thawing, my relationship with your mother isn't that warm."

Amy giggled. "Mostly, mine isn't, either. And *I* feel like a guest in that house, too. It'll never be home."

"Then…?"

"Are you suggesting I move in with you?"

"I'm suggesting—" His hand slid higher, up under the hem of the T-shirt. His touch delicate, he found her core, wet and shivery. He gently rubbed. "A wedding," he finished. "You living here until we can pull that off."

"You want me to marry you." A moment of doubt sliced, scalpel-sharp, but she made herself look at his face, where she saw raw need to equal hers.

I believe.

"Yeah." He stroked her again, but this time he also leaned forward and kissed her, softly and sweetly. "That's what I want."

If she'd been falling, she now knew the landing would be easy. She was floating, her parachute safely opened. "That's what I want, too," she managed to say, her voice small and gruff. "I love you."

His face spasmed. "My Amy."

She kissed him, eagerly. "My Jakob."

"You won't even have to go through the hassle of changing your name on your social security card or your driver's license."

"Who says I would have changed it?"

Jakob laughed. His hands slid down to grip her butt. The muscles in his thighs bunched as he prepared to stand up, lifting her with him. "After food, bed. Right?"

"I love you," she told him, and he quit laughing.

"Sometimes it's hard to believe," he whispered as he leaned in to kiss her, "that I can be so lucky."

This kiss wasn't only tender. It was everything.

* * * * *

LARGER-PRINT BOOKS!
GET 2 FREE LARGER-PRINT NOVELS PLUS
2 FREE GIFTS!

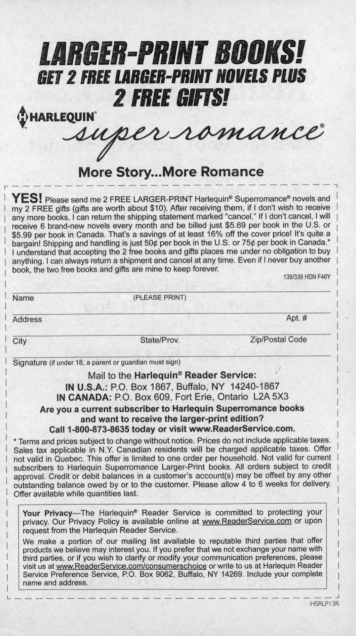

HARLEQUIN
super romance

More Story...More Romance

YES! Please send me 2 FREE LARGER-PRINT Harlequin® Superromance® novels and my 2 FREE gifts (gifts are worth about $10). After receiving them, if I don't wish to receive any more books, I can return the shipping statement marked "cancel." If I don't cancel, I will receive 6 brand-new novels every month and be billed just $5.69 per book in the U.S. or $5.99 per book in Canada. That's a savings of at least 16% off the cover price! It's quite a bargain! Shipping and handling is just 50¢ per book in the U.S. or 75¢ per book in Canada.* I understand that accepting the 2 free books and gifts places me under no obligation to buy anything. I can always return a shipment and cancel at any time. Even if I never buy another book, the two free books and gifts are mine to keep forever.

139/339 HDN F46Y

Name	(PLEASE PRINT)

Address	Apt. #

City	State/Prov.	Zip/Postal Code

Signature (if under 18, a parent or guardian must sign)

Mail to the **Harlequin® Reader Service:**
IN U.S.A.: P.O. Box 1867, Buffalo, NY 14240-1867
IN CANADA: P.O. Box 609, Fort Erie, Ontario L2A 5X3

Are you a current subscriber to Harlequin Superromance books
and want to receive the larger-print edition?
Call 1-800-873-8635 today or visit www.ReaderService.com.

* Terms and prices subject to change without notice. Prices do not include applicable taxes. Sales tax applicable in N.Y. Canadian residents will be charged applicable taxes. Offer not valid in Quebec. This offer is limited to one order per household. Not valid for current subscribers to Harlequin Superromance Larger-Print books. All orders subject to credit approval. Credit or debit balances in a customer's account(s) may be offset by any other outstanding balance owed by or to the customer. Please allow 4 to 6 weeks for delivery. Offer available while quantities last.

Your Privacy—The Harlequin® Reader Service is committed to protecting your privacy. Our Privacy Policy is available online at www.ReaderService.com or upon request from the Harlequin Reader Service.

We make a portion of our mailing list available to reputable third parties that offer products we believe may interest you. If you prefer that we not exchange your name with third parties, or if you wish to clarify or modify your communication preferences, please visit us at www.ReaderService.com/consumerschoice or write to us at Harlequin Reader Service Preference Service, P.O. Box 9062, Buffalo, NY 14269. Include your complete name and address.

HSRLP13R

ReaderService.com

Manage your account online!

- Review your order history
- Manage your payments
- Update your address

**We've designed
the Harlequin® Reader Service
website just for you.**

Enjoy all the features!

- Reader excerpts from any series
- Respond to mailings and
  special monthly offers
- Discover new series available to you
- Browse the Bonus Bucks catalog
- Share your feedback

Visit us at:

ReaderService.com